Summersville *Heat*

N.J. WALTERS

ELLORA'S CAVE
ROMANTICA PUBLISHING

What the critics are saying...

❧

Annabelle Lee

"ANNABELLE LEE has it all, likeable characters, scorching sex scenes and a satisfying happily after." ~ *Just Erotic Romance Reviews*

5 Stars "This story is filled with the most amazingly sensual foreplay. I found myself engrossed with these characters and their plight. […] I will recommend this book to my friends." ~ *ECataRomance*

5 Hearts "The storyline was well written and I loved watching Annabelle go from insecure and reserved to confident and outgoing. I was enthralled from the first page to the last." ~ *The Romance Studio*

Heat Wave

4 Hearts "N.J. Walters is cranking out the books at a fast pace and readers are snapping them up just as quickly. She has written a great book about two people figuring out what it takes to stay together." ~ *The Romance Studio*

An Ellora's Cave Romantica Publication

www.ellorascave.com

Summersville Heat

ISBN 9781419955617
ALL RIGHTS RESERVED.
Annabelle Lee Copyright © 2004 N.J. Walters
Heat Wave Copyright © 2005 N.J. Walters
Edited by Pamela Cohen.
Cover art by Syneca.

This book printed in the U.S.A. by Jasmine–Jade Enterprises, LLC.

Trade paperback Publication September 2007

Also by N.J. Walters

∞

About the Author

ℬ

N.J. Walters worked at a bookstore for several years and one day had the idea that she would like to quit her job, sell everything she owned, leave her hometown and write romance novels in a place where no one knew her. And she did. Two years later, she went back to the same bookstore and settled in for another seven years.

Although she was still fairly young, that was when the mid-life crisis set in. Happily married to the love of her life, with his encouragement (more like, "For God's sake, quit the job and just write!") she gave notice at her job on a Friday morning. On Sunday afternoon, she received a tentative acceptance for her first erotic romance novel, Annabelle Lee, and life would never be the same.

N.J. has always been a voracious reader of romance novels, and now she spends her days writing novels of her own. Vampires, dragons, time-travelers, seductive handymen and next-door neighbors with smoldering good looks all vie for her attention. And she doesn't mind a bit. It's a tough life, but someone's got to live it.

N.J. Walters welcomes comments from readers. You can find her website and email address on her author bio page at www.ellorascave.com.

Tell Us What You Think

We appreciate hearing reader opinions about our books. You can email us at Comments@EllorasCave.com.

SUMMERSVILLE HEAT

 so

ANNABELLE LEE
~13~

&

HEAT WAVE
~139~

ANNABELLE LEE

ജ

Prologue
✆

"I heard you were hot." The voice was male, deep, and husky.

Annabelle turned slightly from where she'd been organizing books in the reference section of the library. The towering shelves filled with hardcover books created a tunnel-like effect, insulating her from the rest of the library. She could see a tall silhouette at the end of the darkened aisle. "You shouldn't be here. The library closed five minutes ago." She used her sternest librarian voice, the one that automatically scolded the recipient for breaking library rules.

The shadow sauntered closer and coalesced into the body of a man. And what a body! Clad in tight jeans and a white tank shirt that emphasized the rippling muscles in his chest, he was every woman's fantasy, but especially hers. The blue material of his jeans clung to his muscular thighs and accentuated the bulge in the front. He was aroused and making no effort to hide it.

"What can I do for you?" Annabelle asked her voice prim and business-like. She could feel the sweat roll down her back, and her nipples were now tight buds against the front of her summer cotton sundress.

"What do you want to do?" came the tantalizing reply.

Annabelle eyed him up and down as she sauntered a little closer. His was a strong face made harsh by the desire stamped on it. His brown eyes scorched her with their lustful gaze. Her fingers itched to reach around his neck and release his long, rich brown hair from its leather thong. She wanted to sift her fingers through it and rub her face in its softness.

Annabelle stopped in front of him. "You should be fined for breaking library rules." She ran her finger up and down the front of his tight shirt, tracing the muscles, feeling them clench tighter at her touch.

"What's the penalty?" His voice was a rough whisper in the quiet of the hushed library. His hands reached to pull her towards him, but she stepped back.

"No. No touching." Annabelle tapped a finger upon her lips, drawing his gaze to them. "That's your penalty." She removed her wire-rimmed glasses, closed them carefully and placed them on top of a thick reference book about the mating rituals of animals.

Taking her time, she reached behind her head and pulled out the pins, one at a time, that confined her long, dark brown hair in a bun. Her dress was drawn tight across her breasts, and they grew heavy with desire as his lustful stare lingered on them. When the last pin was out, she laid them next to her glasses and threaded her fingers through her long tresses, letting them fall softly across her shoulders. She felt powerful and sensual.

"You can look, but you can't touch." Casually, she slipped off her loafers and nudged them aside. He stood as still as a statue before her. Every muscle tensed. Waiting.

She padded towards him, her feet making no sound on the carpet. Clasping one of his hands in hers, she raised it to her lips and placed a kiss in the center of his palm before positioning it on the wood shelf to the right. Then she did the same with the other hand and laid it on the opposite shelf on the left. His hands were slightly rough, the hands of a man who made a living with them. They were broad with long, thick fingers. Capable hands. The thought of them on her body sent a shiver of desire down her spine.

"Don't move," she ordered as she backed away. He was a large man and with his arms spread he filled the aisle. If possible, his gaze got even hotter, a mix of annoyance and lust.

"Annabelle." His jaw was clenched and his voice was harsh. "I want you. Now."

Annabelle gave him a sultry smile. "If you pay the penalty, you can have me. I'll make it worth your while."

She reached down and in one motion pulled her dress over her head and let it slip to the floor. His nostrils flared, and his fingers dug into the wood of the shelves, turning his knuckles white. Annabelle laughed and stroked her cotton-covered breasts with her *own hands.* As he watched her, she drew her fingertips over her aroused nipples.

"You can do that later. If you behave."

"You're killing me."

"We can't have that, can we?" Annabelle reached behind and unhooked her bra. Bending over she allowed it to fall down her arms and join her dress on the floor, all the while giving him an unobstructed view of her full breasts.

"God, you're beautiful. Come over and let me suck your tits," he rasped. His body swayed, but his hands never moved from the shelves. His tongue came out to lick his lips, as if anticipating a feast. "You know you want to."

"Later," she promised. Her heart was pounding hard inside her chest. Her breasts heaved as she took a deep breath, and a confident smile crossed her face. Before he could say anything else, her hands slid to the waistband of her white cotton panties. She could feel the dampness of her crotch area. Slowly, she pushed them down over her legs and kicked them off. Naked and proud, she stood before him, her legs slightly spread. She trailed her fingers up her torso until they were under her breasts. Then she fondled herself, presenting them for his enjoyment.

"Come here," he coaxed. "I want to suck your tits until you come for me. You'd love it. We both would."

She swung her hips as she drifted the few steps necessary to bring her right in front of him. Her hand reached out and cupped the bulge in the front of his jeans. He groaned and moved his hips, rubbing his erection against her palm.

"We can't leave you like this."

"No, we can't. We shouldn't," he agreed hoarsely.

"Take off your sneakers, but don't move your hands." Annabelle watched as he toed off his footwear, his smoldering eyes never leaving her face.

Her fingers undid the snap and then she carefully unzipped his jeans. She peeled both jeans and underwear down his legs at once. "Kick them away."

He made quick work of that and was left naked from the waist down for her perusal. His penis jutted out in front of him and Annabelle licked her lips. He groaned as she went to her knees in front of him and stared at him.

"All this. Just for me." That was the only warning he got before she lowered her head and took his penis into her mouth. She sucked on the tip, loving his musky scent.

He pushed his hips back and forth, desperate for her to take more of him into her hot mouth. Annabelle responded by trailing her fingers over his testicles. They hung heavy and she rolled the sacs gently. Removing her mouth from his penis, she moved her head lower to lick and suck at his balls.

He let out a groan of pure pleasure and then his fingers were tangled in the mass of hair that hung down her back. She no longer cared. She held him in her hands as she licked at the length of him. He was soft and hard all at the same time.

"Give me your mouth," he grated out between his clenched teeth.

Annabelle took as much of him as she could. He held her head gently in his large hands as her mouth slid back and forth over his penis. Annabelle relaxed and allowed his penis to slide back in her throat. Her teeth lightly grazed his length as he slid in and out of her moist mouth. She used her tongue to flick along the underside of his cock and was rewarded as his hands gripped her tighter. Annabelle felt both powerful and weak. Her breasts felt heavy and achy and she could feel her own juices running down the insides of her legs. Her body moved in rhythm with his. She felt empty. Needy.

Annabelle licked at the head of his penis, tasting some drops of his arousal that seeped from the tip. She sat back and drew her tongue over her lips. "You taste wonderful."

"Let me fuck you, Annabelle. You know we both want it." His hands still had a grip on a length of her hair, as if he were loathe to lose contact with her.

Annabelle swayed forward and rubbed her face over his arousal. "Yes." Her breath was hot on him and her tongue flicked out for another lick.

"On your hands and knees, baby. You had your fun. Now I want mine." His fingers released their grip on her hair and he watched, entranced, as the strands slid from his grasp.

She smiled seductively and then turned her back on him. She placed her hands on the floor in front of her and then turned to look over her shoulder. "What are you waiting for?" She rolled her hips as she teased him. She was more than ready for him.

He swore as he tore his shirt over his head and dropped to his knees behind her. His strong left arm encircled her waist and then he pulled her back against him, inserting himself in her until his cock was seated to the hilt. He breathed a deep sigh of relief. "That's much better," he said as he pressed a kiss on her exposed back.

"Mmm," she agreed, rotating her hips slightly. Her breasts hung in front of her and the weight of them made her feel wild. If he was a male animal in his prime, then she was his female counterpart. Her back arched and her mass of hair slid off her back leaving her neck and torso bare. She pushed her bottom snug against his stomach and moved up and down. The motion excited her even more.

He laughed and both hands reached up to cover her breasts. His large hands were filled to overflow with her bountiful breasts. He fondled them for a moment, making her squirm even more. He rolled the tight nipples between his thumb and forefingers. Leaning forward he whispered in her ear. "Payback is hell."

She responded by moving ahead slightly and then pushing back as hard as she could. "It sure is," she panted.

He moaned and his hands tightened on her breasts. He opened his own legs, which spread hers even wider. One hand continued to play with her breasts while the other one wrapped tightly around her waist. Then he moved.

Slowly at first. He pulled himself out slowly until he was almost all the way out and then he eased himself back inside her until she was filled with him. He held her tight and she was unable to control the depths of his thrusts. He kept up the slow steady pace until she was both swearing and pleading for him to finish.

The hand that was toying with her nipples abandoned them and slid down to cover her mound. He held his hand there for a moment.

"You're so damn hot," he whispered behind her. "I love that about you."

He held her still as his fingers combed through her pubic hair. Every other stroke or so, he allowed his index finger to graze her clitoris. Barely touching it. Desperately she tried to move her hips, but he held her tight and continued his erotic torture.

"More. I need more."

In answer, his finger began to move in a regular rhythm. Lightly, he played with her clitoris. Then harder. Then light again. The steady pattern remained the same but the pressure varied.

Annabelle could feel the tension building inside her. She tossed her head from side to side. "Harder."

He continued working her until she almost screamed in frustration. "Come for me," he ordered as he bent down and bit carefully on the side of her neck.

The combination was too much for her and her climax rose up and spilled over. His fingers continued to pleasure her even as she felt herself clenching and releasing around his engorged penis. She rode the sensations to the very end until she collapsed. He held her easily in his arms, his body covered her back and shoulders as he eased her to the carpet.

She lay there feeling replete and satisfied. The bottom shelves needed to be dusted, she noted as the dust tickled her nose. She felt as if she'd just had an out-of-body experience. Little aftershocks shook her. Finally, she sighed and relaxed. His grip immediately tightened around her waist. He still filled her completely and after allowing her this moment of respite, nudged her back up on her hands and knees.

"I don't think I can." She swayed wanting more than anything to just become a puddle on the carpet. He held her until she was back in the position he wanted.

"I'll do the work. Just enjoy." He pulled back slowly, until he was almost out of her and then pushed back hard. He was thick and stretched her as he pushed inside her. Her already swollen and sensitive muscles were stimulated even more. Annabelle felt her body stretch even more to accommodate his length. In and out he stroked. Never hesitating. Not stopping.

Annabelle's arousal grew until his slow, steady assault on her senses was no longer enough. "Harder," she ordered as she pushed her behind back against him.

He responded immediately. His hips moved quickly, hammering in and out of her from behind. Her inner muscles clenched around him as he continued to pound into her. She pushed back as hard as she could to meet his thrusts. The sound of his bare flesh slapping against her bottom made her even hotter. The air was filled with the earthy sounds and smell of sex.

He gave one huge groan and then his cum spurted hot and liquid inside her. His big body heaved and shook as his orgasm went on and on. Her own body reacted to his and she came again, clasping his penis harder even as he rode the wave of his own release.

They both collapsed to the floor, but even then he was careful to roll to the side. He was still inside her, his face buried against her neck as they both shivered and shook with the aftershocks of their lovemaking.

Annabelle loved the feeling of his large body against her. His position was both protective and soothing. His fingers glided up over her stomach and then traced the outline of one nipple before his hand settled reassuringly around one of her breasts. He practically purred with contentment. He radiated a comforting heat, and she snuggled closer, wanting to absorb his warmth. He laughed as her bottom squirmed against him enticing his penis to life again.

"I love your ass," he whispered. Hot kisses traced her neck and his tongue traced the swirls of her ears. "You're a hot piece, Miss Annabelle Lee."

A buzzing sound filled Annabelle's ears. She struggled to hear him even as he began to fade. His solid form disappeared from behind her. She turned, her hands reaching out to hold him to her, but he was gone. Her hands met air as the buzzing grew.

"Stay," she pleaded. But it was too late. The sound of her own voice, added to the buzzing of the alarm clock, woke her completely.

Eyes still closed to keep him inside her head, she reached out and slapped her hand over the snooze button, then flopped back onto the bed. Her hands covered her face in embarrassment even as her body thrummed with the last remnants of her climax. Between her legs was hot and sticky.

This had to stop. She was thirty years old and it was only in the last few months that she'd ever had an erotic dream. They were all about him—Mike Sloan. She rolled over to the side and buried her face in her pillow. Her cheeks felt hot, and she was sure her blush covered her from head to toe. She did things in her dreams that she would never dare in real life.

Pushing her hair out of her face, she squinted at the clock. She definitely needed a shower before work. A cool one to help soothe her heated skin. Leaning over, she plucked her nightgown off the floor and tugged it over her head. Annabelle didn't understand how it happened, but somehow every time she dreamed of Mike she woke up naked.

She swayed as she got to her feet and steadied herself against the nightstand before stumbling to the bathroom. She didn't know what to do about her dreams. The only thing that made them bearable was the fact that she rarely saw Mike Sloan. She groaned at the thought of having to face the man day after day. It was unthinkable.

Her reflection in the bathroom mirror looked as hot and rumpled as she felt, and if the weatherman was correct, this day was going to be another scorcher. Even worse was the fact that the library's air-conditioning had given out yesterday. Harold Keats, her elderly handyman was supposed to try and fix it this morning. Given the sounds it had made before conking out, she didn't hold out much hope. She turned the shower on cold. She needed all the help she could get.

Stepping under the frigid spray, she leaned against the shower wall for support, and forced herself to stand there. The cold water pummeled her aching muscles. She felt as if she'd been hard used last night, even if it was just a dream. It was just the jolt of reality she needed for her body and her mind.

Shivering, she adjusted the taps until the water was a little warmer.

As she lathered her body and rinsed the soap away her sense of humor reasserted itself. She laughed out loud and was rewarded with a mouthful of water. Spitting and sputtering, she turned off the shower and climbed out. Quickly and efficiently, she toweled off and tucked the towel around her body. She was Miss Annabelle Lee Murphy, the old-fashioned librarian. The only chance she had of having a hot encounter in the library stacks was if she caught some hormonal young boy checking out women's naked bodies in the anatomy section.

She dried her hair and pinned it up in its customary style. The woman in the bathroom mirror was the one she recognized. Her equilibrium restored, she returned to the bedroom to dress and plan her day.

Chapter One

ઇ૭

"I heard you're hot."

At the sound of the deep, masculine voice, Annabelle came up from the floor behind her desk so fast she smacked her head on the corner. "Ouch." She sat back on her heels and rubbed the back of her head as she glared at the man standing in front of her.

Mike Sloan. She groaned inwardly resisting the urge to dive back under her desk and stay there. *Might have known.* It seemed that she was doomed to be at her worst whenever he was around. He leaned against the side of her doorway, all six feet and three inches of rugged male perfection. At least in her mind he was perfect. His face was not beautiful, but strong. The bump on his nose suggested that it had been broken, maybe more than once, and his soulful brown eyes were deep-set. His hair was a rich brown and just a bit too long for fashion. He kept it tied back with a leather thong. And his lips. Yum. Not too thin and not too thick. Just right for kissing.

Oh lord, she was just sitting here on the floor, staring at the man. He'd asked her a question. Hadn't he? "What was it you said?" She strove for her best librarian's voice. The one that said, "I'm in charge of the situation". It worked well for six-year-olds. But from the way Mike was grinning, it obviously wasn't working with him. She sighed, disgusted with herself.

His deep voice washed over her. She loved the sound of it, so well suited to seduction. She should know. It was the same voice that seduced her in her dreams several nights a week. She could sit there all day and contentedly listen to him recite the phone book. In fact, she was enjoying listening to him speak so much she'd missed what he'd said yet again.

Striving for dignity, she smoothed back any errant strands of hair that had escaped the strict confines of her bun and tried again. "I'm sorry. The knock on the head must have shaken me up. What was it you said?"

"I heard you're hot, Annabelle." The half-smile on his face was knowing, as if he were somehow privy to her very thoughts.

She could feel the blush cover her cheeks and resisted the temptation to slap her hands over them to hide the telltale color. Oh my lord. Had he seen her watching him whenever she'd run into him in town? Had he guessed that she thought he was the sexiest man she'd ever laid eyes on?

His brown eyes sparkled as they swept her from head to foot. Was it her imagination or had his eyes grown darker since last time she'd seen him? His gaze seemed to linger on her mouth. On her lips. The memory of what her lips had been doing in her dreams hit her full force. Her lips were suddenly dried out. She licked at them, trying to ease their dryness. It didn't help. Her gaze dropped to the front of his jeans before she jerked it back to his face.

Mike stood stock still in the doorway, his eyes intently following the progress of her tongue across her lips. His hands slowly clenched into fists and his whole body tensed as he closed his eyes and tilted his head back. He looked like a man at the end of his patience. Shaking his head, he opened his eyes again and his body relaxed into its former pose. As she continued to stare, that little grin of his curved up once again. The whole tense moment passed as if it never happened.

Now she was just being silly. There was no way he could know about the dreams she had. Hot, steamy, dreams that ended way too soon and left her drenched all over in sweat when she woke. No. At least he couldn't know about those. She'd never told anyone. She'd hardly let herself even think about them, at least not in the daytime. Nighttime was a different story.

She knew he was still waiting, so she summoned up her frostiest smile. It had been tried and tested and was guaranteed to let a man know she wasn't interested or amused. "What do you mean by that comment?"

"Just what I said." He continued to smile as he straightened away from the doorframe and sauntered slowly across the room.

It was only when he was towering over her that she remembered she was still sitting on the floor. It was very reminiscent of her position last night and again her eyes were drawn to the front of his jeans. She wondered if he could possibly look as good naked in real life as he had in her dreams.

This had to stop. Annabelle ran her hand over her face in an effort to gain control of her emotions. This was the first time she had seen Mike after one of her dreams. Usually, it was days before she had to face him on the street or at some local function. This was too soon. Her body was still thrumming with the pleasure from the night before, and it knew that this man was responsible for it. And it wanted more.

Before she could scramble to her feet, he stretched his hand out. "Here, let me help you."

She was powerless to resist the lure of his voice and the excuse to actually touch him. Annabelle placed her hand in his. He gently closed his larger hand around hers tugging her to her feet. She was so close to him now. She could see how sinfully long his eyelashes were. They would make most men look feminine, but on Mike, they were extremely sexy.

His large body radiated a steady heat that made her want to snuggle up against him, even on a hot day like today. The strength and comfort his body offered drew her like a lure. And his eyes. Just like chocolate. Rich, deep, delicious melt-in-your-mouth chocolate. She could quite happily lose herself in those eyes.

She took a deep breath and then wished she hadn't. He even smelled hot. A combination of woodsy soap and masculinity. She realized he was patiently waiting for her to release him. He had opened his hand, but she was still clinging to his fingers.

She hastily stepped back to gain herself some space. Taking her time, she smoothed her hair back again and pushed her glasses high up on her nose. It was time to stop acting like a ninny. She was a take-charge, competent woman. "What do you mean by that remark, Mr. Sloan?"

Mike stepped back and just stared at her for a moment like she was a little dense for not understanding him. "The air-conditioning. I heard it broke down again. I came to fix it."

Now she was really embarrassed. How could she even for a moment have misinterpreted his meaning? A man like him would never be interested in a woman like her. At least not in a sexual way. If she attracted a man at all, she ended up becoming a best buddy. A friend. Someone to talk to. Nothing more. It was time to forget fantasy and get back to business.

"Harold Keats usually takes care of this kind of thing. What are you doing here?" She really was more comfortable with the retired Mr. Keats, who supplemented his income by fixing things for the library. Personally, Annabelle thought he did it more because he was lonely. She didn't mind. He was always cheerful and knew all the goings-on around town. He kept her well informed about town events, but always the facts and never malicious gossip.

"Harold had a slight accident." When Mike saw the look of concern on her face, he added quickly, "But he's fine."

Annabelle sank into her chair and motioned for him to take the one across from her. "What happened?"

Mike settled his large frame into the chair, causing it to creak in complaint. It was more of a casual sprawl actually.

"He slipped getting out of his shower and sprained his foot. He called his sister, Jean, who came and took him to the hospital." Mike crossed his arms over his chest. "Harold will be all right, but he'll be laid up for a few weeks. In the meantime, I'm here to fill in for him."

Annabelle sat back. She had a death grip on the arms of her chair as she stared at Mike. This could not be happening to her. She couldn't take several weeks of close contact with him. He made her hot and uncomfortable when he was just sitting there with his muscular arms crossed across his massive chest. Working with him every day, trying to hide her feelings for him, would be the death of her. He'd be bound to notice her discomfort, and then where would she be?

She could just imagine his look of pity when he realized the old-maid librarian had the hots for him. Not that she was really old. She was thirty. But except for a brief affair in college that had been at best tepid, she had absolutely no experience with men.

"I'm sorry about Harold, but you don't have to take his place. There's really nothing that can't wait until he comes back."

"It's as hot as Hades in here, Annabelle. I figured you and the library patrons would appreciate a little cool air."

He looked at her as if daring her to dispute him, and the worst of it was that she couldn't. She nodded, conceding him his point. "All right, but just the air-conditioning. Anything else can wait."

"We'll see," he muttered ominously.

"You can fix it, can't you?" She didn't know what compelled her to ask, but it was out before she could stop herself.

Mike straightened up in his seat and scowled at her. She squirmed in her chair, not at all comfortable. She had made him very angry and that hadn't been her intention. She'd wanted him to notice her. Well, he was certainly noticing her now and it wasn't pleasant. Which went to prove you should be careful what you wish for.

"I didn't mean it like that." She didn't know why she felt compelled to soothe his male ego, only that she did. "I'm just hopeful that someone can fix it. I've been sitting in a pool of sweat all day."

If she was alone, she would have slapped herself in the head. That knock on the desk must have really scrambled her brains. She should have just blurted out that she probably smelled and was disgustingly damp too. How attractive.

She tried to distract him and make amends for her previous coolness. After all, it looked as if she'd have no choice but to work with him for the next few weeks. "I was just trying to plug in that little desk fan to try and get some relief."

A smile spread slowly across Mike's face. "I wondered what you were doing under your desk. But to answer your question, yeah, I can fix it."

"How come you volunteered for the job? I'm glad you did." She tacked that on quickly when she saw his brows draw together over his eyes. "But why you?"

Mike took his time, picking his words carefully. "Several reasons, actually. First, I'm a friend of Harold and he was worried about leaving you in the lurch. I didn't want him to worry."

Annabelle nodded. This was a reason she could easily understand. Friendship. Loyalty. Both admirable characteristics.

"Secondly, I own my own construction business. We're small, but we're good. I've always been good with my hands and I've been fixing things since I was a kid. This is my town so I consider it my civic duty to help out."

Annabelle nodded again. It confirmed all the tidbits of gossip people had told her about Mike since she moved here six months ago to take the position of head librarian. He was a good man. A solid citizen. A loyal friend. Someone you could depend on. She would just control her wayward thoughts for a few days and everything would be fine. She paid attention as Mike started to speak again.

"The last reason is the most important one."

Annabelle leaned forward in anticipation.

"I want you." Mike stared at her, his eyes hot, his body tense as he delivered his final reason.

Annabelle sat there dumbfounded for a moment. "You want me for what?"

Mike stood slowly and stalked around her desk. He leaned over and placed his hands on the arms of her chair, caging her in. He spoke softly, but plainly. "I want you in my bed."

He leaned down and softly covered her lips with his. She could not mistake his intent as he licked at her lips. She parted them on a gasp and he took advantage and slid his tongue inside her mouth. Slowly, he moved his tongue in and out in a rhythm mimicking lovemaking.

Her hand slid up to cover the side of his face. He needed a shave and the roughness against her hand was stimulating. Annabelle could only imagine how arousing it would be if he rubbed his face over her breasts. Maybe even lower.

His tongue continued to play with hers, teasing her until she moaned. It was that sound that brought her back to her senses. She'd never made such a sound before. Except in her dreams.

When she pulled back, Mike straightened away from her. "That can't happen again." It was an automatic response and Annabelle was almost sorry the moment she made it. How she longed to give in to her feelings for this man. But that way would only lead to heartache. A public affair with this man would not lead to marriage and Annabelle had to live in this town. More than that, she wanted to live here. She was happy here and she didn't want to be an object of gossip and pity.

"It will happen again. That and more." Mike looked arrogant as he towered over her with his arms crossed and scowled at her. "I know you enjoyed that as much as I did."

"That's no reason for it to happen again." When Mike's face took on a smug, satisfied look, she realized her error. She hadn't denied that she liked it. This was like waving a red flag in front of an angry bull.

"I've got my tools in the truck. I'll just go get them and get started." He was almost out of her office when he turned. "We can discuss the rest over dinner tonight."

He was gone before she had presence of mind to say no, because she knew that deep in her heart a part of her was screaming, *Yes!*

Mike Sloan strode towards his truck, just outside the Summersville Library. Only ten o'clock in the morning and already the day was a scorcher. The heat shimmered just above the pavement and Mike could feel the sweat forming on his brow. But no matter how blistering it was outside, nothing even came close to the temperature inside the library. It was hot. And it was all due to Annabelle Lee Murphy.

When he'd walked into her office and saw her tucked under her desk with her butt in the air all he'd wanted to do was lock the door to her office, kneel down behind her, and lift up her long floral skirt so he could gain access to what was underneath. It was hard to tell with the shapeless clothes she favored, but Annabelle had a voluptuous figure. This he knew for a fact. He'd made a study of it. Every time he'd seen her since she moved here six months ago.

At first glance, Annabelle seemed ordinary. She was thirty years old. He'd asked Harold, who knew more about her than anyone else in town. She wore her dark hair in a bun and covered her blue eyes with wire-rimmed glasses. Her figure seemed unexceptional. Her smile was inviting. That was at first glance.

But something had drawn him back for a second glance. And then a third. After a close study, he'd come to realize that for some unknown reason Annabelle hid her sexiness from the world. The hair that she kept ruthlessly tamed was a rich mahogany color. He didn't know if it was shoulder-length, hung to her waist, or somewhere in between. He longed to release it from its confinement and let it flow. He wanted to spend hours sifting his fingers through it and having Annabelle tease him with it.

The eyes behind the glasses were intelligent and kind. Both were pluses in Mike's mind. He couldn't abide silly women, nor did he like those who were cruel to others. Those baby blues were vulnerable, yet inquisitive. He'd seen her watching him. The longing in those eyes, and the fact that she was single and available, had given him some steamy fantasies. She wanted him, even if she hadn't admitted that fact to herself. But she would. He would help her.

Her lips were lush. There was no other way to put it. They were made for kissing and giving pleasure. Having finally tasted them, he knew he wanted more. Much more. As much as she would give him. He could easily imagine those lips working their way down his body and tasting him. *Everywhere.*

He shook his head to clear his thoughts. Walking across the parking lot in full view of the town was not the place to have a hard-on. He was just glad he had pulled on a work shirt over his tank top. The tails of the shirt helped to cover the large ridge at the front of his jeans. It was Annabelle's fault for being so damn sexy.

His fingers itched to strip her out of her prim little librarian's outfit and carry her to bed. He knew she was built like a pin-up model from the forties and fifties, lush and full. Her breasts were large, her hips and butt would be a handful. He grinned at the thought. Good thing he had big hands. She was built for him.

She hid her body under unstructured dress and long skirts with tunic tops. Which was fine by him. He didn't want any other man getting smart and trying to entice Annabelle. In his mind, she was already his, and he aimed to have her. He couldn't wait until she was in his bed and he could spend hours examining and sating himself with her luscious body.

First things first. Pulling his toolbox out of the back of his truck he strode back towards the library. Whistling as he walked, he felt better than he had in a long time. He'd made his move. Now Annabelle knew he was interested, and he would coax her out of her shell. She was a woman made for loving — his loving.

Chapter Two

ဆာ

Annabelle laid out a sandwich and a bottle of water on the counter. Monday, Wednesday and Friday, she ate lunch at the library. She had two part-time employees, but budgetary restrictions meant she was alone until one o'clock on these three days. A lot of people liked to run into the library on their lunch hours, and she wanted it to be open for them. She didn't mind eating at the front counter, and the library patrons didn't mind either. In fact, some of her regulars had started bringing her treats for lunch. She loved Mrs. Casey's apple muffins, and Mr. Johnson's wife made the best scones, with which she always sent along fresh homemade strawberry jam.

Today was different. She just couldn't seem to settle in at the front desk. It was all Mike's fault. She could hear the noise from the back as he worked. The sound of metal on metal, as he tinkered with the air-conditioning unit, followed by the muttering of his voice. Even when he was swearing he sounded sexy.

It all came back to *the kiss*. If she'd been aware of him before, now she was hypersensitive. Her fingers came up to touch her lips. She could still feel the softness of his lips against hers. Taste him. Until this morning, it had only been a dream. A fantasy. Now her body felt hot and achy and she knew it was due to more than the lack of air-conditioning. There was only one cure for what ailed her body. Sex—sex with Mike.

Annabelle recognized that she never really had the opportunity to discover her sexuality before. She'd been an only child, born to an older couple. To say that she'd been a surprise to them was an understatement. They'd loved her, she'd never doubted that, but they'd been strict and set in their ways and she hadn't been the kind of child who challenged their authority.

She'd gone away to college, but when her father had died suddenly of a heart attack she'd moved home. She took a job in the local library and cared for her mother, who never really recovered from her husband's death. When her mother passed away a year ago she'd been sad, but determined to finally start living her own life. When she saw the advertisement for a librarian in Summersville, she sold her childhood home and moved. She wanted a fresh start in a place where no one knew her.

The one problem she hadn't anticipated, which she really should have, was that nothing had changed. Sure, she could move to a new place, but she was the same old Annabelle. Wearing clothing her parents would approve of and not bringing any unnecessary attention to herself. Well, that wasn't quite true. She'd drawn quite a bit of attention to herself. None of it wanted.

It had started the first time she'd seen Mike Sloan. He'd been going into city hall when she'd been coming out. She'd been excited at signing her contract with the town and had run straight into him as she'd hurried out the front door. He'd caught her easily before she had a chance to fall and when she'd looked up to thank him, she'd been struck dumb. Never had she seen a man who seemed to call to her as a woman. Her whole body had gone on alert and she'd tried to absorb everything about him. Unfortunately for her, he'd thought she'd been hurt or was ill and had called out to Dr. James, who had just happened to be walking by.

She could still feel the embarrassment. Annabelle had quickly assured them she was fine, thanked them for their concern, and hurried back to her apartment. She replayed the scene over and over in her head. She wished she were one of those women who could have laughed off the situation with a witty or funny comment. The scene haunted her waking hours for weeks.

From then on it only got worse. She'd spilled her drink on him at the local spring fair when he'd stopped to speak to her. Then there was the time she tripped walking up the stairs at city hall because she'd been too busy looking at him. The only good thing to come out of the incident was that he probably thought she was just clumsy. She'd never have been able to live in this town if he'd know she was ogling him.

Now, for some unexplained reason, he was attracted to her. He wanted her. And there was no doubt that she wanted him. She picked up her peanut butter sandwich and nibbled on it. If there were some way to keep their affair a secret, maybe it would work. It was nobody's business but theirs if they slept together. And if no one else knew, well then, she wouldn't have to be embarrassed when it was over.

This was her chance. A chance to experience everything she'd always been curious about. To try things she'd always wondered about. Dreamed about.

Somehow, she knew that Mike could make her feel things she'd never felt before. And she wanted to feel them. Had waited long enough. This was her time. And better still, she would get full, uninhibited access to Mike's body. There were things she'd always wanted to do. Fantasies she wanted to fulfill. Just the thought of it made her nipples tighten. To cool her thoughts down she reached for the water bottle taking a long sip.

The light brush of something on her neck made her jerk forward. She tried to swallow the mouthful of water that she'd just taken, but ended up choking instead. She coughed and sputtered, trying to regain her breath. A large hand tapped her gently on the back and she knew. Mike.

She turned and glared up at him through watery eyes. He looked thoroughly amused. She jumped to her feet. "What do you think you are doing, sneaking up on me like that?" She placed her hands on her hips and waited for him to explain himself. Her defiant pose was ruined when she coughed once more, and then had to wipe at the tears in her eyes.

"I had to taste that little space at the back of your neck." He reached out and his hand wrapped around the back of her neck, his fingers caressing the small area left vulnerable between her blouse and hairline. "It looked so tempting with you leaning forward that I couldn't help myself."

Annabelle was stunned. She'd never considered her neck to be an erogenous zone before. It was, after all, just a neck. But now, she could feel his fingers moving slowly back and forth across her nape. The caress made her feel tingly all over her body. Against her will, she found herself moving closer to him. Her neck arched to one side. She wanted him to kiss her there again. Lick her. Bite her.

Oh, lord. The man was making her crazy. They had to come to some agreement before she spontaneously combusted. He had started this, but she would darn well finish it. Reaching out she tentatively ran her finger up his chest. His muscles were hard, and his shirt was slightly damp with sweat. His hand stilled at the back of her neck, but his breathing deepened.

"You're asking for trouble, Annabelle." His voice was deep and husky.

"Maybe, I want trouble." She gave him what she hoped was a seductive look. "You started something I want to explore further…"

Before she could say anything more, his arms encircled her and his lips covered hers. There was no tentative seeking this time. This was as carnal as it could get. His tongue swept inside her mouth, laying claim to it. His tongue, hot and moist, dueled with hers in a most primal way.

Over and over his tongue plunged into her mouth, mating with hers. It was all-consuming. Annabelle closed her eyes and gave herself up to the sensations. She was consumed by the maelstrom of desires coursing through her.

His hands moved from around her waist and slid down to cover her behind. He pulled her close and she could feel his arousal. With his hands still covering her bottom, he rocked her hips against his arousal in a seductive motion. It wasn't long before she was moving on her own. Closer, she needed to get closer. Their breathing was labored and hard.

The front door slammed shut and Mike jerked back as if someone had pulled him away. Annabelle started to sway, her balance unstable after that mind-numbing kiss. Gasping for air, she tried to catch her breath. Her head was spinning. Mike reached out with one hand to steady her. They could hear voices closing in on them. Annabelle stared at him in horror.

He pushed her towards the ladies' room in the back. "Go. Hurry and put yourself together and I'll stall them." Grateful, she fled.

She pushed into the bathroom and heard the door shut firmly behind her as she leaned her hands on the cool porcelain sink. She took a deep breath, raised her head and looked in the mirror. The woman staring back at her was not the woman she was familiar with. This was the woman from her dreams.

The woman in the mirror was flushed, her eyes were bright, almost feverish, and her lips were red and swollen. Her breathing was shallow, causing her breasts to push against her blouse. She looked hot. She wanted more. Some of her hair had come loose from her bun and made her look almost wanton. Her body was achy and damp. This was a woman ready for the bedroom, not the library.

Annabelle quickly ran cold water from the taps. Dampening a paper towel, she ran it over her face and neck. As drops of water trickled down her neck, she remembered the feel of Mike's hand and moaned. This wouldn't do. She took off her glasses and laid them on the side of the sink. She threw the paper towel away and cupped the water in her hands and splashed it over her face until she was cooled off.

She quickly dried her face and gave herself a critical stare in the mirror, squinting to get a better picture. She looked more like herself. With years of practice behind her, she quickly took down her hair and twisted it back into its habitual style. She jammed the clip back in to hold it in place. Annabelle tucked her blouse back into her skirt, donned her glasses and gave herself one last glance. Satisfied, she took a fortifying breath and left the bathroom.

As she approached the desk, she could hear ladies' voices followed by Mike's deep rumble. She plastered a smile on her face as she addressed the lady wearing the wide-brimmed straw hat and the long, flowered dress. "Mrs. Casey, how are you today?" Annabelle took her position behind her desk. She didn't glance at Mike, but she could feel his presence. She tried to ignore it.

"And how are you, Mrs. White?" Annabelle gave her attention to the woman in the faded jeans and baseball hat. The two older ladies were as different as day and night, but they were best friends and often came to the library together. "What can I get for you ladies today?"

"I brought you some apple muffins, Annabelle." Mrs. Casey removed her hat, carefully patting her hair her hair into place. "There's more than enough if you want to share."

The aroma wafting from the bag was incredible and Annabelle knew she had no choice. Both ladies were watching her expectantly. "Thank you, Mrs. Casey. You do make the best apple muffins." Lifting the bag, she opened it and held it out to Mike. "Muffin?"

"Don't mind if I do." He took his time and selected a muffin from the bag. Never taking his eyes from her, he bit into the treat. He chewed slowly and licked his lips after he swallowed.

Annabelle could only stand there and stare at him. His actions were blatantly sexual to her. Yet, as she glanced at the older ladies, they seemed to see nothing amiss.

Mike turned to Mrs. Casey. "They're delicious as always."

Mrs. Casey blushed like a schoolgirl, and gave him a big smile. "You're a charmer, Mike Sloan, and that's a fact." She turned to Annabelle. "Did you get those new mysteries in yet?"

Annabelle smiled. This was one of the reasons why she loved being a librarian. Helping others who loved books and reading as much as she did. "I put out some new ones this morning, but I kept this one back just for you." She pulled the latest Janet Evanovich hardcover from under the counter.

Mrs. Casey beamed her approval. "You're an angel, Annabelle. You just keep that here and we'll be back in a few minutes after we look at the other new ones." They nodded at Mike and then hurried off in search of more books.

Annabelle said nothing as she watched them scurry down an aisle. Mike's arms slid around her from behind and his voice was a soft whisper in her ear. "This isn't finished."

She nodded her agreement. It certainly wasn't over. Not by a long shot.

"Have dinner with me tonight." His lips teased the outer edge of her ear, his breath hot on her neck. "Dinner and maybe more. But only if it's what you want." He continued to trace the edge of her ear with his lips and his tongue.

"Yes." She tipped her head to give him better access. She closed her eyes and enjoyed the shivery sensations running through her body for one lingering moment before she reluctantly pulled away.

"We need to discuss the terms of our relationship, if indeed we're going to have one at all." She tried for a brisk tone, and knew she had succeeded when she caught a glimpse of irritation in his eyes.

"We already have one and you know it." Mike reached out for her, but she stepped back out of reach.

"Not here." She glanced nervously around the library, afraid the women would wander back before she and Mike were finished. "We'll talk tonight."

Mike followed her glance and then nodded abruptly. "Tonight. I'll pick you up at your place at seven."

He stood and waited for her agreement. When she finally nodded, he turned away and picked up his toolbox, which she hadn't noticed sitting by the side of the counter. He strode towards the front door. She watched him, unable to tear her gaze from his departing form. At the last second, he turned. "Your air-conditioning is fixed." The door closed behind him.

Annabelle slumped back onto the stool behind her and for the first time noticed the flow of cool air circulating in the room. Her thoughts turned to dinner tonight and she shivered, but not because she was cold. It didn't matter that the air-conditioning was working because Annabelle was still hot.

Chapter Three

જી

Annabelle looked around the room in utter dismay. Clothing was strewn across the bed, on the floor and over the wicker chair in the corner. It was the age-old dilemma of all women as they prepared for that most important date. She didn't have anything to wear. Nothing she owned seemed appropriate for dinner with Mike. The long skirts and dresses were suitable for work, but she wanted something that made her look, if not sexy, then at least nice.

She stomped back to the closet and peered at the few remaining hangers looking for inspiration. Something. Anything. She wanted to be casual enough so that anyone who saw them wouldn't make too much of them having dinner together. In future, she would cook for them. Or maybe they'd just skip food and go straight to bed. Why hadn't she thought of that before agreeing to dinner?

No. They had to come to terms. Experience had taught Annabelle that men weren't attracted to her. Not for long, anyway. So she'd tucked away her dreams of marriage. This was a chance for her to fully experience her sexuality, and she was more than ready to explore that side of herself. Especially with a man who attracted her as much as Mike did. She would settle for a no-strings affair. One that was their business. No one else could know. She didn't think that he'd object. Didn't every man want a woman who was willing to have sex with him, but didn't want a commitment? She thought so. Or at least that's what most of the woman's magazines bemoaned.

She wanted more than sex. She wanted her fantasies fulfilled and she sensed that Mike was the man who would not only make her dreams a reality, but he would enjoy them as well. And to be fair, she'd fulfill any of his fantasies as well.

She closed her eyes and wrapped her arms tight around her waist, envisioning what those fantasies might entail.

She imagined Mike standing behind her. Her naked and him fully clothed. He would gaze at her hungrily as she ran her hands over her own body, lifting and cupping her breasts for his inspection. She would taunt him with her body until he wanted her so much his restraint broke.

Annabelle was a little bit fuzzy on what would happen then, but she knew Mike would think of something. Unfortunately, nothing would happen unless she got some clothes on so that she and Mike could actually go out together. And while the fantasy had been great, the contents of the closet didn't look any better.

Getting through the rest of the afternoon at work had been a chore, but somehow Annabelle had managed to actually get some work done. She'd hid in her office most of the afternoon after one of her volunteers had shown up for her two-hour shift. Annabelle had buried herself in paperwork until closing time, eternally grateful that it was Friday.

Her nerves frayed at the thought of the upcoming evening, she had been driven to her secret vice. Chocolate. It was for emergencies only as it seemed to go straight to her hips whenever she ate it, but sometimes there was nothing else to do but give in to the craving. The heat had made it impossible for her to keep her favorite dark chocolate in her desk. Imported, dark chocolate was her weakness. But thank God for those wonderful makers of candy-coated chocolate that didn't melt. She'd devoured the entire bag while she'd worked. One at a time. Sucking all the candy off until nothing was left but the chocolate.

Closing the library at half past five, she had taken her time and driven home. She'd pulled her little blue compact car into her parking space at the small apartment building where she rented. It was really a converted Victorian home with four apartments of various sizes. Annabelle rented the smaller one-bedroom on the top floor. She would buy a house as soon as one she liked came on the market. For now, her apartment more than suited her needs.

Stopping in the porch, she opened her mailbox and collected her mail. She sorted through it as she climbed the stairs to the top floor. Junk mail and her monthly book review magazine were it, what a sad commentary on her life. She dug her key out of her purse and let herself into her apartment.

The minute she walked through the door, she felt more at ease. She dumped her purse and mail on the small table just inside the front door and retreated to the bathroom, tugging off her work clothes as she went.

She'd run a hot bath with lavender bath crystals and soaked for a good twenty minutes, washing away the stress of the day. She'd shaved her legs and smoothed lotion all over her body in preparation for the night to come. She'd taken pleasure in stoking the lotion up and down her legs, over her belly and breasts and even over her backside. She could imagine Mike running his hands over her body, her skin began to tingle and took on a rosy glow.

There was no choice to be made about her underwear. She only owned white cotton. For once in her life, she wished she'd indulged in satin or silk. Maybe even in blue or deep purple. As she pulled on her white cotton bra, she made a mental note to go shopping for at least a few new things. Even white satin and lace would look better than plain cotton and it would probably feel wonderful against her skin. Sensual. And darn it, she deserved to feel that way, even if she was the only one who ever knew what she was wearing underneath her clothes.

Thigh-high silk stockings would have been quite daring to wear on her date, but she didn't own any. Sensible nylon pantyhose filled her dresser drawers and, with the heat wave they were having, only an idiot would wear them. So her legs were bare, but they were smooth and soft after her bath. Running her hands over her thighs and calves, she pleased with the effect.

Her hair had been a dilemma. She'd contemplated leaving it down, but decided against it. That would bring too much attention if she saw anyone she knew. So she'd reluctantly bundled it back up into a new bun. A touch of mascara and lipstick and she was ready to get dressed.

And now, here she was almost ready, but still undecided about what to wear. A quick glance at her watch reminded her that it was ten to seven. Time was running out. From the rack, she plucked a long skirted dress with yellow daisies printed on a black background. The neck was scooped, but not low and there was a band that ran under her breasts and tied in the back. Nothing spectacular, but she always felt good when she wore it.

Turning first right and then left, she surveyed herself in the mirror. Not bad. On an impulse, she redid the tie in the back of the dress pulling it tighter before retying it in a bow. The top of the dress clung tighter and emphasized her breasts. They were substantial breasts, so she might as well make use of them. She decided she liked the whole effect, as drawing the eye to her breasts made her hips and waist look smaller. It made her look shapely. Who knew? She twirled in a circle and laughed at her own daring.

A knock came on her front door. She stopped spinning and grabbed the dresser for balance before giving herself one last peek in the mirror. A rosy color stained her cheeks as much from anticipation as from all the whirling about. This was as good as it got and actually better than she'd hoped for. She was ready and not a moment too soon.

Annabelle closed the door on the mess as she left her room, and hurried towards the front door. She swung it open and stared as Mike thrust a bouquet of violets towards her and stepped into her apartment. His large presence seemed to fill the room, making it seem smaller.

"For you." Mike offered the flowers, and she quickly took them from him.

"Thank you, they're beautiful." The response was automatic, but heartfelt as she buried her nose in the bouquet. No man had ever given her flowers before. She could feel tears forming in her eyes as she swallowed the lump in her throat, and turned away before Mike could see how much his gift had touched her. "I'll just put them in water."

Hoping she'd have time enough to regain her composure, she disappeared into the kitchen, still clutching the bouquet tightly to her chest. Violets were her absolute favorite flowers. She loved the color and the texture of them and on rare occasion bought them for herself. Had Mike asked at the flower shop or had it been a lucky guess? She chewed her bottom lip as she contemplated the fact that the florist might know that Mike was buying them for her. Better for her peace of mind if she assumed it was a lucky guess.

Reluctantly, she laid the bundle on the counter and pulled a Mason jar out of her cupboard. Carefully, she removed the paper and placed the flowers into the makeshift vase and added water. Using a kitchen towel, she dried her hands and dabbed at her eyes. Taking a deep, fortifying breath she picked up the bouquet. Her emotions firmly under control, she carried the arrangement back to the living room and laid it on the coffee table.

Mike reached out and clasped her hand as she stood back to admire the flowers. "You look beautiful." He used his grip on her hand to twirl her in a circle. The hem of her dress swirled around her legs.

"Thank you." She noted that his eyes were drawn to her breasts and she was suddenly uncomfortable. It was one thing to want to be the center of Mike's attention. It was quite another to actually experience it.

He raised her hand to his mouth and kissed her knuckles. One at a time his lips skimmed over them. Them his tongue slid between each one, licking each finger. His tongue was warm and moist against her skin. Finally, he captured her middle finger in his mouth and sucked on it even as his teeth carefully scraped the side of her finger. In and out. Over and over.

Annabelle was uncomfortable for an entirely different reason. Never would she have believed her fingers were an erogenous zone. They were fingers. Everyone had them, but what Mike was doing to them should be illegal. The sensations from her hand flowed through her whole body until she could feel it in her breasts and between her legs. The pulsing got stronger as Mike kept pleasuring her finger. Closing her eyes, Annabelle allowed herself to enjoy the sensation.

"Nothing will happen that you don't want to happen," Mike murmured in between caresses. "I promise."

Annabelle nodded, unable to speak, and reluctantly opened her eyes. Mike seemed to be totally focused on her face. Seeming satisfied with her response, he released her finger and kissed the palm of her hand before letting it go.

"We'd better get going or we'll be late for our dinner reservations." Mike placed his hand on her back and guided her towards the front door. Annabelle stopped long enough to collect a light sweater, her purse and keys before they left. She shut the door firmly behind her and locked it. With any luck she wouldn't be coming home alone tonight.

Mike seated Annabelle at their table at Gino's, one of the classier restaurants in town. The food was delicious and the atmosphere laid-back. Mike was thankful that he'd had the forethought to call ahead and request a secluded table in a quiet corner. This table suited him perfectly. Tucked away in a darkened corner, lit by soft lighting and candlelight, it had privacy that most of the other tables lacked.

The table was draped with a crisp white tablecloth, which flowed to the floor. Linen napkins adorned the table, set with fine china and crystal. A single red rose floated in a cut glass bowl, while a fat white pillar candle glowed from a silver holder. Annabelle looked right at home in such an elegant setting.

With her hair coiled up and her long flowing dress, she looked untouchable. Almost. The bright colors of the flowers on her dress hinted at the passion she hid beneath the clothing. He had noticed immediately that the dress was pulled tighter than usual, showing her gorgeous breasts to perfection. Most surprising was the impulse he'd had to loosen the belt or cover her with a wrap. He didn't want any other man getting a glimpse of those breasts. In all his years, Mike had never felt this possessive over a woman before.

His own nervousness surprised him. He dated frequently, but not seriously. This attraction to Annabelle felt different. Special. Never in his life had he put so much effort into getting a date with a woman. Well, not since Anna White in tenth grade. But this went way beyond anything he'd ever felt before.

The strange things was, rather than worry about it, he was reveling in it. Maybe it had something to do with the fact that at thirty-four years of age, after years of dating, he was smart enough to look for substance in a woman, not just appearance. Not that Annabelle wasn't pretty, but it was an understated beauty that would only get better with age. Beyond that, she was so much more.

He'd taken it upon himself to learn as much as he could about her, without being too obvious about it. Bringing up her name casually in conversation with friends had given him some information, and all of it confirmed what he felt about her. Annabelle was a kind, intelligent, giving woman. Everyone who knew her liked her, men and women, young and old, and everyone in between.

Right now, she was beginning to look a little bit uncomfortable and he realized he'd been quietly staring at her. That wouldn't do. He wanted her to be relaxed with him. To feel that she could let go and be herself.

"Have you eaten here before?" Casual conversation would put her at ease and besides, he really wanted to know everything there was no know about this fascinating woman.

Annabelle smiled shyly. "No. I've been wanting to try it, but it seemed to be the kind of place you'd wait and go with someone special."

Before Mike could comment, their waiter arrived at their table with menus. After the waiter took their order for two glasses of white wine, he left them alone to peruse the menus. Mike made some suggestions, having eaten here before, and by the time the waiter returned with their drinks and a basket of warm, yeasty bread and fresh butter, they had made their selections.

"We'll both have garden salads to start with and the lady will have the spaghetti." Mike collected Annabelle's menu and handed both of them back to the waiter. "I'll have the lasagna." The waiter took their order and left them alone once again.

Annabelle sipped nervously at her drink. "I hope the pasta doesn't have too much garlic. It makes my breath awful." She laid her wineglass down with a thump and buried her head in her hands. "I can't believe I said that." She looked at him imploringly. "Please tell me I didn't say that."

Mike laughed. He couldn't help himself. "You said it, but I thought it as well." He motioned to the basket of bread sitting in the middle of the table. "Why do you think that's not garlic bread?"

Annabelle giggled and then smiled at him. In that moment, she was the most beautiful woman he'd ever seen. If he lived to be a hundred, he didn't think he'd ever get tired of looking at her.

That exchange seemed to set the tone for their evening. They both relaxed and talked about their work and the goings-on in town. Mike was both surprised and pleased to find out that Annabelle knew his company specialized in custom home building. He found himself telling her about the projects he was working on at the moment. She was so good at drawing him out they had eaten half their meal before he realized she'd said little about herself.

He pointed his fork at her accusingly. "I know what you're doing."

"What am I doing?"

"You're being such a good listener that I'm doing all the talking." He laid down his fork, reaching across the table and took her hand. "I want to know about you."

Annabelle swallowed hard. "There's not much to tell." She seemed apologetic. "I'm not that interesting."

"You are to me." Mike released her hand and sat back to study her for a moment. He knew that she believed what she said, and he could only shake his head in wonder. "I want to know all about you. Your hopes. Your dreams." His voice lowered. "Your fantasies."

Annabelle suddenly seemed fascinated by the food left on her plate. She moved the spaghetti around with her fork, but didn't scoop up any to eat. This was interesting. Had she indulged in fantasies about him? He knew he certainly had. The trick would be getting past her natural reserve to the woman underneath.

Mike sighed. "Annabelle, look at me." He waited until her eyes met his. "Anything we say to each other stays between us. No one else will ever know."

Annabelle nodded reluctantly. She seemed to come to some decision, then squared her shoulders and opened her mouth to speak when the waiter suddenly appeared. Mike wanted to bang his head on the table in frustration, but refrained, knowing that Annabelle would think he'd lost his mind. And maybe he had, because all he could think about was having this woman in his life. In his bed.

Mike hung on to his patience while the waiter cleared the table and brought them coffee. Neither one of them wanted dessert. Mike watched Annabelle add sugar to her coffee and stir it endlessly. He cleared his voice. "Annabelle?"

Annabelle gave him a wry smile. "You don't give up. Do you?"

"Not when it's something I want. And I really want you." He watched her absorb his statement. He could tell she wasn't quite sure if she could believe him or not. Finally, she seemed to come to some inner conclusion as she nodded and began speaking.

"I was an only child to older parents. I was a quiet child, did well in school and went away to college." When Mike nodded encouragingly she continued. "I had one relationship in college, but then my father died and my mother got ill. I went back home to take care of her and after she died, I wanted a new start. I started looking for jobs and found this one." Annabelle finished in a rush.

Thankfully, she'd found this job or he might never have gotten the chance to know her. Then what she'd said sunk in. "You've only been with one man."

Were all the men she'd known crazy? Suddenly, he was glad they'd all missed the gem hiding in their midst. A feeling of possessiveness welled up within him. He'd found her and he was darn well going to keep her.

Annabelle blushed as he blurted out his rather blunt statement. Her cheeks were red, but her eyes were steady as she replied. "Yes. And I wasn't very good at it."

Mike could only stare at her, completely dumbfounded. She was one of the most naturally sexy women he'd ever met. The way she'd responded to his kisses. Her little moans. The way she unconsciously rubbed herself against him. He found himself aroused just thinking about it. If she were any sexier, he'd have burned to cinder.

She'd looked away from him and was now fidgeting with the strap of her watch. She looked so lost and unsure, his heart ached for her. It was his job to let her know how sexy she was and he had a feeling that just telling her wouldn't work. He had to show her as well. She gave him a startled look as he shifted his chair closer to hers.

He reached under the long tablecloth and found her leg. Slowly, he pushed up her dress until he had access to the naked skin underneath. He thanked the lord and the weatherman that it was too hot to wear pantyhose. Mike trailed his fingers slowly up the inside of her thigh.

Annabelle had frozen at the first touch of his hand on her leg, but then she'd relaxed and her legs had actually opened a small amount to give him access. Encouraged, Mike's fingers continued to play over her skin. He trailed his fingers up and down the inside of her thighs, skimming close to the top but not quite touching her panties.

Her skin was smooth and soft, and Mike entertained himself with thoughts of rubbing his face over those amazing legs before he finally buried his face between them, tasting her. To lick her and suck on her clitoris until she screamed her release. Her breathing got heavier and her legs fell open even more. Mike allowed his fingers to gently slide over the crotch of her panties.

Unselfconsciously, as if she couldn't stop herself, Annabelle's hips moved to meet his fingers. Mike could feel his erection straining at the zipper of his dress pants, but he didn't care. The secluded darkness of the corner, and the long tablecloth, shielded them from prying eyes. He was in pain, but the look on her face was so sensual, there was no way he would stop.

Annabelle had tilted her head back slightly and closed her eyes. Her skin had a rosy glow and her lips parted on a low moan. Mike could feel the dampness on his fingers through her cotton panties. She was so wet, so ready. Mike felt his own body clench as his testicles drew tight to his body. He hadn't been this close to losing control of his own body since he was a teenager. And they were in a restaurant.

That thought put the brakes on Mike's advances. He knew she'd be embarrassed if she actually climaxed in a public place. He'd only wanted to make a point, not drive them both over the edge. He carefully pulled his hand away.

Annabelle shuddered and slowly her eyes opened. They were unfocused at first as she looked at him. He loved that he'd made her lose all her inhibitions. All at once she seemed to remember where they were and looked around in disbelief. Hot color shot up her cheeks, but he refused to let her be ashamed of herself.

"You're the sexiest woman I've ever met." He brought his fingers that had caressed her to his nose and sniffed. "I can still smell you. You smell sexy." His tongue reached out and licked the top of his finger. "You taste hot."

Mike could tell she was partly horrified by what they had done, but she was also very aroused by it as well. That was the opening he needed.

"We'd be so very good together, Annabelle. Think about it. We could do whatever you wanted, whenever you wanted."

He groaned inwardly when her tongue slipped out and licked her lips nervously. He wanted to haul her over his shoulder and drag her out of the restaurant. He wanted to keep her in his bed for at least a week, maybe two, before he even considered letting her out for a break.

Annabelle opened her mouth to speak. Closed it. Took a sip of coffee and tried again. "I want to sleep with you. I have things I want to do. To try." She held up her hand to stop him before he could speak. "But I have conditions."

"Anything." Mike agreed readily. They could always renegotiate terms later.

"I don't want anyone else to know about us. That way when we're finished with each other, it's nobody's business but ours." She chewed on her lip nervously, as if afraid he would say no to her terms.

Mike sat back in his chair and crossed his arms across his chest. A deep anger began to simmer inside him. "Let me get this straight. You want to sleep with me, but you don't want to have a real relationship with me."

He felt like he might explode when Annabelle smiled and nodded at him. The muscles in his arms were clenched tight as he resisted the temptation to pull her to her to her feet and shake her until she came to her senses. The fact that she felt relieved only heightened his anger. "Why the hell not?"

Annabelle seemed taken aback by his anger, her eyes widened and she shifted nervously in her seat. So she should, he thought. How dare she try and cheapen what they have together? He said nothing, waiting for her to reply, not willing to lessen her discomfort. Not about this.

"Well," Annabelle looked around to make sure the waiter wasn't around. She chewed on her lip and he sensed her anxiety. Watching her teeth play over her lip, Mike had the sudden urge to nibble on those luscious lips himself. He would need hours to properly explore her mouth. Very pleasurable hours.

"If people know about us, then when you don't want me anymore, people will pity me and talk about me. I know this isn't about marriage, I like my job, and the town…" Annabelle trailed off into silence suddenly becoming very interested in the tablecloth.

Mike was stunned. This wasn't about him at all. This was about her and her insecurities as a woman. What kind of idiot had she been with before that she felt a man would only want her for a short while? Mike had the sudden urge to find the loser and beat him senseless for the harm he'd obviously wreaked on Annabelle's self-esteem. Just the thought of it was enough to make his blood pressure soar. He took a deep cleansing breath to calm his growing anger. The object of that anger was nowhere in sight and a show of temper was the last thing that Annabelle needed.

Annabelle sat across from him, patiently waiting for his answer. The only sign of her agitation was in the slight trembling of her hand as she sipped her now cold coffee. At that small betraying tremor, Mike felt his heart turn over. She still hadn't looked him straight in the face since she'd finished her little speech.

Sureness settled over Mike as he watched her. He knew she wouldn't believe him if he told her he did *indeed* have marriage on his mind. She'd certainly think he was handing her a line. He'd have to show her instead. His actions would prove to her how desirable she was as a woman and a partner. He wanted her to know her power as a woman and then choose him.

The silence between them had lasted for several minutes. It was not a comfortable silence. The very air around them almost crackled with the tension. Mike decided that the first step in his plan was to make her comfortable with him again. So he would agree to her terms, letting her have control of the situation, letting her take the lead. He didn't mind. He was confident now that he would eventually get what he wanted. Annabelle, forever.

"If that's the way you want it, then that's the way we'll play it." He was rewarded when she gave him a shy look, full of promise. Her lips tilted up at the corners until a smile lit her face with a beauty that almost took his breath away. When she nodded, he felt compelled to add. "For now."

Annabelle didn't seem to take exception at this addition. He could tell that she was feeling more confident and in control of the situation. Now that all the terms had been settled to her satisfaction, she looked happy.

Mike felt the anticipation rise up in him. Life was looking very promising at the moment. He intended to fulfill every fantasy she'd ever had and, hopefully, in the process fulfill a few of his own. His whole body clenched in anticipation as he watched her relax even more.

Annabelle began to chat about work. It was only then that he understood just how uptight she'd been during dinner. This was a different Annabelle altogether, and this woman was even more entrancing. She entertained him with her exploits of catching two young twelve-year-old boys ogling naked women in a book on women's health.

"They turned so red when I asked if I could help them with their research," she laughed, "and they ran off just as I was trying to give them a book specifically geared towards the questions young boys have about their sexuality." Her eyes sparkled as she continued. "Honestly, I was just trying to help them become better informed." She paused for a breath. "They were so cute."

Mike laughed at her story, unable to help himself as he pictured the boys in his mind. Having been one himself, he understood their fascination on the very same subject. What Annabelle didn't seem to understand was, that it was something a man never seemed to outgrow. And his own body was making him very aware of the consequences of thinking about such things. It was time to leave. Mike signaled the waiter.

When the waiter presented the bill, Mike paid quickly and escorted Annabelle from the restaurant. He nodded at a few people he knew and saw Annabelle do the same. They didn't stop to speak to anyone, neither of them wanting to linger.

The silence continued as Mike guided her across the parking lot. His hand rested on the small of her back, but instead of just leaving it in one spot, he rubbed small circles on her back as they walked. She leaned back into his hand instead of pulling away and unable to resist he slid his hand around her side and gave her a quick squeeze as they reached the vehicle.

Mike settled her into the passenger seat of his car, making sure her dress was in no danger of being caught when he closed the door. His hand grazed her leg. Her skin was warm and smooth. Annabelle made more of a sweet moan than a gasp. Her leg twitched and moved restlessly. Hastily pulling the seat belt across her he clicked it into place. His fingers grazed her breast and he could feel her tight nipple through the thin fabric of her dress. She moved sensuously against his fingers and her breath quickened. Mike swore under his breath, closed the door, and took a deep breath of evening air before he walked around and climbed in on the driver's side. He put the keys in the ignition, but didn't start the car.

He turned slightly in his seat and reached out to cup Annabelle's chin in his hand. "Do you want to go to your place or mine?"

She licked her lips nervously, but spoke without any hesitation. "Yours."

Mike reached over and gave her a quick kiss on the lips. "My place it is. Relax and enjoy. It's just a short drive out of town." He started the car, put the vehicle in gear, and pulled out of the parking lot and into the night.

Mike was fiercely glad that she had chosen his home over hers. It was a primitive response, he knew, but he wanted her in his home. He wanted her to get used to being there, because if he had his way, she would never want to leave.

Chapter Four

ဢ

Annabelle was quiet on the drive to Mike's home. She was committed to making love with him, but she was still nervous. Her hands clutched at the purse in her lap, giving her something solid to hold onto.

"Almost there." Mike's voice was soft as if he was afraid he would spook her and she would jump out of the car and run away.

She needed to say something. Anything. She cleared her voice. "It's a nice night, isn't it?"

Had she really said that? She buried her face in her hands.

"Yes, you really did say that and it is a beautiful evening."

Annabelle groaned. She hadn't been aware of speaking aloud. She felt the soft touch of his hand as it caressed the top of her head. The contact sent a shiver down her spine.

"Are you cold or just nervous?" Mike's hand never lost contact with her as he spoke.

Mike was waiting for an answer and the time had come for her to stop hiding. She straightened up and turned to look at him. His features were shrouded in the dark interior, but every time they passed a streetlight she could catch a glimpse of him. He was big, solid and gorgeous. And she wanted him.

"I'm nervous, but excited too." Annabelle reached out and placed her hand on his thigh. It was rock-hard. She was encouraged when Mike suddenly placed both hands on the wheel and gripped it tight.

She moved her hand over his thigh. Up and down. The muscles flexed beneath her hand. She loved the feel of him.

Annabelle could only imagine how he would feel without his clothes.

"You're playing with fire," Mike growled. He captured her hand with his and then slid it further in front of him. His erection was obvious and hard.

"Oh, my." Annabelle was enthralled by her effect on him. She'd never realized that a man's arousal could excite her. It certainly never had before.

Mike raised her hand to his lips and kissed it before returning it to the seat next to him. "I want to get us home in one piece, so honey, you have to keep your hands to yourself until we get there." His voice dropped to a husky whisper. "Once we get to my place, you can do anything your heart desires."

The possibilities fueled her imagination, and by the time she could find her voice to speak again, Mike was turning off the main road and into a tree-lined driveway. They were about ten minutes outside of town and most of the area was wooded and secluded.

Annabelle looked out of her window with interest and couldn't stop the gasp of wonder that followed when his home came into her view. It wasn't overly large, but it was absolutely breathtaking. At least what she could see from the porch light and headlights of the car.

Mike parked the car next to his truck, shut off the engine, and sat back in his seat. "So what do you think?"

"It's beautiful." Mike seemed to relax when she spoke, and until that moment she'd had no idea that he was tense too. Oddly enough, that fact helped her to relax.

"Wait for me." Mike got out of the car and came around to open her door. He took her hand as he helped her out; tucking it in the crook of his arm, he led her to the front porch.

Annabelle stopped at the bottom of the steps and looked up in wonder. Mike's home was a two-story log home. The front steps led up to a covered porch, which wrapped around the home on both sides.

"The porch goes around to the back, too." Mike ushered her up the stairs. "And there's a porch swing in the back."

"Can we try it?"

"Not the first time, maybe later." Mike let go of her long enough to unlock the door and usher her inside. It took her a moment to understand Mike's comment about the swing. Her first reaction wasn't prudish like she would have thought. It was intrigue. She wondered what they could do in that swing.

Mike turned on the light and Annabelle looked around with interest. She had to admit she was curious. She wanted to know everything about Mike.

"Welcome home."

Before she had time to think about the implications of Mike's words, he'd bent down and swept her into his arms. Taken off balance by his actions, she grabbed on to him to keep from falling.

Mike stared down at her with a tender look in his eyes, and then he leaned down and kissed her. It started out as a simple kiss. A meeting of lips, slightly tentative and searching at first. Then his tongue swept into her mouth and it became a claiming. He was staking out his territory and didn't care if she knew it. She reveled in it.

Her hands slid up around his neck and she clasped his hair to hold him to her. Her tongue stroked his. The heat was incredible. He tasted so good. He was better than chocolate and twice as sinful. She gave herself up to the kiss. Savoring and enjoying the sensations.

Mike was moving. She could feel him climbing stairs, but she was too caught up in their kiss to care. She could see the house later. For now, all that mattered was Mike. She tugged his hair in protest when he started to pull back from their kiss. He gave a half-laugh, half-groan as he gave her one last hard kiss on the lips before lowering her feet to the floor.

Annabelle was a little unsteady when her feet touched the floor. She swayed slightly, but Mike didn't let go of her. Instead he went down on one knee in front of her. Lifting her right foot, he slid her shoe off. Annabelle grasped his shoulders for balance. He then performed the same service for the other foot.

Still on one knee, Mike wrapped his arms around her waist and just held her. Annabelle was touched by the tenderness of the moment. Her breathing was uneven and tears came to her eyes, even as she blinked furiously to fight them back.

It was a moment she knew she would never forget. Her decision to become his lover was right and she knew, whatever the outcome, she would never regret it. His head was pressed against her stomach and she could feel his breath, hot and moist through the thin fabric of her dress.

"Remember, if I do anything you don't like, just tell me to stop and I will." He kissed her stomach and then stood. "Tell me what you want and I'll fulfill any fantasy I can."

Annabelle could feel her body changing. Her breasts felt heavy and achy. Her stomach was quivering, and she could feel the dampness between her legs. Physically, she wanted this man. Of that, there was no doubt. She now realized she wanted all of him—heart, mind and body. But she'd take what she could get.

Mike left her for a moment. A soft light flicked on. Annabelle flinched as if a spotlight had hit her. "Do we have to have the lights on?" She bit her lip nervously.

"Not if you don't want to, but I really want to look at you." His heated gaze traveled the length of her body from the top of her hair to the tip of her bare toes. "I want to see every part of you, naked." He moved closer to her. "I want to see you, touch you, taste you."

"Oh, yes," Annabelle sighed. The visions his words brought to her mind sent her heart racing.

Mike couldn't take his eyes off Annabelle as she moaned. She had the look of a woman in the throws of an orgasm. Her head was tilted slightly back, her eyes were closed and her lips were parted slightly. At that moment, he knew he'd never seen a more beautiful woman in his life.

The feelings she brought out in him were extreme. On the one hand, he wanted to treat her with care and carefully make love to her all night long, pleasuring and pleasing her. On the other hand, he wanted to toss her on the bed and fuck her every way possible until they were both exhausted sweaty heaps on the bed.

Then he wanted to do it all over again.

Mike sauntered across the bedroom until he stood directly in front of Annabelle. "Let's just get this dress off you." Mike reached out and turned her around until her back was to him. He gripped the ties of her dress and pulled slowly. They parted and the dress loosened around her.

Annabelle hunched her shoulders a little. "I didn't think about getting out of this dress when I put it on tonight. It's got to come off over my head."

"No problem." Before she had time to worry herself too much, he reached down and grasped the skirt of the dress and pulled it up and over the top of her head. She raised her arms to help him, and in less than a second it was off.

Mike reached around Annabelle and cupped her breasts through her sensible cotton bra. Annabelle was quite a handful. He molded her large, soft breasts with his hands and gently teased her nipples with his fingers. She moved with his hands, thrusting her breasts deeper into his palms.

Her nipples puckered to sharp points beneath the cotton and Mike increased the pressure slightly as he rolled them between his thumb and forefinger. Annabelle moaned and her head fell back against his chest. Her neck was too much temptation and he bent to taste it. He licked her skin and savored the salty flavor before nibbling his way up to her ear.

Tracing the curves of her delectable ears with his tongue was a turn-on. Annabelle was a moaner and her cries got louder when his tongue swirled inside her ear. His dick was hard as a rock and he eased himself by rubbing it against her sweet little ass. The sensation was amazingly stimulating through the fabric of their clothing. Mike almost lost his control imagining how it would feel skin to skin.

When her hips started to undulate, he kept his right hand on her breast, but allowed his left hand to slide down her belly. He pulled her back even closer and ground his erection between the cleft of her behind. Annabelle pushed back against him and he tortured himself by sliding himself up and down her bottom. Her neck beckoned him again and he nipped his way down to her shoulder.

Needing to feel more of her, his hand slipped past the waistband of her underwear until he came to the curls hidden within. He didn't stop.

His fingers combed through the curls in search of her clitoris. He allowed his index finger to slide back and forth. "Open your legs and let me in."

Annabelle didn't hesitate, instead parted her legs. He immediately slid his middle finger straight inside her. Annabelle moaned and moved against his hand. He could feel her wetness on his fingers. Unable to stop himself, he continued to grind his erection into the softness of her cotton-covered ass. It took all of his willpower not to come there and then.

He gritted his teeth together and concentrated on Annabelle. He continued to play with her breasts as his finger continued to thrust in and out of her. He could feel her body tightening on his finger. "Let go and come for me, sweetheart."

Mike kissed the side of her neck and bit it slightly just as he thrust his finger back inside her. He felt her suddenly tense and then she let go. She moaned and started to slide to the floor, so he abandoned her breast and wrapped his arm around her waist instead, while his fingers finished their work.

"You're so sexy." Mike reluctantly slid his fingers out of her panties and hugged her from behind. He held her tight against his erection, loving the feel of her pressed so tight against him.

Annabelle suddenly buried her face in her hands and tremors shook her whole body. Mike was instantly alarmed. He lifted her into his arms and sat down on the side of the bed with her cradled tight in his embrace.

"It's all right," he muttered as he rocked her back and forth and kissed the top of her head. "Did I hurt you?" He waited for some sign, but Annabelle said nothing. She continued to shake in his arms.

Unable to wait any longer, he gently pried her hands away from her face. Tears fell down her cheek, but she was laughing as well.

"I didn't know. I just didn't know."

Instant relief flooded him. This he could deal with. So his Annabelle had never had an orgasm before. "There's more where that one came from." Mike grinned at the stunned look on her face and just nodded when she looked uncertain.

He wasn't prepared when she threw herself at him and they both tumbled back onto the bed. Annabelle peppered his face with kisses. "Thank you. Thank you. That was absolutely amazing."

He pulled her on top of him and savored the look of pure enjoyment in her eyes. The fact that he had made her feel this way filled him with pride. It was also a huge turn-on, and his dick twitched beneath his pants as it felt her softness above him.

The moment she felt his erection push into her stomach, she stilled and looked at him quizzically. "But you didn't..." she trailed off uncertainly.

"No, but I will," he assured her. "That was only the beginning." Unable to resist, Mike reached behind her and unhooked her bra. When it came free he quickly tugged it down her arms and threw it to the floor.

She was more amazing then he'd even imagined. Her breasts were full, her nipples large and dusty rose in color. Her skin was soft and supple under his hands as he shaped and kneaded her breasts.

He watched her as he teased her nipples, enjoying her uninhibited display of delight. Her head was thrown back and her chest heaved up and down as she panted in rhythm to his touch. He could feel the heat from her sex on his belly. She was so responsive to him as if she had been fashioned specifically for his enjoyment. He could spend all night just looking at her. On second thought, he would rather taste her.

He positioned her so that she was straddling him and her breasts were level with his mouth. He reached out and licked slowly around her nipples, but not touching them. Like licking around the edge of an ice cream cone without sucking on the top. Round and round he traced the edges of her nipples.

Annabelle squirmed over him, but still he did nothing but tease her. Mike knew what she wanted, but he wanted her to ask for it. To demand it as her due. He could feel the wetness of her orgasm through her panties as she rubbed against him. Her breath was as ragged as his was.

"Suck on them," she ordered as she tugged on his head.

Mike obeyed instantly, drawing her nipple into his mouth and sucking hard. Annabelle groaned and ground her body against him, her movements becoming more frantic as he continued to suckle her hard. He couldn't believe that she was this close to coming again. Damn, she was hot.

Mike grasped her hips and moved her so that she was covering his arousal. And although it was almost too painful to bear, it was also the most pleasurable thing that he'd ever felt in his entire life.

Her heat surrounded his erection even through the layers of her panties and his pants. Gripping her tighter, he worked her back and forth against his erection as he continued to suck on her breasts, alternating back and forth between them.

He was one second from coming in his pants for the first time since his early teens when he felt her orgasm begin within her. She simply gave herself up to the pleasure. His Annabelle was a moaner, and she came long and loud. When it was over, she collapsed on top of him.

Mike pulled her to his side and hugged her. He had to have her or he would either go insane or come in his pants. When he started to ease himself off the bed, Annabelle tugged him back. He gave her a quick kiss and pulled back. "Let me get my clothes off."

Annabelle froze. She looked at him as if seeing him for the first time. "You're still dressed." She looked at herself. "And I'm… Well, I'm not quite undressed all the way either."

Mike ran his hand over the top of her head. She looked so bewildered. "But you will be." He rose from the bed and started to remove his shirt.

Chapter Five

✍

Annabelle lay on the bed and watched Mike unbutton his shirt. As it gaped open, she was rewarded with the sight of his muscular chest. He pulled his shirt off and tossed it over the chair in the corner. Her mouth went dry. She knew he was well built, but without clothes, he appeared massive. The muscles in his arms rippled with each movement he made. He was a perfect specimen of masculinity, and she wanted him.

He bent over and undid his shoes. Taking his time, he removed them and laid them by the chair in the corner. Then he turned and faced her.

Unselfconsciously, he unzipped his pants and slid them off. They joined his shirt in the corner. His underwear and socks followed. Then he stood before her, allowing her an unrestricted view of him.

He fascinated her. He was all rugged male, from his long dark hair, which was kept tied back, to his large feet. His shoulders were wide, his stomach flat and muscled, his thighs rock-hard. A light sprinkling of dark hair covered his chest, and her fingers itched to touch it. He was impressive. Almost intimidating. He was a healthy male animal in his prime. His penis jutted out in front of him, giving no doubt as to his readiness.

She swallowed hard. This was all for her. He was standing there for her perusal to allow her the time to get used to him. To accept him. She reached out her hand and he came toward her. He took her hand in his and kissed it before lowering himself to sit beside her.

It was then she became aware of her own vulnerability. Her nakedness. Instinctively, her hands covered her breasts.

She was glad for the presence of her underwear. As little protection as it provided from his heated gaze, it was something.

"Hey, don't hide from me." Mike reached out and coaxed her hands away from her breasts. Bending down he kissed them both. "They're so lovely."

Annabelle relaxed in spite of herself. Her body remembered the pleasure he had already given her and wanted more. Encouraged by unspoken assent, he sat up and reached for the waistband of her panties. Slowly, giving her time to stop him if she chose, he tugged her them off. She was left lying naked on the bed before him.

Part of her felt terribly exposed. The other part of her was fiercely proud that he wanted her as much as he obviously did.

Mike stretched out beside her. Propping himself up on one arm, he gathered her close with the other. His dark head dipped towards her and all thought fled. There was only Mike, and the magic of his touch. His lips sought hers in a searing kiss. There was no hesitation now. He thrust his tongue inside her mouth, teasing her, enticing her. His breathing was harsh, his kiss all-consuming.

Annabelle ran her hands over his shoulders, loving the play of his muscles under her fingers. Reaching up, she did what she had been dying to do for days. She pulled at the narrow strip of leather that confined his hair until it came away in her hand. She tossed it aside and then threaded her fingers through his hair. It was so soft, and incredibly sexy.

Mike groaned at her touch and broke away from her mouth. He kissed a trail down her neck, stopping to nip hard on her neck. It stung a little, but drove her wild. She clasped his head to her as he licked the sting away.

He worked his way down her body, licking and nipping at her breasts until she was panting hard. Her legs moved in a restless dance on the sheets. He threw one of his legs across her to pin her to the bed while he continued to play with her breasts.

"I can't take much more," she gasped.

"You can. And you will." It was a threat and a promise all at once.

He watched her as he gripped both of her thighs in his hands and slowly spread her legs to make room for him. He shifted so he was sitting between her legs with her thighs draped over his.

When she started to protest, he leaned over and placed a finger over her lips. "Shh, let me do this for you." He rubbed his fingers across her lips until she opened them. He slipped his finger inside her mouth. "Suck." It was a one-word command that she obeyed.

She sucked and licked his finger. This was something she wanted to try later with his penis and from the look in his eyes, he would let her. Without warning, he withdrew his finger and held it in front of her. It was large and damp.

"Open your legs wide for me." His voice was mesmerizing and she did as he asked. He rewarded her by sliding the same finger that had been inside her mouth into her vagina. It was shocking and erotic all at once. He kept his finger still, not moving it at all. Annabelle moved her hips trying to encourage him to move inside her. Instead, he removed his finger totally and she moaned in protest.

"Shh," he whispered and his finger slid over the lips of her sex. He parted her with his other hand so that he had a better view of her. "You're so pink and lush and hot." His finger flicked over her engorged clitoris and Annabelle moaned and twisted her hips. His words and his actions were bringing her to the brink again.

"I want more." Her head thrashed back and forth on the pillow as her hips pumped wildly into the air.

Mike slid his finger inside her. He withdrew it and then plunged in again. The rhythm was steady and intoxicating.

Annabelle instinctively tried to close her legs when his finger entered her. He quickly withdrew it from her. "Keep your legs open. It will be better that way. I promise."

Annabelle thrust her legs as far apart as she could. Anything to get him to finish. She was so close now. Mike continued to move his finger back and forth within her. The sensations built inside her.

Annabelle could feel herself coming again. She gave herself over to the powerful release. Her legs instinctively closed over Mike's hand keeping it close to her. He didn't disappoint her, but kept up the steady pressure until she was spent. When it was over, she sunk back into the mattress in a sated stupor. Her entire body felt boneless.

Mike pulled away from her and reached over to the bedside table. Pulling open the drawer, he thrust his hand inside, and pulled out a condom. Ripping it open, he quickly sheathed himself and then moved back between her legs.

Shifting her slightly for a better angle, he slowly pushed himself inside her. The feeling was almost overwhelming. She was tight, the delicate muscles within already swollen from her releases, and he was so big. She squirmed a little in an attempt to get comfortable.

"Relax, honey. Just relax." He was trying very hard not to move. The muscles of his arms stood out in relief as his hands clenched tight. His head was thrown back and his teeth were clenched.

The longer he was inside her, the better it got. She was amazed at his self-restraint and knew it was all for her. The fact that he would exercise such self-control made her want him even more. "You feel so big and hot inside me." She wanted him to know how much she wanted him, but didn't know what to say. Instead, she grabbed onto his butt and wrapped her legs around his waist.

It was all the encouragement he seemed to need and his control finally snapped. His hips pumped back and forth, getting faster and harder with each thrust. His breathing got harsher and she could feel beads of sweat roll down his back.

Surprisingly, she could feel her own body come to life again. The sensation started low in her belly. Every time he thrust forward she tilted her hips up to meet him and the friction against her clitoris soon had her moving her hips in rhythm with his, straining to reach orgasm again. Her head tilted back on the pillow and her hands gripped the sheets. Her whole body was alive and reaching for that explosive feeling again.

Mike's grip on her waist grew tighter as he drove into her, again and again. She dropped her feet to the mattress and drove herself up to meet his thrusts. He came on that stroke. He groaned and slammed his body into hers one more time. His whole body tensed as he emptied himself. The sensation drove her over the edge and she came once again. Her inner muscles clasped his penis tight inside of her. Mike swore and ground himself against her. Her body tightened on his once more and he gave one final groan before he collapsed on top of her.

She lay there totally exhausted and replete. Annabelle had never felt such contentment in her entire life. Her body was sprawled, open and naked and she just didn't care. Her limbs were heavy and so were her eyes, so she closed them and actually dozed. She didn't know how much time had passed before she woke and found the energy to turn her head and look at Mike.

Face down in the pillow next to her head, he didn't move. His eyes were closed and his features were relaxed. His hair tangled around his face and as she watched a bead of sweat rolled down the side of his temple. Annabelle became aware of just how sweaty and sticky she was herself. She'd do something about it, just as soon as she could gather enough energy to move.

As if he felt her gaze, Mike shifted until he was looking straight at her. "That was amazing." His hand came up to push aside a strand of hair that had fallen from her bun. "I can't believe your hair is still up."

He sounded amused by that fact, but she was in too good a mood to mind his teasing. With some effort, he levered himself off the bed and padded into the bathroom that was part of the master suite. She heard water running and a moment later he returned to the bed, the used condom disposed of.

She didn't notice the washcloth in his hand until he nudged her thighs open and started to wash her. The cloth was wet and cool. The sensation was surprisingly comforting and sensual all at once. His whole concentration was on what he was doing. He traced the lips of her sex and dipped in around the opening. When the cloth grazed her sensitive clitoris, Annabelle's hips moved even as she groaned in embarrassment. Seemingly satisfied with what he'd done, Mike removed the cloth from between her legs and laid it on the bedside table.

"Let's get you more comfortable." Mike grasped her hands and pulled her into a sitting position. Reaching behind her head, his large hands pulled the remaining pins from her hair.

He combed through the long length of hair with his fingers. "It goes all the way to your waist." He brought a lock of her hair to his face and ran it over his lips. "I want to feel your hair all over my body."

She nodded her agreement. She wanted to drape him in her hair and tease him with it. There was a temptress inside of her who longed to get out. She yawned in spite of herself. The spirit was willing, but the flesh was tired.

"Later. Sleep now." Mike murmured to her as he tugged back the covers and tucked her beneath the cotton sheet. He turned off the bedside lamp, slipped into bed beside her, and drew her into his arms.

She drifted off to sleep feeling better than she'd ever felt in her life. The last thought in her head as she drifted off to sleep was that there was still so much she wanted to try.

Annabelle was having the most wonderful dream. Her lover was lying behind her and his arms were wrapped around her. His nimble fingers played with her breasts while his lips nibbled on her neck. She sighed and arched herself into his embrace, thrusting her breasts into his large, capable hands.

"God, you feel so good."

The sound of a male voice growling in her ear woke her. This was no dream. She was wrapped tight in Mike's arms and he was no phantom.

She gave herself over to the sensations he aroused in her. After tonight, there was no doubt in her mind that she was a sensual woman. Her one dismal encounter in college had not been because of any defect in her, as she had always feared. Mike had made sure that she would never doubt her desirability again.

Armed with a new sense of power and determination, she slipped from his grasp and turned to face him. It was her turn now.

The look in his eyes was tender and loving as he smoothed her hair back from her face and down over her back. His hand followed a lock of her hair all the way to her behind, caressing, testing and teasing.

"Stop that." The command came out sharper than she intended and he stilled instantly. His gaze lost its sleepy, sated look and became concerned.

"Did I hurt you?" Mike caught her chin in his hand until she looked at him. "Are you sore?"

Annabelle could feel herself blush. Not exactly the image of a sex goddess. "No, I'm not sore." Annabelle bit her lip, unable to stop herself from being totally honest. "Not too sore anyway."

"We don't have to do anything else." Mike kissed her softly on the lips. "Just stay with me." He continued to cover her face in kisses.

"I want to stay." Annabelle hesitated, wanting to make her own demands but not sure what to say.

Mike sensed her hesitation. "What is it, honey?" He pulled back and waited. "You can tell me anything."

"I want my turn." She blurted out her demands before she chickened out.

"Your turn for what?" Mike seemed more perplexed than concerned.

Annabelle took a deep breath. She wasn't explaining herself very well. She tried again. "Before. When we..."

"When we made love," Mike added encouragingly.

"Yes. You got to do things for me. I want my turn. I want to do things for you." Annabelle finished in a rush and waited with her breath held for his reaction.

"You want to do things to me?" Mike looked intrigued by her statement.

"Yes."

Mike flopped back onto the bed and tucked his hands under his head. "I'm all yours."

"Really." She couldn't believe it was this easy.

"You can do whatever you want." His smile was relaxed. "As long as you remember that I'll get my turn again later."

Annabelle sat up in bed and looked at him lying there. He really was gorgeous. She hardly knew where to begin. She licked her lips in anticipation and was rewarded by the flare of desire in Mike's eyes.

Slowly, she eased the covers back until he was totally uncovered. It said something about how comfortable she was with Mike that she was more concerned with the fact that he was naked than with her own nudity. It felt natural and right to be sitting here next to him covered in nothing but her hair.

Bending down, she slowly licked his lips and was rewarded with a groan. He tried to deepen the kiss, but she pulled away. "If I let you kiss me, I'll never have my turn."

"I'm at your disposal, honey." Mike was fully aroused now and she had no doubt that he wanted her. She wanted more.

Annabelle nibbled her way down his neck and across his chest. Her fingers threaded through the hair on his chest and she rubbed her face against it, loving the soft feel of it against her skin. Taking her time, she used her tongue to play with nipples that were flat and brown. When his hand wrapped around the back of her head to encourage her, she got bolder. Using her teeth, she carefully bit him.

"Annabelle," he groaned.

She abandoned his chest and kissed his stomach. She could feel the muscles flex as he stiffened at her touch. Sitting back a little, she caught his gaze. She gathered her hair in one of her hands and trailed the end of it over his stomach, letting it glide over his chest and stomach, down his legs and across his thighs. She avoided his penis, which was fully aroused and swollen.

Mike started to reach for her, but she pulled back. "No. You promised me my turn." She waited for a moment and was relieved when his hands dropped to the mattress beside him.

Annabelle knew that Mike's patience wouldn't last much longer so she did what she'd been dying to do all evening. Without warning, she bent over and took Mike's penis into her mouth and sucked. Hard.

Mike almost shot off the bed. "Annabelle!"

She sat back, her eyes huge and uncertain. "Did I do it wrong?" She bit her lip as she waited. She so wanted to do this right. To be the temptress like in her dreams.

His eyes blazed with desire, but when he reached out to touch her cheek, his touch was tender. "No, honey. It was great. You just took me by surprise is all."

"Can I try again?" Annabelle looked at him hopefully.

A snort of laughter escaped from Mike. "You can try it. I may not survive, but at least I'll die happy."

Annabelle bent over him again. This time she was determined to go slow. She licked the length of his erection, learning his shape, texture, and taste. He was large and thick, but the skin covering him was soft and smooth. She took a deep breath, loving the musky scent of his sex. Her fingers teased the skin of his testicles, gently testing their weight. Her hair flowed as she licked and kissed his length, hoping to add to the sensation.

Judging by Mike's moans of encouragement, Annabelle felt she must be good at this. This time when she took him into her mouth, his large hand cupped the back of her head to keep her there. *As if she'd stop now.*

She loved the taste of him. Slightly salty and spicy. And while her hands played with his testicles, her mouth found a rhythm that pleased them both. She was enjoying herself immensely.

"Stop." Mike's command was a hoarse whisper as he tugged lightly on her hair.

Reluctantly, she stopped. The moment she released him, he pulled her up so she was sitting on his stomach. She heard the sound of a package ripping and a second later he had the condom in place. He lifted her and slid right into her. The new position caught her off guard and as she sat back he slid in even deeper.

"I couldn't wait." Mike gripped her hips and started to move her.

"That's all right," she panted. She caught on to the new rhythm and took over. She rose and fell on him. She moved slowly and then more quickly as she could feel her own body start to strain.

Mike released her hips and placed his hands on her breasts. While he played with her nipples, she moved at a faster pace. She was so close now. She could feel it.

"Help me," she moaned.

One of Mike's hands slid down her body and between her legs, where their bodies were joined. His fingers barely touched her when her climax was upon her. She started to collapse as the sensations swept over her, but Mike's hands grabbed her hips and held them as he pumped himself into her. Her climax went on and on.

Mike thrust himself one last time and then she could feel him coming. She could feel the release inside her and it made her shiver even more. His grip on her relaxed and this time she just slumped on his chest. His arms came around her, holding her tight to him, as if he would never let her go. Annabelle snuggled against his chest and with her head cushioned against his body drifted off to sleep.

Chapter Six

ଚ୍ଚ

When Annabelle awoke the next morning, the sun was streaming into the bedroom. Groaning, she rolled over onto her back. All the muscles in her body protested the move. Her eyes were gritty and she scrubbed at them with the back of her hand. Prying her eyes open took her a few minutes and she squinted as she read the time on the bedside clock. Annabelle bolted upright in bed. She'd overslept. Her alarm hadn't gone off.

She had the sheet tossed back and was half off the bed before she realized she was stark naked. Grabbing the sheet, she quickly dragged it to her chin. A fast survey of the room assured her that this was not her bedroom. In fact, this was not her bed. Memories of last night's activities flooded back to her.

"Oh, my lord," Annabelle gasped and fell back onto the pillows, covering her head with the sheet. Her aching body protested the movement. She felt as if she'd run in a marathon. Muscles she hadn't known existed ached this morning. Details flooded back into her mind. Images of naked limbs in seemingly impossible positions. No wonder she was sore. Had she really been that wanton woman the night before?

She'd barely slept all night. Mike kept waking her with mind-numbing kisses. And one thing led to another. She'd lost count of the number of times they'd made love. She'd never had to face a morning-after before and she wasn't ready. What did one say or do after the activities of the night before? She wanted it to be night again, to lie in Mike's arms once more and not have to think about anything but the touch of his body on hers.

Annabelle rolled over in bed and moaned. The excesses of the night before were making themselves known. She needed a shower desperately and she would have one just as soon as she could summon the energy and the nerve to drag herself out of bed.

The mattress dipped next to her and she froze. Annabelle knew she was being a coward, but she really didn't know what to say to Mike. She felt completely tongue-tied.

"I know you're in there." His hand smoothed the covers over her back and then started to tug on them.

Annabelle could hear the amusement in Mike's voice. She scrunched the covers tighter in her hands, but she could feel them being pulled from her grip. Reluctantly, she rolled onto her side, and peeked above them.

Mike sat next to her, looking more handsome than ever. There ought to be a law that stated that a man couldn't look that good first thing in the morning. Obviously, he had already showered as he looked fresh and alert, while she felt about as fresh as last week's laundry. He had pulled on a pair of faded jeans and had donned a crisp white shirt, but hadn't buttoned it. His rich, brown hair hung free to his shoulders and looked as soft as silk. His eyes were filled with humor as he smiled at her.

"Let go, Annabelle," Mike coaxed her. "I have coffee." He picked up a cheerful yellow mug from the bedside table and waved it in front of her.

"You don't play fair," she wailed as the scent of fresh brewed coffee reached her nose. Reluctantly, she released her death grip on the covers and sat up in bed, but she took care to make sure the sheet was tucked firmly under her arms. She leaned back against the headboard, grateful for its support.

Mike passed her the coffee and waited until she'd taken a sip. "Not when it's something I really want."

Annabelle choked on the hot liquid, bending at the waist. Mike patted her on the back while she coughed and sputtered.

It took her a moment to get her breath back. "What do you mean by that?" she glared at him as she resettled against the pillows.

"We'll talk over breakfast." Mike leaned over and gave her a quick kiss before standing. "Right now, I'd say you'd like a shower."

Annabelle nodded. She ducked her head, embarrassed. It was one thing for her to know she desperately needed a shower, but it was quite another for Mike to know just how badly.

"There's fresh towels in the bathroom. Help yourself to anything you need." Mike started to leave and then turned back to the bed. "Oh, and I left one of my shirts hung up on the door for you to wear."

Annabelle watched him leave, unable to think of anything witty to say. He was so matter-of-fact about it all she wondered how commonplace this sort of situation was to him. Just thinking about Mike with another woman gave her a headache. She laid her coffee mug down on the bedside table and started to pull back the covers when Mike poked his head back around the door.

"Breakfast will be ready when you are."

She stared at the doorway until she was sure Mike wasn't going to sneak back again and surprise her. Sliding cautiously from the bed, she wrapped the sheet around her and padded to the bathroom. She stopped long enough to pick up her bra and panties, which were lying in a tangle on the floor. It took her longer than she thought it would to bend over and then stand up straight again. Her dress, she noted had been hung across the back of the chair.

She'd worry about her dress later. Right now she needed a hot shower to work some of the stiffness out of her body. Annabelle closed and locked the bathroom door. She didn't want any interruptions during her shower. Turning, she caught a glimpse of herself in the mirror. She screamed.

The underwear slipped from her grasp and fell to her feet, forgotten. Leaning against the vanity, she stared at her reflection through bloodshot eyes. Her face was pale and her lips were swollen. She noted that her hand was shaking as she raised it to her head. The long mass of her hair looked as though rats had played in it. She rested her head against the cold glass. Mike had seen her like this.

Pounding on the door made her jump. Her leg hit the corner of the cabinet and she bounced off the wall. Reaching out, she grabbed a towel rack for support.

"Annabelle, are you all right?" Mike sounded alarmed.

"I'm fine." Her voice was barely a whisper, so she tried again this time much louder. "Really, I'm fine."

"Are you sure? I heard you scream." Mike jiggled the handle of the door.

"I saw myself in the mirror." Annabelle slapped her hand over her mouth the minute she spoke. What was it about Mike that made her lose her common sense?

Mike's laughter filled the air. "Shower, Annabelle." She could hear Mike's footsteps as he retreated to the kitchen.

Thoroughly disgruntled, Annabelle turned on the hot water with more force than necessary and jumped back when the water splashed her. She rubbed her poor abused thigh as she waited for the water to heat up. Muttering to herself about men and life in general, she adjusted the water temperature and the spray. She dropped the sheet and climbed into the shower and allowed the water to work its magic.

Annabelle took her time. Standing under the spray, she let the hot water pummel her poor body. The pounding spray felt good against her tender skin. Once the heat had loosened up her sore muscles, she washed and rinsed her hair, twice. Then, she lathered her entire body with Mike's soap. The smell reminded her of him and for the first time in her life, the act of bathing became an erotic experience.

It was just like rubbing against him in bed. The soap was hard and smooth in her palm and when she ran it over her breasts her nipples automatically puckered in response. Annabelle moaned, she'd never done anything like this in her life. She was actually arousing herself. But it felt so good.

Unable to resist, she slid the slick bar between her legs and moved it back and forth. The nub of her clitoris hardened and Annabelle dropped the soap as her body responded to the stimulation. She swayed in the shower and put out a hand to support herself against the wall. She had to stop before she had an accident in the shower. She shuddered in horror as she imagined trying to explain the situation to the responding paramedics. The thought was too horrible to bear.

Reluctantly, she let the rushing water clean the soap from her body. Gritting her teeth, she blasted the water cold for a full half minute before turning it off. She'd never needed a cold shower in her life. One night with Mike had turned her into quite the brazen hussy.

Stepping out of the shower, she wrapped herself in the big bath towel that Mike had left there for her. Using her finger, Annabelle brushed her teeth as best she could. Filling the cup that sat on the sink, she rinsed her mouth twice and then drank a full glass of water.

She helped herself to his comb and hairdryer and in no time had her hair tamed. Annabelle started to twist it up, but stopped and let it fall free. It stroked her bare shoulders, making her feel sensual. Sexy.

She picked up her underwear from the floor and rinsed it in the sink. There was no way she could put on yesterday's underwear. Draping it over the towel rack, she prayed it would dry quickly.

Annabelle patted her skin dry and then hung up the damp towel to dry. She wished she had some of her own moisturizer and even her own toothbrush. She made a note to start carrying a small bag of supplies in her purse. Her mental check list included toothpaste, toothbrush, moisturizer, and as much as it made her blush, clean panties. If she was going to conduct an affair she might as well be prepared. The drugstore might even carry trial sizes of products that would fit nicely into her large purse. It was definitely something to check on.

As Mike had promised, one of his shirts hung on the back of the door. She slipped it on, loving the feel of it against her skin. The material was soft from many washings and the blue denim had faded to almost white. It was big on her, hanging to just above her knees. She rolled up the sleeves and buttoned it right to the top. Peering into the mirror, she studied her appearance.

She looked much better. Her face had some color and her eyes were a little clearer. The shirt covered her as well as a dress, but she was well aware of the fact that she was naked beneath it. The fabric seemed heavy against her skin and she tugged it away from her body and flapped the ends. The slight breezed cooled her for the moment and she dropped the tail of the shirt again.

She'd delayed long enough and she was as ready as she'd ever be. Gathering her courage, she left the bathroom. She stopped long enough to grab her now cold coffee and followed her nose towards the smells from the kitchen.

Mike was standing at the stove scrambling eggs when he sensed that he was no longer alone. Although she'd made no sound, he was very aware of her presence. The atmosphere in the room felt different. More complete somehow. "There's more coffee if you want it." He motioned to the coffeemaker sitting on the counter as he spoke.

Annabelle edged into the kitchen, tugging down the hem of the shirt she wore as she walked. He could have told her it was a waste of time. The shirt covered her as much as any respectable dress would. It was the woman under the shirt that made the difference. And Annabelle looked good enough to eat for breakfast.

Quickly and quietly, she dumped the coffee from her cup into the sink and poured herself a fresh one. After taking a fortifying swallow, she worked up enough nerve to send a glance his way. Annabelle had obviously had too much time to think about last night and had made herself nervous.

Mike shook his head and smiled with amusement when she automatically refilled his mug as well. That was Annabelle, always taking care of others. He wanted the right to take care of her.

When she stood, hovering uncertainly by the counter, he motioned her towards the table. "Sit down. Breakfast will be ready in just a minute."

Annabelle padded to the table with her hands wrapped around her coffee mug. Carefully, she sat down, taking the time to make sure the tails of the shirt were tucked safely beneath her. When she was settled to her satisfaction, she glanced around the kitchen with undisguised interest.

The room was large and the table was set in a nook with comfortable bench seats on either side. Both the table and benches were constructed of pine, and the benches were covered in a sturdy forest green fabric. The walls were pine halfway up, and the top half was painted an off-white color. The cupboards were forest green as well, and the appliances were the same color as the walls. The whole effect was masculine without being overwhelming.

Mike enjoyed watching her as she took in the room. He was unable to keep himself from asking. "What do you think?" It suited him just fine, but it was more masculine than frilly and he wasn't sure if Annabelle would like it.

Her eyes met his and the look of wonder was plain on her face. "I love your home, Mike. It's absolutely beautiful."

"So you won't mind spending a lot of your spare time here?" Mike turned off the stove to let the eggs finish cooking and popped the four slices of whole wheat bread into the double toaster.

Annabelle bit her lip and hesitated. "You don't have to say that. I understand that last night was about...well, sex."

Mike turned to face her slowly, his fists clenched at his sides. He was normally a very even-tempered guy, but Annabelle's stubbornness about their relationship was quickly becoming a sore spot with him. He took a deep breath to calm down. When that didn't help, he took another. Mike didn't think he'd ever been this angry in his life. "Last night was not a one-night stand."

"No." Annabelle hunched over her coffee cup, not looking at him. "What was it then?"

Mike stalked over to the table. He just stood there a moment unable to speak. Taking yet another deep breath, he let it out slowly, trying to shake off his anger. He understood that Annabelle was insecure and for that reason he forced himself to be gentle as he reached down and tenderly gripped her chin in his hand. He tipped her head up until her eyes met his. "This is the beginning of a long relationship. Do you understand?"

Annabelle nodded hesitantly. "I didn't know if last night was all you wanted."

Mike closed his eyes and prayed for patience. How Annabelle could even ask that question after last night was beyond him. He'd been all over her last night, barely giving her time to rest before making love to her again. Did she think that was normal? He opened his eyes and Annabelle was watching him with a hopeful look in her eyes. Obviously, she did.

"I want a heck of a lot more than last night." He spoke slowly wanting there to be no doubt in her mind. "Last night was just the beginning."

Annabelle's face flushed and her eyes took on that sultry, sexy look that told him she was pleased and aroused by his statement. One look from her and he was horny again. By all accounts a hard-on should be impossible after last night. But the bulge in the front of his jeans left no room for doubt. He wanted her. Now.

Reaching down, he gently pulled her up from the bench. His hands threaded through her hair and held her in place as he leaned down and covered his lips with hers. She tasted even better this morning than she had last night. As he licked her lips he tasted mint toothpaste and coffee. It was addictive.

He nipped and nibbled at her lips until she lost all patience and grabbed him by the hair and tugged him closer. He laughed but was soon lost in the heat of their kiss. Her tongue dueled with his as he swept into her mouth and claimed it for his own.

This woman was becoming as necessary to him as breathing and it was time she knew that and accepted it. "I want you." Mike muttered as he peppered her face with kisses. "I want you now."

"Yes," Annabelle moaned. Her hands clutched at his back, urging him closer.

"Here," he insisted. "Now."

"Whatever you want." Annabelle nibbled on his neck as she gave him her answer. It was all the permission he needed.

His hands slid down her back and back up, pushing under the shirt that she wore until his hands met with bare flesh. His heart pounded harder when he realized she wasn't wearing any underwear. Mike covered her bottom with his large hands and massaged both cheeks, loving their plump fullness. "I love your ass," he murmured as he continued to move his hands over them.

"It's too big," she wailed as she tried to squirm away from him.

Mike pulled back in surprise, unable to believe what she'd just said. Annabelle tugged on his arms trying to move them off her behind, but he refused to give up his grip on her delectable bottom. When he looked at her in disbelief, she just nodded at him as if confirming her absurd notion. He growled at her in frustration. "It's perfect."

Annabelle just shook her head and buried her face against his chest. Reaching down, Mike tilted her face up and kissed her nose, her chin, and finally her lips. He lingered over her mouth, tasting and teasing her. All the while his hands continued to rub and caress her behind. "It is perfect," he whispered in her ear as he trailed kisses down her neck.

When Annabelle went still in his arms and gazed at him with an uncertain look in her eyes, he knew he had to show her. "Trust me?" he asked and waited patiently for her reply.

Annabelle nodded without hesitation. Mike gently turned her in his arms so she was facing away from him. He heard the toaster pop in the background, but ignored it. He had to fill this appetite first. Food would come later.

"Bend over and put your hands on the end of the table." Mike waited to see if she would do as he asked. She quivered for a moment as if undecided, but then slowly bent at the waist and placed both hands flat on the table. Mike wanted to howl in triumph. Instead, he flipped up the tail of the shirt so that her bottom was exposed to him.

Annabelle flinched when he exposed her, but stayed as she was. Her body was tense, but Mike was pleased and encouraged by her show of trust. "I love the feel of your skin. So soft. So damn sexy." He reached out and slowly ran his hands over the exposed globes of her bottom. He moved closer rubbing his denim-clad erection against the cleft of her ass, at the same time moving his hands around her waist.

Annabelle moaned and her whole body went rigid before she softened and began to move against him. Her bottom slid over his erection and Mike closed his eyes enjoying the sensation. She was so naturally sensual, she took his breath away. But if she didn't stop, he was liable to come in his jeans. He gripped her waist and held her tight to stop her. "Don't move."

"I have to move," she panted. She fought against his hold on her and pushed back against him.

Mike gritted his teeth and struggled for control. "Trust me. It will feel even better if you don't." He could feel Annabelle struggling against her natural inclination to move. Mike tightened his hold on her waist and waited until Annabelle was still in his embrace. Slowly, he slid one of his hands down her smooth belly, pausing to rub little circles around it, and loving the way it curved slightly outward. Annabelle had exquisite curves. Finally, his hand delved between her legs, his fingers tangling through the thick curls. He could feel that she was already damp and felt his erection grow even harder. To torture himself even further, he rubbed his fingers over the lips of her moist core and then brought his fingers to her lips.

"Taste how good you are." Mike almost came in his pants when her tongue licked his fingers. He closed his eyes as the sensations of her lips sucking on his fingers flowed through him. Her lips were soft and her mouth was hot and moist as she drew his fingers into his mouth and ran her teeth lightly over them. Annabelle's mouth was a thing of beauty and if he was extremely lucky, she might be tempted to use that mouth on his penis again.

His cock pushed harder against the zipper of his jeans at the thought. But for now he wanted to take Annabelle from behind so he could enjoy her beautiful ass. Mike's whole body was alive. Nothing was more important than making love with this woman.

Urgent to be inside her, he forced himself to pull away and yanked out a condom that he'd tucked in his back pocket earlier. Carefully, he unzipped his jeans over his straining erection and pushed them down around his hips. His cock sprang free of the confining material and he quickly sheathed himself before sliding into Annabelle's waiting warmth. Her channel was hot and wet and he filled her easily.

She shifted slightly away from him and he forced himself to be still. He knew that his entry had been abrupt even if she was ready for him. "Am I hurting you? Do you want me to stop?" It might just kill him, but he knew he would stop if she didn't want this.

"Don't you dare stop." Annabelle moved back against him. "Move."

He did as she commanded. He slid his hands under the shirt until he found her breasts. Cupping them in his hands, he played with them as he moved in and out of her from behind. Her nipples were hard points and he rolled them between his fingers. It was incredible, but it was time to further Annabelle's education.

Mike cupped her breasts in his large hands and then moved his legs between hers. He spread his legs, forcing Annabelle to spread hers further. She gripped the table harder for support and Mike knew he was now in control of their lovemaking. "I want you to stay as still as you can."

Annabelle tried to squirm and move against him, but was unable to move in the position she was in. "I need to move," she panted.

"No, you don't." Mike buried his penis to the hilt and then slowly withdrew from her until only the tip of him was inside her. Slowly, one inch at a time he entered her until he was as far as he could go. As he repeated this several times, he could feel Annabelle's internal muscles clenching around his cock. The feeling was incredible. He withdrew once again and then entered her quickly and followed with three hard, quick thrusts.

Annabelle's head was thrown back as she moaned and squirmed. Mike stopped moving and just held her still. His fingers teased her taut nipples and played with her breasts. Moving his legs slightly further apart forced Annabelle to balance on her toes. "Every time you move, I'll stop."

"That's not fair." Annabelle tried to move but couldn't.

Mike continued to tease her breasts, loving the way Annabelle's inner muscles were contracting and her breasts heaved as she panted. "No, it's not fair, but you are enjoying it, aren't you? I can feel how excited your body is." Mike pulled out and thrust back into her body. "Let me have you my way."

Annabelle nodded, unable to speak as her whole body quivered with desire. Mike set a rhythm of short, slow strokes and long, quick thrusts. Annabelle's body responded as he could feel her body clench his cock even harder. Mike gritted his teeth and recited his work schedule in his head. He wanted Annabelle to come, but he wasn't ready to let go just yet. There was more he wanted to do.

Annabelle struggled to keep her balance as her whole body clenched. Mike could feel her orgasm as it hit her full force. Her inner muscles clenched his so tight, he thought he might lose control. He kept thrusting inside her and rode out her orgasm until he could take no more. Withdrawing from her, he kept his arms wrapped tight around her as she collapsed in his arms.

Murmuring endearments in her ear, he turned her and held her in his arms. He buried his face in her hair, content just to hold her until she was ready for more. When Annabelle relaxed in his arms and laid her head on his chest, he leaned down and whispered in her ear. "No more negative thoughts about your beautiful behind."

She looked up at him and smiled, looking both sated and sleepy. Her hand came up to brush a lock of hair off of her cheek and her face was solemn as she nodded her agreement. "My ass is beautiful."

Mike threw back his head and roared with laughter. God, this woman was amazing. She took him from hot and horny to laughter and contentment within seconds. He was totally captured by her spirit.

Annabelle nestled closer to him, rubbing her belly seductively against his erection. "You didn't come."

"No." He enjoyed her sensual movements. "I wanted you to come first."

"Do you want breakfast now?" Annabelle started to move away from him, but Mike pulled her back into his arms unable to believe she could leave him like this. One look at her face told him that the little imp was teasing him.

"Yes, I want breakfast now." The downcast look on her face was priceless. "But you're on the menu," he growled as he picked her up and plunked her bottom on the table. Annabelle laughed with delight as he tickled her sides and nuzzled her breasts. He continued to tickle her until she screamed for mercy.

Annabelle lay on the table with Mike draped over her shaking until the laughter died away. Her hand came up to tenderly stroke his face and he turned his head and kissed the palm of her hand. His eyes stared into hers, deep and dark with desire. "Take me inside you."

Reaching down, Annabelle guided him to her and when he was deep inside her, she wrapped her legs around him and held him tight. Bracing his hands on the table by her head, Mike leaned down and kissed Annabelle. It was a kiss filled with a slow burning passion that quickly got out of control. He feasted on her lips, as if only she could sustain him.

He tore his lips from hers and kissed his way down to her breasts. His tongue laved her distended nipples before he drew one into his mouth to suck and tease. Moving his arms, he unlocked her legs from his waist and draped them over his shoulders, opening her further as he began to thrust once again.

Annabelle moved with him and set a rhythm that she liked, and Mike let her. Just being in her like this and having her trust him was incredibly erotic. The smack of their skin as they thrust towards one another was the only noise besides the sound of their panting. Annabelle was straining hard now and he knew he was close. His balls were tight against his body, screaming for release.

Forcing himself to stand, he gripped her waist and drove into her harder and faster. "Let go, baby." He panted as he tried to hang on.

Suddenly, it was too late. His own orgasm was upon him. He pumped into her, prolonging it as much as he could and was rewarded when she cried out and her whole body shivered. He could feel her inner muscles closing on his penis and his own pleasure was increased. The feeling was incredible.

When it was over, he collapsed on top of her and felt her legs slide off his shoulder and just hang off the end of the table. He could feel her heart pounding in her chest, but didn't have the energy to move. Her hand moved over his head and caressed it briefly before falling back to the table with a thud. Mike started to laugh as he imagined the totally debauched picture they made.

"What's so funny?" Annabelle asked weakly, sounding mildly interested.

"We are." Mike managed to raise his head from the cushion of her breasts. He braced his weakened legs and slowly slid out of her. Holding her around the waist with one arm, he reached out and snagged some napkins off the table and used them to wipe away the traces of their lovemaking from her.

Annabelle was totally limp as he sat her down on the bench seat before he went to the garbage and disposed of the condom and the napkins. The shirt still hung on her shoulders and her hair draped over her face covering it as she rested her head on the table. Mike shook his head as he walked back to the table and hunkered down next to where she sat.

He pushed back the long, thick curtain of hair and she opened her eyes and looked at him, her smile tired but beautiful all the same. "I don't want you to ever think that I don't want you. This is more than a one-night stand. Much more. Do you understand?"

Annabelle nodded as she pushed herself away from the table and sat back on the bench. Glancing at the table, her face turned red. Mike knew she was embarrassed, but she was also well satisfied, if the look in her eyes was any indication.

Mike turned her so she was facing him, buttoned the shirt, and adjusted it until she was completely covered. Her hand came out and covered his, squeezing it for a moment before releasing it. Unable to stop himself, Mike dropped a quick kiss on her swollen lips.

"I understand." She took a deep breath and then spoke again. "And thank you. It means more to me too."

Mike was more than pleased. At this rate it wouldn't take long to convince Annabelle that they belonged together forever. For now it was a start. Mike's stomach chose that moment to emit a huge growl. Annabelle looked at his stomach, her eyes wide, and started to laugh.

"We need to feed you to keep up your strength." Annabelle started to get up from the table, but he stopped her.

"You just sit there and keep me company. It will only take me a few minutes." He scraped the now cold eggs out of the pan and into the garbage. The soggy slices of toast followed.

Mike found that Annabelle was an easy person to just be with. Once she'd decided to accept the fact that he wanted to cook for her, she sat back and enjoyed it. She teased him as he cooked, but he could tell she was pleased by his efforts.

When they finally sat down to a breakfast of scrambled eggs, toast, orange juice and coffee, Mike was in a contented state of mind. He'd never enjoyed a breakfast more. By the time they'd finished eating Annabelle was yawning. He'd kept her up most of the night before and she'd already had quite a workout this morning.

Mike tossed the dishes in the sink and when Annabelle objected, he kissed her soundly, picked her up and carried her back up the stairs to bed. "You need a nap. We'll do the dishes later. Much later."

Annabelle smiled and cuddled into his arms and allowed him to carry her to bed. Mike smiled smugly. She was putty in his hands.

Chapter Seven

ဆ

The man was driving her crazy. Her nerves were frazzled and she was at her wit's end. Mike Sloan didn't know the meaning of the word discreet. He'd been to visit her at the library every day this week. People were starting to notice. Soon they would start asking questions. And Annabelle just didn't have any answers.

Just thinking about last weekend brought a blush to her face. She'd had no idea that people really made love *that many times* and in *so many ways*. Annabelle didn't think she'd ever be able to look at Mike's kitchen table as just a place to eat. Forever, it would be the site of one of her most erotic experiences.

The entire weekend was filled with sensual memories. But it had been more than that. Much more. Mike had been a tender and considerate lover, but he'd also been wild bringing out a side of her that she hadn't known was there. There was a part of her that reveled in his loss of control when he'd just had to have her. She understood those feelings, because he made her feel the same way.

It was the quiet times that had meant even more to her. After Mike had carried her to bed again Saturday morning, she had fallen asleep exhausted from all the unaccustomed activity. When she'd finally awakened, the sun was sinking in the sky and Mike was lying next to her.

Propped up on one arm, he was running his free hand through her hair that trailed down over the covers, but it was the look on his face that made her want to weep. He was watching her as if there was nothing else he would rather be doing. As if she was the most important thing in the world to him. He'd made her feel cherished.

They'd shared a long, hot bath that had helped ease much of the soreness she'd felt, but they hadn't made love again that evening. The master bathroom had a huge tub that you had to climb up a step before you actually stepped down into it. There was a wide ledge all the way around the rim of the tub and Mike had lit candles and poured them each a glass of white wine. Annabelle had never had such a decadent experience in the bathroom before. Mike climbed into the tub and pulled her back against his chest where she'd been content to just loll about in the water and sip her wine.

When her fingers started to prune, Mike had soaped a thick, cotton cloth and washed her from head to toe. He finally had to tug her out of the water, as she would have been content to stay there all night. He'd wrapped her in a thick white towel, given her a kiss and left her with orders to dry herself off.

When she'd dried off and pulled on another clean shirt belonging to Mike she joined him on the patio. He had been busy and already had steaks grilling on the barbecue. Annabelle rummaged around in the kitchen and soon had potatoes baking in the oven. The refrigerator produced enough greens and vegetables for a garden salad. Annabelle was famished her stomach growling, reminding her that she hadn't eaten a thing since breakfast.

The back deck was private, so Annabelle carried out dishes from the kitchen and they sat at a wooden picnic table and ate their food and sipped their wine. Never had dinner tasted so delicious. Lingering over coffee, they talked and shared stories about themselves.

After the dinner and the breakfast dishes had been cleared away, Mike had taken her on a tour of his home. She loved all the wood and the simple lines of his home. It was typically male, without much to make it cozy, but the potential was there. Annabelle could envision plants, throw pillows, and a comfortable chair or two. It was all too easy to picture herself there as well. That thought worried her, but she was in too mellow a mood to let it take hold in her mind.

They'd finished the tour in the living room where they'd ended up curled up on the sofa watching old movies on television. The comedy had made her laugh, but the love story had made her cry. Mike had just wrapped his arm tighter around her and pulled her into his lap. Annabelle had never been so content in her life and it scared her.

Sighing, she shuffled the papers on her desk for the tenth time, and then pushed her chair away from her desk. She rubbed her temples to try and stop the pounding in her head. It didn't help much. Sleep hadn't come easy this week and her days had been stressful. Mike had kept her on edge; she just didn't know when he was going to show up or what he was going to do next.

He had promised her that they would keep their affair a secret, but that was proving to be impossible. Mike showed up at the library first thing Monday morning with coffee and muffins from Sammy Joe's Bakery. The coffee had two sugars, just the way she liked it, and the muffin had been oatmeal raisin, her favorite. He'd delivered it along with a long, lingering kiss before he'd headed off to work, whistling all the way out the door.

Tuesday, a bouquet of wildflowers had found their way to her desk. There had been no card, but she hadn't needed one. Several people at work had noticed them and teased her about her secret admirer.

Wednesday afternoon Mike had dropped by with a small bar of imported chocolate, a weakness of hers that she'd admitted to last weekend. Closing the door to her office, he had made himself right at home, pulling her down onto his lap and feeding her pieces of chocolate until the wrapper was empty. Then he'd kissed her senseless, announced that the chocolate was delicious, and left her bemused and on a sugar high for the rest of the day.

Thursday at lunchtime, he'd dropped by with a huge garden salad from her favorite deli. Extra cheese and tomatoes and no onions. Iced tea with lemon, in a large take-out cup, and a warm oatmeal cookie had rounded out the meal. He'd delivered it with a flourish and a kiss and then was gone again. He'd passed Mrs. Casey on the way out and had just smiled and said hello. Annabelle had been so flustered she hid in her office away from the woman's knowing gaze.

Now it was Friday and she was on pins and needles, not knowing what was going to happen next. They had made no plans for this weekend. She didn't know if she should ask him to come over to her apartment after he got off work or if she should wait to see if he asked her back to his place. She tilted her head back and rested it against the comfort of her chair. Closing her eyes she took a deep breath and tried to release the tension. Having an affair was more stressful than she'd anticipated.

Annabelle was not a deceptive person by nature and keeping a secret of this magnitude was hard. Annabelle rubbed at the knot in her stomach.

She concentrated on taking one deep breath after another, and she finally felt the tension of the week begin to melt away. It was late Friday afternoon. Whatever else happened, she was finished work for the week and had two whole days off to rest and relax. She'd take a hot bath, eat something healthy and have a good night's sleep. That was the plan.

Annabelle hadn't heard a sound, but the feeling in the room had changed and she knew she was no longer alone. She didn't have to open her eyes to know that Mike was standing next to her chair, so in tune had she become with him. She felt his breath on her face just before his lips touched hers. Softly, he kissed her, his lips firm and warm against hers, and she yielded completely to his caress. He took the unspoken invitation and deepened the kiss. Annabelle could hear nothing but the sound of their breathing, deep and heavy. She could feel nothing but the movement of his lips over hers. She could taste only Mike. It was heavenly.

A door slammed in the distance and Annabelle's eyes popped open as she pulled away from Mike and glanced quickly at her office door. Closed. She closed her eyes and sent up a prayer of thanks. When she looked back at Mike, he had a scowl on his face.

"What's wrong?"

"Why would anything be wrong?" Mike pulled back, sat on the corner of her desk, crossed his arms over his chest and glared at her.

Annabelle wasn't quite sure how to respond to him. Could Mike be in a bad mood and still kiss her the way he just had? "Did you have a good day? Did everything go all right on the new job site?" She wanted to reach out and just touch him, to reassure him that everything was fine, but she didn't feel that she had the right to do so. Instead, she gripped the sides of her chair to keep from reaching out to him.

Mike stared at her for just a moment. Hard. As if he was looking for something in her face. Whatever he was looking for she wasn't sure if he had found it or not. He unlocked his arms from over his chest and gave a deep sigh. He rubbed his left hand over the back of his neck. He looked tired.

Annabelle could resist no longer and reached out and took his right hand in hers. She wanted to fix whatever was wrong, but not knowing what it was, she did the only thing she could. She offered comfort instead.

"It's been a long week. How about I cook us supper and we relax?" Annabelle waited for his reply, unable to believe she was being so bold, but her uncertainty had vanished. He needed her and if he wanted to be with her she wasn't going to waste a moment of their time together.

Mike's lips tilted up at the corners until he was smiling at her. "I'd like that a lot." Raising her fingers to his lips, he kissed them before releasing her. He stood and dug into his front pocket. A key dangled from his fingers as he held it out to her.

"What's that?" She eyed the plain silver-colored key curiously, but slowly reached out her hand.

"Take it." He waited until she had accepted the key. "I've got to go back to work for an hour or so, but you go on out to the house when you're ready." His eyes went dark and his voice was husky as he spoke. "Pack a bag for the weekend."

He seemed to be waiting for a reply so she nodded her acceptance. "Okay," she replied, swallowing back the lump in her throat.

Mike leaned down and kissed her again. This kiss was different from the first one; this was a kiss of possession. Mike's lips devoured hers as if he was trying to brand her with his touch. Throwing herself into the moment, she wrapped her arms around his neck and kissed him back with all the emotion she felt churning up inside her. The kiss went on and on until Annabelle felt lightheaded and completely out of breath.

Still, she gripped him even tighter when he pulled her out of her chair and wrapped his arms around her waist. She reached up and clutched his hair in one hand to hold him close. He squeezed her so tight she couldn't take a breath. Breathing was very overrated anyway.

Mike was the one who finally found the strength to tear himself away. "Later," he gasped. "We'll finish this later." He planted one last quick kiss on her lips before he stormed out of her office. The door swung wide and bounced off the wall before swinging shut again.

Annabelle was frozen to the spot. Her right hand hurt and when she looked down she realized she had the key Mike had given her clenched tight in her fist. She forced her fingers to open until she could see the key in her palm. Such a small item, but it meant so much. Mike trusted her with the key to his home.

Annabelle knew she was grinning like an idiot but she couldn't stop herself. She gave a little shriek and spun around in a circle. She danced all the way to her purse and carefully tucked her treasure inside. Mike was obviously in this affair for the long term. She knew he cared about her and for now that was more than enough.

Annabelle danced back to her desk and in five minutes had cleared her desk for the weekend. She spent another five minutes making lists of food and clothes she would need for the two days. Taking her time, she slipped her purse over her shoulder and left her office. She turned off the lights and locked the door behind her.

Sedately, she walked out to the front desk and informed her part-timer, Betty Andrews, that she was leaving for the weekend. As soon as the front door of the library closed behind her, she scurried to her car. She had a lot to do and not much time in which to do it.

Mike was grateful to be home even though he could feel the familiar tension rise within him. The tension headache he had been fighting all day was throbbing behind his eyes. Pulling the truck into the driveway, he just sat there with his arms resting on the steering wheel. He stared at the house but made no move to go inside. It had been a long, frustrating week. The closer he tried to get to Annabelle the more she pulled away. Not physically. No, physically she gave her all to him. She was completely uninhibited in their lovemaking. He had no complaints in that department. But emotionally, well that was another matter altogether.

When they were alone, Annabelle was a warm, giving woman. It was in the way she touched him constantly with small caring gestures, like stroking his hand or playing with his hair. He didn't think she was aware she was even touching him half the time, but unconscious or not, Annabelle showed her emotions in a physical manner. She gave of her affection generously and without thought.

When they were in public, everything was different. Annabelle treated him with an offhanded courtesy that made him grind his teeth until his head ached. She acted as if they were no more than acquaintances that barely knew each other. She smiled and chatted but she held herself physically separate from him. And it hurt. He wanted so much more from her than a great time in bed.

He laughed at himself, but the sound held no humor. Mike was well aware of the fact that most of his single male friends would think he was nuts. After all, he had a beautiful, giving, sensual woman who wanted a hot affair with no strings attached. Most men would get down on their knees and give thanks. But, Mike wasn't most men. Only he knew how much Annabelle had to offer a man, and he was greedy. He wanted it all.

Mike prided himself on his patience, but he freely admitted to himself that he was quickly reaching the end of it with Annabelle. He had no idea why she wanted to keep their relationship a secret. At first, he'd wondered if she was ashamed to be seen with him for some reason. He was a rough-looking, hard-working man. He could wear a suit when need be, but he was more at home on a construction site. Annabelle Lee Murphy, on the other hand, was every inch a lady. But, he'd quickly dismissed that thought after spending time with her. She was such a down-to-earth, caring person, and she held nothing of herself back from him when they were alone together.

Whatever the reason, he hoped that her reservations and her need for secrecy would be gone soon. It had only been a week, but already he was tired of skulking around. He wanted everyone to know that this lady was his. Mike admitted to himself that the situation left him feeling insecure. He didn't like it and, damn it, he was going to change it.

Filled with a new determination, Mike collected the bags perched next to him on the front seat and climbed out of the truck. Using his hip, he slammed the door shut and hurried up the front steps. Before he could put his key in the lock, the door opened in front of him as if by magic and Annabelle stood there looking so beautiful it made his heart ache. She had a warm, welcoming smile on her face. And it was all for him. For the first time since he'd moved into his house, he felt like he was really coming home.

He kept moving forward until Annabelle was forced to back up into the house. The smile fell from her face and uncertainty filled it instead. Mike dropped his parcels on the hall table and pushed the door shut. It closed with a solid bang and he turned the lock. He didn't want the outside world to intrude upon them.

"Is everything all right?" Annabelle's voice held concern and her beautiful blue eyes were filled with worry.

Mike moved forward and wrapped her in his arms holding her tight against him. Her body relaxed into his and he could feel her heart pounding against his own chest. The tension of the week slipped away from him. Spending their nights apart during the workweek had been hell. He often found himself rolling over in the middle of the night looking for her, missing her lying next to him. He would never admit it out loud, but he loved the way she cuddled into him when they slept. It made him feel as if he belonged.

"It is now," Mike murmured in her ear. He relaxed even more as he felt her arms slide around his waist and hold him tight. He sighed deeply as he felt contentment fill him. This is what Annabelle did to him.

"I made supper." Annabelle slowly tugged away from his embrace, and reluctantly, he let her go. "I hope you'll like it." She wrung her hands together in front of her as she spoke.

Mike placed a single finger on her lips. "I'm not picky, I like just about anything." Leaning down he gave her a quick kiss. "Besides, I'll never say no to a meal cooked by you."

Wrapping one arm around her waist, he snagged the parcels with the other and herded her back towards the kitchen. She walked easily beside him, fitting perfectly next to him. He deposited the bags on the kitchen counter and began emptying the contents for her inspection.

"I didn't know what you were making for supper, but I figured this bottle of white wine would go with just about anything." Mike handed her the bottle and reached back into the bag.

"It'll go great with the chicken and potatoes that I've got baking in the oven." Annabelle rummaged around in the kitchen drawers until she found a corkscrew. She pulled down a couple of wineglasses from the cabinet and carried all of it to the table. "You can open the wine when you're ready."

"This is for you. For dessert." Mike produced the covered container with a flourish.

"Chocolate chip cookie dough ice cream. Mmmmm." The look Annabelle gave him was almost sensual. "It's my favorite."

"I know." He also knew that he'd had to make two stops on the way home to find the kind she liked. He also knew it was worth the effort when she gifted him with a soft smile and kissed him on the cheek.

"Thank you." Her voice was a whisper against his skin. He wanted to drag her into his arms and up to bed, but he held himself back. Later.

"Have I got time for a shower?" He really needed a cold shower to get a grip on himself. And besides that, he definitely smelled as if he'd been working on a construction site in the sun all day long. He smelled ripe.

She gave him another of her seductive smiles. "You've got plenty of time."

Taking her at her word, he went upstairs pulling off his dirty clothes as he went. The shower was quick and as cold as he could stand it. He soaped his body, scrubbed it and rinsed in record time. Wrapping a towel around his waist, when he stepped out of the shower he then inspected himself in the mirror. Running a hand over his jaw, he knew he could use a shave, but decided against it. He could always shave later. He pulled on clean jeans and t-shirt and headed downstairs.

Less than fifteen minutes later, he was back in the kitchen, clean and with his libido under control. She'd been busy while he'd been gone. The table was set just like a restaurant with all the correct dishes and utensils. There were even cloth napkins on the table and he knew for sure he didn't own any. The vase holding the wildflowers on the table didn't belong to him either. He eyed both of them, liking the fact that Annabelle felt comfortable enough to bring some of her things into his home. It gave him hope that she was beginning to think of them as more than just an affair.

Annabelle had opened the wine and helped herself to a glass. She watched him as he took in the table and snagged his own glass of wine. Raising his glass, he proposed a toast. "To a beautiful table, a tasty dinner, and an even more delicious lady."

She reached her glass out to tap his even as she blushed at his words. "You don't mind that I brought a few things over?" She straightened the napkins as she spoke.

"Nope, looks great." He took a deep drink of his wine to fortify himself. Mike wanted nothing more than to scoop her up and take her to bed, but she'd obviously spent a lot of time preparing this for it. There was no way he'd disappoint her.

"It smells great." It sounded cliché but he really meant it. Taking a deep breath, he inhaled and just enjoyed the scents permeating the air. The aroma of fresh chicken and yeasty bread filled the kitchen. His stomach growled in anticipation.

"Sit down and eat before it gets cold." Annabelle's face was suffused with pleasure as she ushered him into his seat at the table. The plates had been filled with golden brown chicken, steaming baked potatoes with rosemary and melted butter, and baby carrots. A basket of warm rolls sat in the center of the table with a fancy little dish filled with butter sitting next to it.

"This is amazing," Mike said as he reached out and snagged a roll. He slathered butter on it and took a bite. "I missed lunch, so I'm starving," he said around his mouthful of food.

"You're welcome." Her face was red, but Annabelle seemed pleased by his compliment. "It's only chicken."

He reached over and took her hand. "It's more than just food. You took the time to make this for me." He raised her hand to his lips and kissed her knuckles. "Thank you," he paused for effect, "now dig in."

Annabelle laughed, as he'd hoped she would, and they settled in to enjoy their supper. The conversation flowed easily as they both covered their week at work. He told her about the homes his company was working on, the delays due to materials not being delivered, problems with some of his men all being ill with some stomach virus, and all the other small aggravations that came with running your own business.

Annabelle shared stories of interesting things that had happened at the library. She also talked about her own problems with budgets for books versus computer software, having to depend heavily on volunteer staffing, and the constant battle to provide all the services the community demanded. Mike had never thought about how demanding her job could be and how much skill it took to balance everything. It gave him even more respect for her abilities and intelligence.

After dinner, they worked easily side by side as they cleared away the dishes. After everything was washed and put away, they carried their coffee and ice cream into the living room where they curled up on the sofa. It was a very relaxed and ordinary evening.

It all changed with one simple statement.

Mike had been toying with the ends of Annabelle's hair, which she'd taken down at his request, after they'd finished cleaning up after dinner. He finally got the courage to ask her something that had been on his mind all week. "I want to take you to the end-of-summer fair next week."

Annabelle, who had been comfortably settled in his arms, sat forward as if alarmed. "I don't know if that's a good idea." She tugged her hair from his grasp and sat picking at the skirt of her dress as she spoke, not meeting his eyes.

"Why the hell not?" Each word was spoken slowly and carefully enunciated.

Her blue eyes widened and filled with fear as she glanced at him and for that reason he almost relented. Almost. When her gaze skittered away from him, he stiffened his resolve and asked again. "Why the hell not?" His voice was louder this time and filled with anger. Each word got louder until he was shouting by the end. She flinched as he spoke.

Jumping up from the sofa, Annabelle began to pace the room. "Because, people will see us together and have expectations..." Annabelle trailed off as if she didn't know what else to say. She was moving back and forth around the room with her arms hugging herself, as if she was in pain. The pace was quick, almost frantic.

Mike slowly got to his feet and crossed his arms across his chest to keep himself from reaching out to her. He hated himself for causing her such agitation, but this was too important to them. "What's wrong with expectations?"

Unable to stand it any longer, he reached out and stopped her when she paced by him. Gently, he turned her to face him. "I've got expectations of my own." He kept his voice low and even, but it didn't help.

Tears filled Annabelle's eyes. "But you know it won't last." The words seemed to gush up from somewhere deep inside her.

"What won't last?" he thundered. He knew she was referring to their relationship and all thought of being gentle fled, as he was flooded once again with anger at her words.

"Us." That one word she whispered was filled with such anguish and despair that Mike closed his eyes and prayed for divine intervention.

"Not when you have that attitude." Mike cupped her cheeks with his hands and used his thumbs to brush away the tears that fell from her cheeks. "When have I ever given you the idea that this was temporary?"

"Never," Annabelle whispered. She leaned into his touch as if searching for reassurance.

"No. Never." Mike bent down until his forehead was resting against hers. "It's you that's made this a secret affair. Not me. I've always been honest with you about what I want. It's you who's been dishonest with me and with yourself."

He gave her no time to reply before his lips covered hers in a tender kiss. He licked the salty tears from her lips and coaxed them open. Sliding his tongue into her mouth, he kissed her using every bit of skill and experience at his disposal. His hands cupped the back of her head and angled it for better penetration. Eagerly, she invited him inside. His tongue tasted the inside of her mouth before coaxing hers to play with him. He retreated and as he'd hoped, hers followed.

As her tongue swept into his mouth, he captured it with his teeth and nibbled on it. She rewarded him with a moan of pleasure. Mike could feel his erection straining against the front of his jeans. This woman made him hotter than when he'd been a hormonal fifteen-year-old.

His hands swept down her back, molding her body to his. Her breasts pressed against his chest and he could feel her hardened nipples. He rocked her back and forth in his arms, loving the feel of her breasts against him. Annabelle responded by rocking her hips against his erection. The more she yielded, the more he wanted.

Mike grasped her hips in his hands and rubbed his penis hard against her pelvis. Both of them were frantic with need, and time lost all meaning. Mike knew he was in danger of losing all control if he didn't stop and he didn't want this to end. He would make love to her until she wouldn't even think of leaving him. The kiss had gone on and on, but both of them knew it was more than a kiss. It was a declaration of his intent.

It was Mike who finally tore himself away. "I'll take as much as you give me until you give me everything I want." Before she could respond to that cryptic statement, Mike lifted her into his arms and strode out of the living room.

She felt safe and treasured within the confines of Mike's embrace as he carried her upstairs to the bedroom, but her mind was a mass of confusion. Had she been lying to herself, as Mike claimed? And what did he want from her? She opened her mouth to question him but he stopped her before she could speak.

"Shhh. Don't talk. Just feel." He let her legs slide out of his arms until she was standing in front of him. "Take what I give you and know that it's real."

She waited to see what he would do next. Annabelle might be uncertain about the nature of their relationship, but she trusted Mike implicitly.

Slowly, his eyes never leaving her, he reached for the first button at the top of her dress. His nimble fingers slid the button through the hole and glided down to the next one. He continued working his way downward until her dress gaped open, revealing a glimpse of a pale blue satin bra. It was the first time she'd ever owned lingerie that wasn't serviceable white cotton. Mike had given her the confidence to test her womanly wiles and if the burning look in his eyes was any indication, she had more than succeeded.

"Pretty." His fingers pushed open the dress, which now hung loose around her, and he traced the satin cup of the bra before sliding his fingers up over the strap. His hands continued up over her shoulders and slid the material down her arms. The dress pooled at her feet, and she was left standing in front of him wearing only her panties and bra.

Mike seemed to be in no hurry. His fingers glided over the slippery satin, outlining her breasts. The darkness of his hands was a sharp contrast to the paleness of her skin. She loved his hands. They were large and capable, strong yet incredibly gentle. When they'd made love before, his hands had been callused and a little rough, which had been unbelievably arousing. Her breathing quickened and she felt her nipples harden. Annabelle's body swayed towards him, trying to get closer to his touch, but he held her away from him.

His hands skimmed down over her sides and around back to cover her behind. The matching panties were the same pale blue satin and lace, and Mike's hands slid easily over the fabric as he cupped her behind.

"You are so incredibly sexy." His voice was low and harsh with need as he continued to touch her. He put those wonderful large hands to work, shaping and squeezing her bottom. When his fingers skimmed the crease between the tops of her legs and her bottom, she shivered.

Annabelle could wait no longer. She stepped over the dress that lay bunched at her feet and slipped her arms around Mike's neck. Reaching up, she buried her fingers in his dark, silky hair. She slid her fingers through the dark, thick hair letting it glide over his fingers. The next time she ran her fingers through his hair, she held on and tugged him down so she could reach his mouth. Then she kissed him. All that she was feeling, she poured into the kiss—confusion, apprehension, and love.

In the darkness of his bedroom, with his arms wrapped tight around her, she finally admitted it to herself. She loved Mike. Acknowledgement of that emotion brought with it a sense of relief and freedom. Their relationship might be for a short while, but while they were involved she would give it her all. No longer would she hold back. She would gift Mike with all the love that she had to offer.

Mike leaned away from her and stared at her as if sensing something different about her. "You take my breath away."

Feeling bold, Annabelle reached behind and unhooked her bra. Stepping back she leaned forward, exposing her cleavage for him to view and gave her arms a little shake. The satin slithered down her arms and she let it fall to the floor. Mike's breathing was harsh as he watched her. Waiting.

Annabelle never took her eyes off him, as she slowly stood straight. Her breasts thrust out in front of her, and his heated gaze devoured them. Skimming her hands down her sides to her waist, she tucked her fingers into the waistband of her panties and shimmied them down her legs. Stepping away from them, she used her foot to kick them aside. Boldly reaching out, she took Mike's hand and led him to the bed.

Mike followed her and reached around her and tugged back the covers on the bed. Bending his head, he brushed his lips against hers. "Get in bed, sweetheart." He urged her onto the cool cotton sheets.

He pulled his shirt over his head and let it drop to the floor. Annabelle lay on top of the sheets, rather than crawling beneath them. No longer did she want to hide from him. She was proud of the fact that he wanted her. Propping herself on her arms to get a better view of his chest, she was unaware of just how provocative she looked lying there in the middle of Mike's bed.

His nostrils flared and his chest heaved as he made quick work of shucking his jeans. She was surprised and then excited to note that he hadn't been wearing any underwear. It made her wonder just how often he went without them. The image made her shiver with delight. Then he stood before her, every muscle tense, naked and fully aroused. It was a sight guaranteed to make any red-blooded woman weak with wanting.

She licked her lips in anticipation. He was all hers for the duration of their affair. There was no doubt in her mind that Mike would see no one else while they were together. Just as he knew that he was the only man in her life.

Mike groaned as he watched her mouth. Suddenly he moved and was on the bed with her, pulling her into his arms. His arms banded around her, as if to keep her from escaping him, and then he kissed her.

His kiss was ravenous.

Almost desperately, he possessed her mouth with his own. Tongues dueled. Lips and teeth teased. Annabelle lost all track of time and thought as he consumed her. He nipped his way down her neck, spreading hot kisses on her flesh as he worked his way towards her breasts.

"Tell me you want me," he murmured as he laved her nipples with his tongue.

"Yesss." Annabelle clutched him to her breast. Wanting more. Needing more.

"Tell me." Mike ordered as his fingers delved between her legs. She was wet and ready for him. His fingers wasted no time, but slid straight inside her. "Tell me," as he worked two long fingers in and out of her body.

Annabelle thrust her hips up as her legs fell open, urging him closer. "I want you. Only you," she panted as he continued to tease her heated flesh. His fingers thrust in and out and then withdrew and he spread her own wetness over her clitoris making her moan and thrust her hips higher.

Mike swore and pulled back. He ripped open the drawer of the bedside table and grabbed a condom. He was sheathed and inside her before she could form a coherent thought. And then she didn't think at all.

Their lovemaking had been fun and playful. It had been drawn out and intense. But this time it was raw. There was no more foreplay and no more talk. Mike draped her legs over his arms and then planted his palms by her shoulders. She was open, exposed and vulnerable. Mike hesitated only a moment. She gave him a small nod. That was all the permission he needed.

Mike thrust in and out of her. He varied his rhythm. At first it was shallow and light. Then he thrust deeper, pulling back and almost out of her before he thrust into her again.

Annabelle was soon frantic with need. Mike pulled almost out of her and stopped, holding himself rigid and away from her. "Don't stop," she pleaded.

"Tell me what you need."

"You," she cried. "You."

Mike's control broke and he drove into her so hard that she moved up the bed. He wrapped his hands around her shoulders and continued to drive into her. Her hands fisted in the sheets as she matched him stroke for stroke. Their bodies were both slick with sweat as they both moaned and panted. The slapping of skin on skin made her even wilder.

Annabelle's climax went on and on as Mike continued to drive into her. One last thrust and Mike went rigid. He groaned as he emptied himself and then collapsed on top of her. A few seconds later, he slowly pulled himself out of her, rolled out of bed, and headed to the bathroom.

Annabelle just lay there, letting the air cool her heated flesh. What they had just shared was amazing. It was more than just sex. She had a feeling that Mike had just branded her in the most primitive way possible. And she had done the same to him.

The mattress dipped as Mike settled next to her. He wrapped his arms around her and pulled her into his arms. Neither of them spoke. What they'd shared was beyond words. They lay in the dark, listening as the sound of the wind rustling the leaves of the aspen trees drifted in through the open window. Finally, sleep came to them both.

Chapter Eight

ɞ

Annabelle bit her lip as she concentrated on coiling her hair into a neat bun. Sticking the pins in carefully, she peered hard into the mirror, but the image didn't change. She still looked the same as she had this morning when she'd dressed for work. Ordinary and presentable.

Sighing, she reached for her purse, which she had laid on the vanity in the library bathroom. Her hand shook as she reapplied the light pink lipstick that she had chewed off. Satisfied that the color was where it was supposed to be, she took a deep breath and released it. Tossing her lipstick and brush back into her oversized purse, she slung it back over her shoulder and left the safety of the ladies' room.

Knowing that she wouldn't have time to go home to change after work, Annabelle had dressed with care this morning. Her skirt was long, but it was a light cotton of turquoise blue and swished when she walked. It made her feel young and flirty. She had topped it with a plain white tank top, but she had one of her sensible white bras underneath it and had covered it with a light cotton cardigan for work.

Feeling daring, she stopped in her office long enough to unbutton the sweater so that the scooped necked tank top was visible. She had the strap of her purse in her hand when she muttered a curse and dropped it to the floor. Before she could talk herself out of it, she pulled her sweater off, picked up her purse and strode out of her office. But, she couldn't quiet shake the sensible Annabelle, so she stuffed the sweater into her bag. Just in case.

Her shoes were flat and had soft soles and made no sound as she hurried towards the front door of the library. Not that it mattered. Everyone was gone for the day and she was there alone. Most of the town would be at the fair tonight. There would be food of all kinds to eat, booths where you could win prizes, charity groups would be selling goods and raffle tickets. There were carnival rides for the kids and later tonight a band would set up and play.

Annabelle had never been to a fair with a date before. Back in her hometown, she'd helped out at various charity booths, always watching the fun, but never a part of it. Not this time. For the first time, she was going to the fair to have fun. And if her stomach didn't calm down, she'd throw up before she even ate a bite of food or had a spin on one of the carnival rides.

She closed and locked the door behind her. The walk to the fairgrounds would give her time to calm down. After all, women went on dates every day. It was no big deal. She was calm.

"Ahh!" Annabelle jumped when she felt the hand on her shoulder. Her foot hit the library stairs and she felt herself falling. Her purse went one way and she went another as she flailed her arms out to try and catch herself. She didn't fall. Instead she was pulled into a pair of arms that she recognized well. She sighed and let herself sink into Mike's embrace.

"Are you all right?" His voice was a husky whisper in her ear.

Annabelle nodded, her nose rubbing against the soft cotton of the t-shirt he wore. She caught a whiff of his scent and took a deep breath. He smelled like soap, sunshine, and sexy male, and it was more calming than fresh air. And what that meant she really wasn't sure and didn't have time to investigate as Mike was holding her at arm's length so he could look at her.

"Are you sure?" Mike stared at her, trying to gauge her mood. "I didn't mean to scare you. I finished work early so we could walk to the fair together." He ran his hands up and down her arms, as if to assure himself that she was indeed fine.

"Sure... Yeah... All right." She could feel the blush stealing up her cheeks. Part of her wanted to run back inside the library, to safety, rather than face a public date. Groaning inwardly, she tried to pull herself together. She was acting like a complete idiot and couldn't blame it on the near fall, because she hadn't hit her head. "That would be nice."

Mike gave her an odd look, but reached out and took her hand in his. "If you're sure..." and trailed off as she nodded her agreement. When she just continued to stand there, he gave her hand a tug to get her moving down the sidewalk.

It was a perfect summer evening. The day's heat still lingered in the air, but Annabelle was comfortable in her cotton outfit. She glanced at Mike out of the corner of her eye. The man looked good enough to eat. But then he always did. He'd obviously gone home after work and showered and changed. He was wearing a clean pair of jeans and plain white t-shirt; he filled out both to perfection. She wondered if he was wearing any underwear, and made a note to find out later tonight. The thought made her smile.

It was a moment Annabelle knew she would remember forever. All the sights and sounds were etched on her brain and all her feelings and emotions were captured by her heart. Her hand and Mike's fit together perfectly, despite the size difference. Sort of like when they made love. She sighed again, contented with the moment. Unfortunately, Mike misunderstood her sigh and started to question her.

"Did something happen at work today?" Mike turned his soulful brown eyes on her and gave her his complete attention as they strolled towards the fairgrounds. The sounds of children shouting and people laughing filled the air. Recorded music was piped over loudspeakers. The smell of hot dogs, cotton candy and French fries wafted on the light breeze.

Annabelle put away any misgivings she had about this evening. This was her night to enjoy with Mike and she didn't want to waste it wallowing. She summoned up her brightest smile and squeezed Mike's hand. "I'm fine. I'm exactly where I want to be," she added honestly.

"Me too." He raised her hand and kissed her fingers, his face solemn. Then he laughed out loud and swung their clasped hands between them, just like a couple of teenage kids on their first date might.

With that statement Annabelle fell completely and utterly in love. The world continued to move around them, but she felt apart from it. Annabelle realized she had been denying the truth from herself to protect herself, but the fact was that it was too late to worry about giving too much of herself to him. She loved him heart and soul. If they were together for a short while or a long time, it didn't matter. When they parted, the pain would be the same.

That realization was freeing and with it came a new determination. Annabelle was suddenly greedy. She wanted to experience as much as possible in their time together. She wanted every memory they could make together, because she knew she would never love another man like she loved Mike. She had waited thirty years to find him and it had been worth the wait.

"Let's eat. I'm starving." Mike let her pull him along behind her, laughing as she hurried to the food concessions.

"I'm hungry too, but I won't get what I want until later." The sexy gleam in Mike's eyes let her know that she was on the menu for later.

Annabelle tossed her head back and laughed out loud. "Feed me first. I have to keep up my strength." As little as a few weeks ago, such a statement would have been impossible for her. Mike had helped her to change and she was fast coming to realize that she liked the changes.

Pulling some bills from his pocket, Mike addressed the lone teenage male running the hot dog stand. "Two hot dogs and two sodas, please."

The tone was set for the evening. It was everything Annabelle had wished for and more. Who knew that sharing a container of fries could be an erotic experience? But with Mike feeding her the tasty golden morsels, it was only fair that she lick the salt off his fingers. He'd paid her back in kind when she'd given him a taste of her pretzel.

The rides had been the best. Mike had wrapped his arm around her as they rode the Ferris wheel and the some other ride with twirling cars. The exhilaration as they spun around was amazing and she'd laughed and clapped like a child. If the smile on his face was any indication, Mike was enjoying her enthusiasm.

They strolled the grounds hand in hand and Annabelle knew that people were watching them. Mrs. Casey and Mrs. Johnson smiled and waved from the church charity booth they were manning. Dr. James stopped and spoke them. The mayor smiled and said hello as he passed by with his wife and children. Annabelle hated to be the center of attention, yet tonight she felt proud. She and Mike were together and it felt so good and so right to be part of a couple.

The sun finally sank and the night sky was filled with hundreds of twinkling white lights that had been draped over the trees at the edge of the park where the bandstand was located. The band was finished tuning up and the mayor took the stage and thanked everyone for coming. He encouraged them to enjoy themselves and to support the various charities and fundraisers. Then the music started.

The first dance was a fast one and before Annabelle could even think, Mike had spun her out onto the dance floor. She'd never danced much before, but tonight she felt like she was floating on air. Mike kept her close to him, to the dismay of a group of women who had been giving Annabelle dirty looks all evening, and when the band began to play a slow ballad, Mike just eased her into his arms and kept dancing.

"Are you having a good time?" Mike's voice was a rumble against her ear as he leaned down to whisper in her ear.

"I'm having the best time." She snuggled closer to him as she spoke and he responded by wrapping his arms tighter around her.

And she realized she was having the best time of her life. In fact, the last two weeks had been the happiest of her entire thirty years. Mike had opened her eyes to life and to the real her. A woman who was passionate about love and life.

Annabelle didn't want the music to end, but all too soon it did as the band took a break. She was startled to realize that she and Mike had been dancing for forty minutes straight.

Mike kept his hand on the small of her back as he escorted her from the dance floor. He led her to the shadow of a large oak tree beside the bandstand and stole a quick kiss before he spoke. "Would you like something to drink? Some lemonade?"

She looked up into his warm brown eyes, so full of life and caring. "I'd love some."

"Wait here and I'll be back in a minute."

Annabelle watched as he disappeared into the crowd. People were milling about, laughing and talking, as they waited for the band to begin again. She drew back further into the shadows as the group of women who had been giving her the evil eye all night walked by. They hadn't noticed her and she didn't want to draw their attention her way.

"Who does she think she is keeping her claws dug into Mike all night? It's obvious he's too polite to break away from her." The tall blonde tossed her hair over her shoulder as she spoke.

"It must be a charity date or something," a pretty brunette responded.

"There's no way he's interested in a dowdy creature like her when he could have one of us." A stunning woman with short black hair and a figure any woman would envy uttered this last statement.

Annabelle stood there frozen in place as they continued on past her. She had hidden so well, they hadn't even seen her. The food that had tasted so good earlier now churned in her stomach. A wave of humiliation washed over her as she realized what people were saying about her and Mike. And even if some of them were too nice to say it they must surely be thinking it or something similar.

"Here's your drink, honey."

Annabelle automatically took the frosty cold beverage from Mike, but the cup shook in her hand and he quickly took it back from her.

"What's wrong?" Mike laid the drinks on the ground and then tilted Annabelle's face up so he could see it in the glow from the lights.

"We are." Her statement was stark and to the point. Mike jerked in shock and his hand fell away from her face.

"What the hell do you mean?" His hands were fisted as they hung by his sides and his whole body was rigid. It was a far cry from the relaxed, happy man from a moment ago.

"People are talking about us. They don't know what you see in me at all or why you're here with me. Sometimes I'm not sure why you are either." Annabelle waited, hoping he would reassure her. She needed it after what those women had said. She waited. And waited.

Mike closed his eyes and just stood there. When he finally opened his eyes, Annabelle almost wished he hadn't. Pain. There was nothing but pain in those beautiful, expressive eyes. When he spoke, his words were like daggers to her heart.

"I've told you how I feel about you and I've shown you." He stepped away from her when she held out her hand. "You care more about what complete strangers might say about us than what I say about us. If that's how you really feel, I'll leave you in peace."

Mike stared at her as if waiting for her to speak. Annabelle was tongue-tied, wanting to say so much, but not knowing what to say. Caught up in her own torment, she took too long.

"I guess that's my answer." Mike turned to leave, but turned back at the last second. "I love you, Annabelle. I just wished you could love me, trust me." Then he was gone.

"Don't let him go."

Annabelle jumped as the voice came from behind her. She whirled around to find Mr. Keats standing behind her. His weathered face was sad as he leaned on a cane for support.

"I've known that boy his whole life and he's in love with you." His kindly gaze took in the torment on Annabelle's face. "And I think you love him too."

"Oh, I do and I've hurt him so much."

"Then tell him," Mr. Keats advised, "before it's too late."

Annabelle understood then that she had allowed her own insecurities to hurt not only her, but also Mike. He had given her nothing but respect and love and she had tossed it back at him in public. She had to stop him.

Annabelle didn't give herself time to think. She ran to the bandstand and grabbed the microphone. "Mike Sloan, don't go. I love you."

Silence descended upon the park. Everyone stopped and stared at her. It was like inhabiting her worst nightmare, but she didn't care. "Did you hear me, Mike? I love you."

Nothing. She stared out at the faces that watched her. Some were filled with pity and others, like the group of women she'd overheard earlier, were filled with scorn. She almost gave up and ran, but then she noticed other faces. Faces of people she knew. These people were smiling.

"Mike's already gone."

Annabelle felt hollow inside as she recognized Mrs. Casey's voice. She knew that it was too late.

"Don't just stand there, child, go after him." Mrs. Casey's voice filled the night air and was soon joined by others urging her on.

Annabelle jumped off the stage and ran after Mike. The sound of people clapping kept time with the rhythm of her feet as she flew past them and down the sidewalk. Her skirt flew around her, showing off more leg then she ever had in public, but she didn't care. Nothing mattered but Mike. She grasped her purse in her right hand and pressed it against her stomach to keep it from hitting her. Soon there was nothing but the sound of her heavy breathing and the pounding of her feet on the sidewalk.

When she finally reached the library parking lot the only vehicle there was hers. Undaunted, she dug her keys out of her bag and unlocked the car door. A few seconds later she was headed out of town. Pride be damned, she wasn't going to give him up without a fight.

Chapter Nine
❧

Annabelle crept through the darkened house. She knew Mike was here because his truck was out front and the hood was still warm. Using the key he'd given her, she'd let herself in. Truthfully, she'd been afraid to knock. Afraid he might not let her in. She reached her hand out in front of her to guide her as she searched the downstairs. The moonlight provided her only illumination.

Careful, to make no sound, she checked the living room. Even before she was all the way inside, she knew he wasn't here. She couldn't sense him in the room. Backtracking, she hesitated at the bottom of the stairs, but followed her instincts and headed towards the kitchen. Her eyes, now adjusted to the dark, showed her that the back door was open. As she eased closer, she could hear the squeak of the porch swing as it moved back and forth.

Taking a deep breath, she turned the handle, stepped out onto the back porch, and spoke, all in one motion. "I told the entire town I loved you."

"Did you?"

Mike sounded almost uninterested and for a moment her fears almost got the best of her. She thought about running, for about two seconds, but she was no coward and Mike deserved no less then her total honesty. What he did after that was up to him.

Obviously, he wasn't going to make this easy for her. Sucking up her courage, she continued to explain. "I ran up on stage, grabbed the microphone and called out to you not to go, that I loved you."

The swing continued to sway back and forth. Annabelle was unable to see Mike in the darkness as his face was shrouded in darkness. She bit her lip and watched Mike for any response. A bead of sweat ran down the side of her face, but she made no move to wipe it away. She stood motionless. Waiting.

Annabelle almost jumped out of her skin when Mike's boots came down hard on the back porch and the swing came to a halt. He leaned forward and a beam of moonlight illuminated his face. His eyes were grim and his face was serious when he spoke.

"Did you really mean it?" Mike's voice was harsh in the quiet night.

Now it was her turn to close her eyes in anguish. She now understood how painful a blow she'd dealt to Mike. It had taken all her courage to speak the words and he doubted them. Just as she had doubted him. But, if she was honest with herself, he had every right to question her commitment to him.

Her knees were shaking, so she leaned against the porch railing for support. It wasn't much, but right now she needed all the help she could get. The corners of the railings dug into her hands as she gripped them tight and gathered her courage to speak. What emerged was a croak, so she swallowed hard and tried again.

"I allowed my own insecurities to blind myself. I doubted myself and therefore you, even though you never gave me any cause or reason. I can only promise that I'll never doubt that your feelings for me are real." Before she continued, she took a deep breath to help fight back the threatening tears. "And if you're willing, I'd like us to have another chance."

Her fingers retained their death grip on the railing. She was afraid to look away from him as she waited for him to respond. Had she thrown away the best thing that had ever happened to her?

"Come here," he ordered, his voice little more than a rasp.

Mike held out his hand to her and she tumbled forward into his arms. Her momentum started the swing rocking, but she was not afraid. She was cradled securely in Mike's lap with his arms wrapped around her.

"I'm sorry." Annabelle suddenly burst into tears, surprising not only Mike but also herself. "I never cry," she wailed, unable to stop the flow of tears.

"Of course you don't, honey." Mike held her as she cried, waiting patiently for her to subside. He gently wiped her eyes with the tail of his shirt. He kissed her eyelids, her nose, her cheeks and, finally, he brushed a kiss across her lips.

Annabelle responded instantly. Every fiber of her being was crying out to show him how much she loved him. Her hands burrowed into his hair, freeing it from its leather tie. She kissed him with every ounce of feeling she had inside her. She was surprised and a little hurt, when Mike suddenly pulled back from her.

"Do you remember the first night you came out here?" As he spoke, Mike lifted her gently until she was astride him. He adjusted her skirt so that it covered his lap like a blanket, giving his hands easy access to what was underneath.

Annabelle felt her face flush when she recalled her innocent comment about trying out the swing and Mike's reply that they would try it later. Now his meaning was clear. "Yes." It was a moan that was both affirmation that she recalled the conversation and permission to proceed.

Mike needed no more urging. His hands came up to cup her face as he leaned forward and kissed her. It was a gentle caress, filled with tenderness and love. Everything he felt for her was evident as his lips trailed over her lips.

When his tongue slid along her bottom lip, she opened her mouth and used her tongue to coax his inside. Mike groaned and tightened his hold as he kissed her now with a passion that took her breath away. His tongue laid claim to her mouth, devouring her.

He left her mouth and trailed hot kisses down her neck, pausing to nip her shoulder. "I have to have you. Now."

His words were stark, but so was her reply. "Yes."

Mike sat back in the swing. His gaze never left hers as he tugged the tank top over her head and dropped it onto the back porch. For a moment, he paused and just stared at her. Her white bra shone like a beacon in the moonlight. He traced the lace covering her nipples and was rewarded as they hardened instantly. Mike swore under his breath and reached behind her to unhook her bra. Dragging it down her arms, he tossed it onto the porch.

Slowly, reverently, his hands cupped her breasts. He then leaned forward to lap at her nipples. Annabelle moaned and squirmed as she tried to get closer to him. Mike gave both breasts one last lick before sitting back. His eyes were hot as he stared at her wet nipples. "Give me your hands."

Annabelle was unsure what Mike wanted her to do but offered him her hands. Guiding her hands to her breasts, he positioned them so she was supporting her own breasts. She felt awkward when he leaned back to survey his handiwork.

"You look like a pagan goddess offering herself to me in the moonlight." He clamped his hands around her waist to hold her steady and then took what she offered. His fingers traced her nipples. Softly at first and then with more pressure. He caught both nipples between his thumb and forefinger and squeezed gently.

Annabelle felt pagan and wild, half-naked in the moonlight. The light evening breeze was warm on her heated flesh, making her feel like a temptress. Her hands cupped her breasts tighter, offering them to him.

Leaning forward, Mike replaced his fingers with his mouth. He sucked her nipples shifting back and forth from one to the other. Annabelle gave herself up to the sensation. The hot tug of his mouth on her nipples, the feel of her own hands on her breast, and the summer breeze, was incredibly erotic.

But she soon wanted more. Needed more. She had to feel his skin against hers.

Her hands fell from her breasts and she reached out and tugged at his shirt until he lost patience and pulled it off over his head. Pleased, she ran her hands over his muscled chest. She loved the feel of his muscles as they rippled under her touch. Placing a palm over his heart, she could feel its pounding rhythm. Her fingertips traced a pattern lightly over his nipples and were rewarded with his moan of pleasure.

Mike's arms encircled her as he devoured her lips. He drank from them like a man dying of thirst. Her hands slid around to his sides so that she and Mike were chest to chest. Annabelle moved her body from side to side, loving the feel of her soft breasts against the hardness of his chest. The rasp of her nipples against the light covering of his chest hair was incredible.

He pulled away and his lips blazed a path down her neck to her breasts. He cupped them both with his hands and feasted on her. His movements were not the caring touches of an accomplished lover, but those of a desperate man. She'd never felt this needed in her life or this needy either.

"Mike, hurry," she encouraged. "I need you."

In answer to her plea, Mike lifted her off his lap and in one motioned stripped off her skirt and panties.

He paused only long enough to open his jeans and release himself. His penis was hard and straining as he pulled her back to him. He pulled her astride him and impaled her at the same time. "Take all of me." It was more of a plea than a command and Annabelle responded immediately.

Annabelle spread her legs wider, using his shoulders for support. She felt him slide deep inside her. The pleasure was more intense than anything she'd ever felt in her life was. And then Mike used his foot to set the swing swaying.

It was incredible. As he pushed the swing forward he pulled her to him. The momentum drove him deep. Annabelle was open and vulnerable as she hung on to Mike's shoulders for support. He held her as they swung back and then pulled her harder against him as the swing moved forward again.

Annabelle felt wild and free for the first time in her life. There was a bond she shared with Mike that enabled her to let go of all her inhibitions and just explore all aspects of herself. Sitting naked on Mike's lap, making love in the back garden and on a swing, no less, she should have felt vulnerable. Instead, she felt powerful and sexual. It was intoxicating.

Her fingers dug into his shoulders as she slid up and down his penis. Her inner muscles were clamping down hard on him as she could feel her own climax building. Mike's grip on her tightened as she reached her peak. Annabelle screamed as the intensity of her climax washed over her. It went on and on.

Mike continued to swing, prolonging her climax. Finally, he gave one more push and emptied himself inside her. She could feel the hotness of his ejaculation inside her. It gave her a moment's pause that for the first time, they hadn't used a condom. Strangely enough, the thought of having Mike's baby didn't bother her at all. In fact, Annabelle was quiet proud of the fact that she had caused Mike to lose all control.

Annabelle fell forward and rested against Mike's chest. He held her there, lightly running his hands over her back and around her naked bottom. Contented, they slumped together on the swing as it slowly rocked back and forth before finally coming to a halt.

"That was incredible." Mike tenderly kissed her forehead, as she stayed snuggled up against his chest. "You're a wild woman, Annabelle."

"Only with you." Annabelle could feel the pounding of both hers and Mike's hearts as they gradually slowed back to normal. "I'm glad you don't have neighbors."

Mike burst into laughter. She tried to look disgruntled with him, but his humor was infectious and she began laughing with him. It was a release of a whole other kind to be able to laugh with Mike. She felt him slip out of her as they continued to laugh. They were both sweaty and sticky, but Annabelle felt no hurry to clean herself up. She felt natural and comfortable and was still chuckling when Mike spoke.

"Marry me." Mike was suddenly very sober. "Share my life with me."

All thoughts of laughter fled as Annabelle sat there stunned by his proposal. She sat back on his lap so she could see his face and was startled when she felt his growing erection flex against her belly.

He gave her a boyish grin. "You do that to me, honey."

"You really want me to marry you?" Annabelle wanted to make sure she'd heard him correctly.

"Yeah, I really do." He watched her, waiting patiently for her reply.

The smile started deep within Annabelle. A warmth filled her and she realized that it was love for this man and that there could be only one answer.

"Yes, I'll marry you."

"I'll make you happy," Mike promised before he kissed her. It was a kiss full of tenderness and promise.

"I know you will," she whispered. Before she knew what he intended, Mike slipped inside her again. Then she felt the swing started to rock once again. The thought crossed her mind that she'd answered the question she'd wondered about earlier. He certainly hadn't been wearing any underwear. Then she was too busy making love with Mike to think at all.

Chapter Ten

∞

"I heard you were hot." The familiar voice was male, deep, and husky.

Annabelle turned from where she'd been returning books to the reference section before she left for the evening. She raised her eyebrows and gave him what she hoped was a haughty stare. "You shouldn't be here. The library closed five minutes ago." It was delivered in her best librarian's voice, but instead of leaving, he crossed his arms over his chest and leaned against the shelf at the end of the aisle.

She gave an inward sigh. She'd known it wouldn't work, but still she'd had to try. Her eyes ran over his form as he waited patiently for her next move. And she knew better than anyone did just how much patience he had. He looked amused as he watched her stare at him.

Still, he was quite a figure to behold. He was the man of any woman's dreams, but especially of hers. He was tall, with a strong face and a nose that had been broken more than once. It had a little bump in the center that always made her want to kiss that spot every time she saw him. His rich brown hair was kept tied back, except when he was relaxing at home. Then it was wild and free. Her fingers itched to release it from its confines.

His body. Oh, how she loved his body! The arms crossed over his chest, bulged with muscles even when he was at rest, as he was now. His shoulders looked a mile wide and his chest rippled with muscles beneath his shirt. Jeans covered legs that were long and sturdy. Just looking at him made her body ache with need.

Just looking at him raised her body temperature several degrees. The sensible denim dress she'd worn to work this morning suddenly seemed way too warm. Maybe, she mused, the air-conditioning was faulty. But she knew better. It was him.

"Like what you see?" His voice sent shivers down her spine.

It was a tone she knew well. Her body reacted immediately and she could feel the moisture gathering between her legs. Her dress felt too tight and her breasts felt heavy. Trying to act nonchalant, she shrugged and returned her gaze to his face.

"You can't fool me, Mrs. Sloan. I not only heard you were hot. I know you are." Pushing away from the shelf, he walked slowly down the aisle towards her. He was a male animal who had scented prey and knew that there was no reason to hurry the hunt.

Annabelle, however, was no easy prey. She held out her hand and stopped him in his tracks. "Stop right there." He stopped, but the look in his eyes was one of a man who was sure he would have the prize. Maybe he would, but it would be her victory as well.

Reaching slowly up to her head, she started pulling out the pins that held her hair in their customary bun. The heavy tresses fell to her waist and she smiled as his nostrils flared in response. She tossed the pins on top of a book about the mating habits of wild animals. Laughing out loud, she ran her fingers through her hair.

Suddenly, she was glad she wore this dress today. It was a light denim dress, but it had buttons from hem to neckline. Her fingers slipped one button from its hole. Then another. And another.

He watched her fingers as they moved leisurely down the front of her body. His hot gaze made her feel as if she was already naked. When the last button was undone, she slipped the dress off her shoulders. It pooled around her feet, and she kicked it aside. Then she slipped out of her shoes and nudged them after the dress. Dressed only in her underwear, she faced him proudly.

She was so glad that she'd chosen to wear her new lingerie this morning. It was a pale lavender bra that was nothing but stretch lace and underwire with a matching thong. She knew he could see her dark pubic hair beneath the lavender lace, so she ran her fingers along the thin straps at her hips to draw attention to that fact.

Mouth hanging open in disbelief, he watched her. He swallowed hard, opened his mouth, and then closed it again. Clearing his throat, he tried again. "Annabelle...." He trailed off.

"You heard right." She ran her hands up over her sides and cupped her breasts, running her thumbs over the tights nubs. "I am hot." Sauntering a little closer she lowered her voice to a sultry whisper. "I think you're man enough to handle me."

"You're damn right I am." Advancing forward, he tore his white T-shirt over his head and dropped it to the floor. He didn't slow until he was standing right in front of her.

He towered over her, but Annabelle felt no fear. She would trust him with her very life. Running her fingers over his chest, she taunted the savage beast that lurked beneath the man.

Trapping her hands against his chest, he scowled down at her. "I'm the only man who is ever going to handle you." He looked fierce as he stared at her.

She nodded and gave him the reassurance he needed. "Yes." It really was that simple. No other man aroused her like the one in front of her. He was all she'd ever wanted and he was all hers. "And I'm the only woman you'll ever need."

"You got that right." Raising her hands to his mouth, he kissed all of her knuckles, one by one, before dropping her hands and stepping back from her.

"Let me look at you." He used more than just his eyes to "look" at her, for he used his hands as well. His large, rough hands covered her lace-covered breasts, weighing them in his palms. "I love your breasts." He spoke almost reverently as he bent down and took a lace-covered nipple into his mouth. He stroked it with his tongue until he was satisfied that the nipple was as hard as it could be, and then he gently worked it with his teeth.

Annabelle rubbed her body against his, even as she clasped his head to her chest. But he wasn't finished. His clever mouth continued to play with her breasts while his fingers slid to the waistband of her thong. He traced the lace triangle that covered, but didn't conceal, her pubic hair. "Did I ever tell you that I love how thick your hair is?" He slid his fingers beneath the fabric and combed his fingers through the curls there.

When she shook her head, he continued. "I love to taste and smell you." He pulled his fingers out of her panties and brought them to his nose and sniffed. "You smell hot."

She reached down between them and traced the hard ridge of his arousal. "You feel hot." Her palm covered him, testing his readiness.

"You're asking for trouble," he warned, even as he pushed his erection harder against her hand.

"Maybe, I want trouble," she taunted him, squeezing his erection.

The flaring heat in his eyes was the only warning she got. He opened his jeans and pushed down his shorts enough to release his penis. It was large, thick, and throbbing. Pushing her back against a bookshelf, he reached down and hooked one of her legs over his hip. Impatiently, he pushed away the thong and guided his cock into her waiting wetness.

Her inner muscles squeezed him tight as he entered. Even though she was aroused, it was a tight fit. She flexed her hips slightly and he sunk even farther into her. He grabbed her ass, left bare by the thong, and pulled her tight to him. Burying his face in her neck, he took a deep breath as he struggled for control.

She didn't want him to be controlled. "Fuck me," she whispered the command in his ear. His head jerked back quickly. He opened his mouth to speak, but she flexed her hips again and all that came out of his mouth was a long groan.

"Hold on tight," he ordered as he began to move. Using his hold on her ass for leverage, he plunged in and out of her.

She hooked her leg as high as she could over his hip and urged him on. "Harder," she moaned as she flexed her own hips to meet his thrusts. He worked her up and down his penis, thrust after thrust. Suddenly, he banded one arm around her waist and wedged one finger between them. His finger sought and found the front of the lacy thong and he rubbed her clitoris through the lace. The rough fabric and his finger stimulated her even as he continued to thrust inside her.

Holding on to the shelf behind her with one hand and grasping his shoulder for balance with the other, she felt her inner muscles tighten around him. Squeezing him. His finger pressed harder on her clitoris and she came apart in his arms. Convulsing, she let go and let her orgasm wash over her. As she squeezed his cock, she felt him come deep inside her.

He stiffened, but didn't stop thrusting until the last tremor of her orgasm finished. Her leg slid down his hip and her foot flopped to the floor. Her hand dropped from the shelf and she fell against his chest. "I love you, Mike." She nuzzled his chest and allowed herself to sink into his warmth.

"Love you too." He absently kissed the top of her head while his hands soothed her tired body.

"Hey, anybody up there?" The voice came from below, shattering the moment.

"Oh, my god," Annabelle whispered in shock. "It's Mr. Keats."

Mike held her tight, refusing to let her move. "It's Mike."

"Is Annabelle up there with you?" The disembodied voice floated up from the bottom of the stairs.

"Yeah, I'm just waiting for her to finish up so I can take her home." He pinched her bottom and nipped at her neck.

She squeaked, unable to stop herself. She'd never made a sound like that in her life.

"Are you sure you're all right?" The voice sounded a little closer.

Panicked, Annabelle took charge. "Every thing is fine, Mr. Keats." She took a deep breath and continued. "I'll be a little longer, just make sure the door is locked behind you, and Mike and I will turn off all the lights when we leave."

"Have a good evening." His tone now sounded more amused than worried.

"Goodnight, Harold," they both replied in tandem. They both held their breath until they heard the sound of the front door closing.

Slumping against him in relief, she mocked him. "I'm waiting for her to finish up. I'll finish you, all right." She made good on her threat by using her secret weapon. She tickled his sides.

"No," he yelled, but it was too late. She attacked his sides and was ruthless until he dissolved into laughter. He fell to the floor, but pulled her with him. In moments, he was tickling her as well and they both laughed and played until they fell back exhausted.

Annabelle had ended up lying on top of Mike. It was an extremely cozy position. "Do you give up?" Propping herself up on his chest, she peered down at him, awaiting his surrender.

"I gave up a long time ago," He hooked a long tress of her hair behind her ear. "And I'm glad I did." The look on his face was one of a man very satisfied and content with his life.

"Me too." Annabelle placed her head on his chest and dozed to the comforting rhythm of his heartbeat. She didn't know how much time had passed before he roused her.

Sitting up, Mike cajoled her off his lap and leaned her against a shelf so she wouldn't slide back to the floor. He struggled to his feet, snatched up his T-shirt and pulled it over his head, and tucked it into his jeans. He zipped his jeans and then ran his hands through his hair which had come loose during their vigorous lovemaking. He took a moment and retied the leather thong around it.

She sat tousled, sleepy, and content and watched him. Her dress looked even more delicate in his masculine hands, but those hands shook her dress out and brought it to her.

Shaking his head at her debauched sprawl, he helped her to stand and then dressed her. Patiently, he redid all the buttons on her dress for her and then went down on one knee in front of her and, one at a time slipped her shoes on her feet.

He stood in front of her and eyed her hair, clearly at a loss. "I can't do anything about your hair, sweetheart."

Annabelle scooped her pins off the shelf and handed them to Mike. "Just hold these." Bending at the waist, she combed her fingers through her hair and then expertly twisted it. In seconds, her familiar bun was in place on her head and she reached out and plucked the pins from Mike's hands and poked them into place.

Mike admired the result. Except for the flush on her face and her swollen lips, she looked exactly like she did when he first got here. "I still don't know how you can to that."

Smiling coyly at him, she responded. "A woman has to have some secrets."

"I don't know about most women, but you continually surprise me." Clasping her hand in his he led her towards the front of the library. "Let's go home."

The lights clicked off behind them and a door slammed as they left the empty library. The only sign that they'd been there was a single pin that lay on the floor, forgotten.

HEAT WAVE

஋

Dedication

∞

To my wonderful husband, whose continuous love and support is invaluable to me. And to Pamela, whose hard work makes my stories shine. Thank you both!

Chapter One

ഇ

The minute the door closed behind them, he bent down and kissed her. His lips barely grazed hers as he moved them from side to side. Unconsciously, she leaned forward, wanting to deepen his touch. A whimper of need escaped her as he pulled just out of her reach.

She opened her eyes and stared up at him as he smiled down at her. Well, maybe not a real smile. More of a slight upturn of the corners of his mouth. It was the look of male satisfaction in his face that set off the first warning signal. But it was faint, and before it could take hold of her, he slowly bent down and covered her mouth again.

Sighing, she parted her lips and invited him in. The man certainly knew how to kiss. Taking his time, he lazily tasted her lips before delving inside. Her purse fell to the floor with a thud as she raised her hands to his shoulders, gripping them tight. She could feel the play of muscles under her fingers.

When he finally slipped his tongue inside her mouth, she sighed with relief. Still, he took his time, slowly stroking her tongue with his before exploring every crevice of her mouth. He didn't challenge her or try to overpower her. It was more an invitation to share with him. Emma Howard couldn't resist.

Her hands crept up the side of his neck and tunneled through his short, spiky black hair. Gripping the back of his head with her fingers, she angled his face so she could deepen their kiss. She felt the heady surge of power as he moved as she wished. Then she was lost in the sensations assaulting her. She couldn't get enough. Coffee, peppermint and Tucker.

Her brain registered the fact that she was moving backward, but she didn't care. She was so wrapped up in their kiss that nothing else mattered. She felt the door against her back as he surrounded her with his sheer size and bulk.

Tucker Martin was six feet tall, but looked much larger as he towered over her five-foot-five frame. His shoulders and chest were wide, his waist lean. His legs were long, his thighs thick with muscle.

Usually, large men made her uncomfortable, but somehow Tucker managed not to intimidate her with his size. Until now. Now, she was very aware of the difference between them. But instead of alarming her, it only served to send a torrent of sexual awareness zinging through her entire body.

Moisture pooled between her thighs and she had to fight the urge to rub her crotch against the bulge she could feel in the front of Tucker's jeans, but it wasn't easy. She knew it would feel so damned good and help ease the throbbing ache.

Tucker still hadn't touched her except for where their mouths were joined. His hands were flat on the door on either side of her head. She was the one who had moved closer to him, so their bodies were barely touching. She couldn't stand it any longer. She needed his hands on her.

"Touch me." Her voice sounded strange to her own ears. Breathy and low, not the usual no-nonsense, well-modulated tone that she'd cultivated over the years.

His lips left hers and he nuzzled her sensitive skin around her ear. "Are you sure?"

If she was any surer, she'd explode with the amount of heat her body was generating. Instead of answering him, she leaned forward and rubbed her breasts across the broad planes of his chest. Even through the fabric of her blouse and his shirt, the pressure of his body on her swollen nipples made her moan with pleasure.

Tucker's large hands cupped her face as he swooped down and captured her lips. She'd thought his earlier kisses were devastating, but they'd been nothing but a small taste of the real thing.

This time, he took total control and claimed her. His tongue stroked hard, demanding a response from her. Unable to do anything else, she gave him what he wanted. She rubbed his tongue with hers and sucked it deeper into her mouth.

Groaning, his hands slid down over her neck, his thumbs tipping her chin higher. She arched her neck towards him as his hands continued their descent. His fingers lightly traced her collarbone before moving down the center of her chest, unbuttoning her blouse.

When his strong hands cupped her lace-covered breasts, she totally lost control. Need rushed through her body as she struggled to get even closer to him. Digging her fingers into his shoulders for support, she angled her lower body towards his, rubbing her pussy against his hard erection.

Tucker stroked his thumbs over the silky fabric of her bra. He traced the outline of her swollen nipples, keeping his touch light and undemanding, until she thought she might go mad. She craved more of his touch. "Harder. Touch me harder," she managed to gasp out.

She fought him when she felt him pulling away from her, not wanting to lose her grip on him. Then she struggled to help him when he murmured, "I want to see you naked."

Her blouse and bra hit the floor, leaving her naked from the waist up. The cool air from the air conditioner wafted across her nipples, making the tips pucker even tighter. Goose bumps skittered across her skin. Usually she was self-conscious about the small size of her breasts, but Tucker's eyes were filled with pure unadulterated lust as he stared at them. She was proud that her breasts turned him on, and she arched her back slightly, the small movement thrusting her chest towards him.

"I've got to see you naked." His words, so blunt and unadorned, thrilled her. But it was obvious that she wasn't stripping fast enough to suit him. When his hands reached for the button on her pants, she didn't utter a word of protest. He quickly undid the button of her black slacks, slid down the zipper and pushed them down over her hips, taking her lace panties with them. Going down on one knee in front of her, he lifted her feet, one at a time, removing her shoes, sliding her clothing off.

Emma could barely breathe as she looked down at the man kneeling between her spread thighs. The hum of the air conditioner and Tucker's heavy breathing were the only sounds she could hear over the pounding of her own heart.

As she watched him, he undid several buttons on his shirt before just giving up and yanking it over his head and tossing it aside. His chest was magnificent. Bronze and heavily muscled, it had a light sprinkling of hair that spread from nipple to nipple before angling downward and disappearing into the waistband of his jeans. Her fingers curled into her palm, longing to stroke him.

"You are so beautiful." His words were low and his voice thick with need as he reached out and wrapped his hands around her ankles, encircling them both in his grip. Inch by inch, he slid his hands up over her shins, past her knees, finally coming to rest on her thighs. He slipped his hands to the inside, his touch featherlight as he silently encouraged her to spread her legs wider.

Emma couldn't tear her eyes away from him as he looked up at her, his green eyes glowing with desire. She'd never seen anything so erotic or beautiful in her life as the sight of him sitting between her thighs, his mouth just inches from her swollen pussy. She spread her legs wider, inviting him to taste her.

Lowering his gaze, he brushed his thumbs over the swollen folds of her labia. She was wet and swollen with a need unlike any other she'd ever experienced in her life. She'd had lovers before, not many, but enough to know that this was something far outside her own experience.

She held her breath as his head dipped between her thighs. His breath was hot on her flesh as he flicked his tongue out, rasping the small nub of desire. Her entire body clenched with need as he continued to stroke her with his fingers and tongue. All her concentration was centered on her pussy and the wondrous sensations he was making her feel.

Her hips undulated towards him, urging him to deepen his caress. She gasped when he picked up one of her feet and draped her leg over his shoulder. It opened her wider to him and he slipped his tongue inside her slit.

Emma clutched his hair with both hands, holding him tight to her as she arched into his touch. There was no way she was letting him stop now. His laughter vibrated through her pussy as he suddenly grasped her other leg and lifted it over his shoulder. Totally off balance, she felt herself starting to fall. "Tucker," she cried as she dug her fingers into his back for support, her fingernails lightly scoring his flesh.

"I've got you." His strong hands gripped her hips, holding her steady, as he buried his face in her pussy and devoured her.

With her legs spread wide and draped over either of his shoulders, Emma had no control over what he did. And she no longer cared. Nothing mattered but reaching completion. She bucked her hips against his face, as he licked and sucked at her. She was so close. Her feet thumped against his back as she closed her eyes and held on tight to him.

Tucker released her hips and slid his hands up over her rib cage, not stopping until his hands were covering her breasts. He kneaded them, plumping them in his grip before gently rolling the tight buds between his thumbs and forefingers. At that exact moment, he sucked her clit into his mouth and lapped at it with his tongue.

Emma screamed as an orgasm, unlike anything she'd ever experienced in her life, shot though her body. Heat exploded within her, spreading to every part of her, as her body convulsed. She dug her heels into his back, desperately trying to get even closer to him, even though she knew that was physically impossible. She wanted to take him inside her and never let him go.

When she finally recovered her senses, she was slumped back against the door and her feet were flat on the floor. She had no memory of him moving them off his shoulders. The sound of something tearing caught her attention and she blinked, trying to bring the world back into focus.

Tucker's jeans were undone and he'd shoved them partially down over his hips. As she watched, he pushed aside his underwear as well and released his swollen cock from its confinement. He was big. Much bigger than any other lover she'd ever had. And thicker. Fascinated, she watched as he sheathed himself in a condom.

It belatedly occurred to her that she had come, but Tucker obviously had not.

He surged to his feet in one smooth motion, cupped her bottom in his hands and lifted her high. Wedging his body between her thighs, he held her with one hand as he reached between their bodies and guided his cock to her moist, humid opening.

She could feel the broad head push into her still swollen flesh. He stretched her wide as he pushed his hard length inside her, not stopping until he was seated right to the hilt. She struggled, trying to accept him, but he was so large and her pussy was sensitive from her own orgasm. She whimpered and Tucker held himself still, burying his face in the curve of her neck.

She could feel him struggling for breath and sensed his control was tenuous at best. "Just relax, honey." Tucker licked her neck before nipping at it. "You can take me." His grip tightened on her, but other than that, he didn't move.

His cock pulsed deep inside her and her inner muscles squeezed his hard length as her body responded to his. She ran her hands over his slick shoulders and, as if that was the signal he'd been waiting for, he flexed his hips, pulling his cock almost all the way out until only the tip was still inside her. Then he thrust himself back in.

At first, Emma found it slightly uncomfortable. But after a few thrusts, her body relaxed, eagerly accepting his, and she began to anticipate the feel of his hard length as it plunged deep, arching her hips to meet him.

"Emma." That was all he said as he trailed a path of hot, stinging kisses across her chin before claiming her mouth. His tongue thrust into her mouth, keeping time with his cock.

Each stroke was faster and harder. She locked her ankles together and levered her pelvis towards him with each thrust. As he plunged into her, she could feel his balls slapping against her. She gripped him to her as tight as she could, digging her fingers into his shoulders.

The musky smell of sex wafted around them as the sounds of sex filled the air. Moans and groans were punctuated by the sucking noise her body made as Tucker pulled almost all the way out of her wet pussy.

As her inner muscles began to convulse around him, she tore her mouth from his, gasping for breath as she cried out. She shook her head from side to side, trying to deny the power of their coming together, but nothing could stop it.

As she spasmed around him, she could feel the heat of his cum as he filled the condom. He let out a yell and thrust himself hard one final time.

Emma felt totally drained. She was surprised by the lack of control she had over her own body. She'd never known that she was capable of such explosive orgasms.

Her body shook with the occasional aftershock as she unhooked her ankles from behind Tucker. Her legs slid down over his flanks driving him even deeper inside her. Moaning, she clung to him for support.

"Hmm," he agreed as he thrust his hips once again.

"Tucker," she panted. "You have to stop."

He froze at her words and she felt his entire body tense. "Are you all right?" His concern washed over her as he carefully withdrew from her. She shuddered at the separation, feeling empty without him.

She nodded, although she wasn't really sure she would ever be okay again. Tucker wrapped his arms around her and hugged her tight. Burying her face against his chest, she returned his embrace with a fierceness that surprised her before forcing herself to release him.

Leaning down, he dropped a kiss on the top of her head. "I've got to get rid of this." He gestured towards the condom. "I'll be right back." Hitching his jeans up, he turned and walked away.

She watched as he disappeared down the short hallway. He'd never been in her apartment before, but he knew where to find the bathroom as she had the exact same layout as his. A shiver racked her as she watched him disappear. He hadn't even taken off his shoes and she was totally naked.

That thought galvanized her to action. Grabbing her underwear, she hauled it on, ignoring the sticky, wet sensation between her legs. She pulled on her slacks and grabbed her blouse, pulling it on and buttoning it quickly. Picking up her bra, she stuffed it in her pants pocket just as Tucker came back down the hall.

His eyebrows came together in a scowl when he saw that she was dressed. Ignoring him, she picked up his shirt and handed it to him. Not saying a word, he yanked it over his head, not bothering with the rest of the buttons.

"I think you should go." The words came automatically to her lips. Part of her wanted him to stay. Desperately. She wanted to explore this explosive sexual chemistry that ran between them. It was for that very reason that she asked him to leave.

Tucker, more than any other man she'd ever known, threatened her peace of mind. He rocked her world, destroying the carefully cultivated control that she'd worked so hard to protect. He made her feel reckless, stirring up all kinds of deep and powerful emotions that she'd kept buried deep inside her. He could easily become very important in her life and that would give him power over her. She couldn't bear the thought of that.

She needed time to think. Straightening her shoulders, she ignored the part of herself that was telling her she was making a huge mistake. She listened instead to the part that urged her towards the safe, sure path.

"What did you say?" Tucker was staring at her as if he couldn't quite believe the words coming out of her mouth.

"I said, I think you should go." She was getting angry now, but most of that anger was aimed at herself. It was only their third date, and she'd not only had sex with him, she'd encouraged him. She had no one but herself to blame for the situation. "I don't think we should see each other again."

"You've got to be joking." Tucker moved towards her, his hands outstretched to gather her into his strong embrace.

Emma flinched backward, afraid that if he touched her, she'd melt into his arms again.

He stopped dead in his tracks. "You know I would never hurt you." He slowly lowered his arms back down to his sides.

He said it with such sincerity that it brought unwanted tears to her eyes. He might not mean to hurt her, but Emma knew it was inevitable. She opened the door to her apartment. "I think you should go now."

Tucker's fingers opened and closed reflexively as he stalked to the doorway. His eyes narrowed as he pinned her with his laser green eyes. "This isn't over. I know you want me and for some reason that scares you."

Before she could react, he leaned down and planted a single hard kiss on her lips. Even as she felt herself leaning towards him, he was already pulling away.

"I'll be waiting when you're ready."

She stood there with her mouth open as he sauntered across the hall and let himself into his apartment. It was only when the door closed behind him, that she was able to shake herself out of her trance. "Of all the nerve," she said, because she felt like she should say something. Slamming the door shut, she glared at it, but it didn't give her any satisfaction. Tucker's words still rang in her head, mocking her.

Leaning her forehead against the door, she closed her eyes. What had she done?

Chapter Two

✖

Tucker winced when he heard the door to her apartment slam shut. Damn, he'd finally thought that he'd made some headway when Emma invited him into her apartment after their date.

Kicking off his shoes, he headed to his bedroom to change.

He knew it was a mistake to make love with her this soon, but he'd been unable to resist kissing her. And when she whispered *touch me* in that soft, sexy voice, he was lost. Sex with Emma was even better than he'd imagined and he'd imagined plenty.

Running his fingers through his hair, he heaved a sigh as he walked into his room. He knew he'd lost what little ground he'd gained in the last few weeks. She was so darn skittish around him and he wasn't quite sure why. He'd done his best to keep his actions laid-back, mostly coming around her so she could get used to him. His time and patience had been rewarded when she'd agreed to go out to dinner with him. This was their third date, but he had a sinking feeling that it would be their last one for a while.

Stripping off his shirt, he flung it on the bed. He was still pissed off at how quickly she'd kicked him out of her apartment. He'd been looking forward to a long night in her bed. The first of many such nights. But in the time it had taken him to clean up in the washroom, she'd changed from a sleepy, sated woman to one who had all her defenses up.

She was afraid of him. Tucker tipped back his head, closed his eyes and took another deep calming breath. He hated seeing her close up right before his very eyes. The open, smiling woman was gone, replaced by one he couldn't read. The hardest part was that he had no idea what she was afraid of.

He knew that she wasn't physically afraid of him. She'd have never made love to him if that were the case. And thank God for that. At least she knew that he would never hurt her.

But he sensed that she was very afraid of what he made her feel. That, at least, gave him hope. It meant that she at least felt something for him. And he hoped that that something was deep and meaningful. Or maybe he was simply deluding himself into believing what he wanted too.

He'd wanted Emma from the moment he'd laid eyes on her. She might not be society's idea of beautiful, but there was something about her that had struck a chord deep within him.

There was a calmness about her that appealed to him, a steadiness of character that shone through in everything she did. Her brown eyes were expressive, showing every emotion. And, when she smiled, it lit her entire face, making her glow. Emma was beautiful from the inside out and her beauty was the kind that only got better with age. His entire body had gone on alert at their first meeting and nothing had changed since then. He still wanted her.

But it had changed and developed into something even deeper since then. The more he'd gotten to know her, the more he wanted her. And not just for sex. He wanted her in his life on a permanent basis.

It had been easy to find out more about her. Dropping her name in conversation here and there, he'd learned a lot about her. She was honest, hard working, friendly and people liked her. They'd both been on the fundraising committee for the local library. He'd enjoyed working alongside her. She was smart, organized, and had a sense of humor that complemented his own.

They'd spent time together at local functions, but they'd always been around other people. Emma was a different person then, more open and friendly. It was only when they were alone together or when she sensed that he was trying to get closer to her that she became nervous and closed off.

Pulling off the rest of his clothing, he tossed them aside and hauled on a pair of faded jeans, zipping them, but not bothering with the button. Padding back down the hall, he went to the kitchen and got a beer. Opening the can, he took a swig before wandering into the living room, slumping down on the sofa, and propping his feet up on the table.

She'd avoid him now. He knew that as sure as he knew that the sun would rise tomorrow morning. It would take time and effort to get back to the place they'd been in their budding relationship. But Tucker was in this for the long haul. He'd never met a woman who suited him so well.

It was for that very reason that he'd moved into her apartment building. He'd never tell her that. It made him sound like some kind of stalker, which he wasn't. But he was smart enough to know that everyday contact was the only way to win Emma. She had to get used to him being around in order to lose her irrational fear of him.

He'd actually been getting ready to buy a house, but he'd put that on hold for a few months. Right now, getting close to Emma was priority. If everything worked out the way he wanted, they'd be looking for a house together in a few months. Better to wait and get something that he was sure she would like.

Taking another sip of his beer, he enjoyed the cold liquid as it slid down his throat. Holding the can between his hands, he tilted his head back and closed his eyes. Tonight had been absolutely amazing. The sex had been incredible, but it was the connection he'd felt with her that had made it even better. She'd been so open and giving. Now that he had a taste of how it could be between them, he wanted it even more.

Failure just wasn't acceptable. In all his thirty-two years, he'd always known his own mind and had planned and worked for what he wanted. He had a good life, plenty of friends, his own electrical contracting business, and was financially secure enough to purchase his own home. And he knew he wanted a chance at a life with Emma more than he'd ever wanted anything in his life.

He'd just have to be patient. She'd never have given herself to him so completely tonight if her feelings weren't involved. She rarely dated and never seriously, so for her to have sex with him was a huge deal for her. And that suited him just fine.

His cock stirred as memories from earlier flickered through his mind. She'd looked breathtaking when she'd finally come. The expression of surprise and delight on her face would haunt him for many nights to come. No, she certainly hadn't held anything back from him. He was starting to sweat just thinking about it.

Sighing, he swung his feet back to the floor and stood. He stopped in the kitchen long enough to pour the remaining beer down the sink and toss the can in the recycle bin before heading to the bathroom. Right now, he needed a cold shower or he'd never get any sleep tonight. Not that he really expected to get any.

He had to view this as a small setback. There was no way he was giving up on his and Emma's burgeoning relationship. In fact, he was just beginning.

Emma managed to go almost one whole day before she ran into Tucker again. She'd practically run out of the building this morning, skulking down the stairs instead of waiting for the elevator, which was known to be ridiculously slow at times. She couldn't risk bumping into him while she was waiting.

She'd breathed a sigh of relief when she'd finally pushed her way out the front door and hurried down the front steps and away from the building. But then, she kept looking over her shoulder all the way on her walk to work. And being at work hadn't helped. She'd jumped every time someone had come into the gallery, certain it would be Tucker demanding some explanation for her behavior last night.

And she had no explanation. Sex with Tucker had been unlike anything else she'd ever experienced in her life. Physically, she hadn't known it was possible for her to have an orgasm that intense and certainly not several within the space of a few minutes. Her nipples puckered against the thin silk sheath she was wearing under her summer cotton blazer. She had to bite her lip to keep from moaning aloud. Her panties were already damp.

Tucker seemed almost too good to be true. The man always seemed to be prepared for anything. When Mrs. James down the hall had problems with her sink, Tucker fixed it easily. Have a flat tire? No problem, Tucker can change it for you so you can get to the garage. It had gotten to the point that, if the superintendent of the building wasn't around, everyone looked for Tucker to take care of any problem they had. And the thing that surprised her most was that he usually handled all their minor household crises and did it with a smile on his face. The man exuded charm and appeal.

She knew it was perverse, but that was why she didn't trust him. He was too handsome and charming for her peace of mind. There was a small voice in the back of her head that whispered that anyone who seemed too good to be true probably was. That had certainly been her experience.

By the time she left work for the evening, she was feeling better about things. Locking up the building for the evening, she hitched her purse over her shoulder and started her short walk home. If he were going to confront her about last night, she reasoned, he would have done so before now. In fact, Tucker probably wasn't thinking about it at all. They'd dated, had sex and now it was over. Her stride lengthened as she walked and thought.

The more she thought about it the more she was convinced that she was right. There was no way he'd have spent the entire day agonizing over what had happened last night. Most men only wanted sex. Now that he'd had it, Tucker would probably just move on to some other woman. Just the thought of that made her stomach clench, but she ignored it. Whatever he did it was no concern of her. Not anymore.

She was being silly, working herself up over nothing. Still, her heart started to pound the closer she got to her building. She could see him standing on the front lawn with Mrs. Jacobs. The older woman was gesturing to something on the ground and Tucker was hanging on her every word and giving her the occasional nod.

She still wanted him. Swallowing hard, she willed her feet to keep moving forward. Just the sight of him made her break out into a sweat. Her hands were clammy and her legs unsteady as she put one foot in front of the other and headed up the walkway.

Deep in the pit of her stomach was the nagging doubt that she'd given up on something very special before it had a chance to even begin. Her head continued to remind her about the unreliability of men like Tucker and that she was better off without him.

Rubbing her temple with one hand to try and stop the headache that was forming behind her eyes, she placed the other one over her churning stomach, trying desperately to settle it. All she wanted right now was to get to her apartment, strip off her work clothes and lie down.

"Are you all right?" The low, concerned rumble brought her to a complete halt. Slowly, she raised her eyes and was struck by the concern in his. "Emma?"

"I'm sorry," she shook herself, realizing she'd been caught staring at him. "I'm fine."

"You don't look fine." His blunt words had her back stiffening and the beginnings of anger running through her veins. If she didn't look good, then it was his fault. He was the one who'd upset her entire well-structured life.

She opened her mouth, but quickly closed it again. No, it wasn't his fault. She couldn't blame anyone but herself for this mess.

"I don't think she looks well, Tucker." Emma felt Mrs. Jacobs' hand on her arm. Forcing herself to smile, Emma turned her attention away from Tucker's intense stare to focus on the older woman. "Really, I'm fine. Just a hard day at work." She decided it was time to try and change the subject. "What are you two doing?"

Mrs. Jacobs looked unconvinced, but patted her arm and thankfully dropped the subject. "Tucker is helping me put in some flowers. It looks so stark and bland out in front of the building that I thought it needed some color."

Reaching out, she patted Tucker's shoulder. "He convinced the owners of the building to pay for some of the cost of the soil and the flowers by telling them that he'd do all the labor." Mrs. Jacobs laughed. "Then he took me shopping for flowers. The poor boy didn't know what he was getting himself into when he volunteered for this."

Tucker wrapped his arm around the older woman's shoulders and bent down, planting a kiss on her cheek. "I'm having a great time and learning quite a lot from you. It will come in handy when I get my own home."

"Oh? Are you buying a house?" Emma wanted to swallow back the words as soon as they passed her lips. It was none of her concern. But the thought of Tucker moving away and not seeing him anymore started her stomach churning again.

"Not yet. Right now I need to get a few other things straightened out in my life."

She couldn't quite decipher the strange look he was giving her.

"But I'm hoping to start looking at houses soon."

Not knowing what else to do, Emma gave him a polite nod. "Well, I'll leave you to your work." Turning, she headed up the walkway and into the building without looking back. But she couldn't resist a quick glance behind her before she was out of their sight. Tucker was still standing there with his hands on his hips, watching her.

Swallowing hard, she broke away from his gaze and trudged towards the elevator. She was too exhausted to even consider the stairs and there was no need now that their first meeting since having sex was over.

They would go back to being just friendly acquaintances and she would forget all about the amazing evening they'd spent together. When the bell rang, she stepped into the elevator, pulled the old iron gate across and watched the door close. She had no idea at the time that she'd be still trying to convince herself of that two months later.

Chapter Three

ဢ

Emma tilted her head to the side and stared at the picture she'd just finished hanging on the wall. As the owner and manager of Art Inspired, she took a keen interest in every aspect of the business, but it was the art itself that she loved. And this painting was exceptional.

It seemed simple enough at first glance. Nothing more than a man repairing a fence. But closer inspection revealed layers of meaning. The man was pictured side-on, but he had his face turned away so that the viewer caught only a hint of the strength stamped there. The tilt of his chin gave him a slightly arrogant, self-assured look.

His body was strong, a tool to be used much like the hammer he held in his hand. He'd stripped his shirt off and had hung it over a fence post. He was naked from the waist up, wearing only a pair of worn jeans and work boots. The muscles in his arms seemed to ripple with movement as he held the hammer poised to strike the nail on the fence.

The day was hot, the heat seeming to rise around him. There were insects on the grass and in the air around him. A bead of sweat was poised to roll down his muscular back. Indeed, his entire torso seemed to shimmer with a light sheen of perspiration.

But it was his hands that held her spellbound. Encased in a pair of leather work gloves, they held a wood post with one hand and the hammer with the other. The gloves came just to his wrists, which were thick and strong and tanned.

Closing her eyes, Emma swallowed. A bead of sweat trickled down her temple in spite of the air-conditioning that cooled the gallery. She licked her dry lips as she imagined what his hands would look like outside the gloves.

Strong. They would be strong and hard and calloused. These were hands used to hard labor, as hard as the man who owned them was. But they would be gentle too, as they skimmed over a woman's softer flesh.

A shudder racked her body as her breasts swelled and began to ache, the hard nubs pushing against the silk camisole she wore under her linen jacket. She could practically feel the rough pads of his fingers as they stroked across her nipples. Her body swayed forward towards an unseen hand.

In her mind, the man turned his head towards her, his green eyes glittering with undisguised lust. Tucker. Just the thought of him was enough to have her pussy throbbing with need. She shifted, trying to ease the ache, but it was useless. Her body knew what it wanted even as her brain screamed at her to stop. Moisture dampened her panties as her body prepared itself for him.

Yes, Tucker could easily be the man in the picture. He held himself with the same kind of confidence. He knew who he was and what he wanted. And, he'd made it abundantly apparent months ago, what he wanted was her. His every look and word were designed to seduce her.

The very first time she'd laid eyes on him, she'd wanted him. And that had never happened to her. He evoked unwelcome feelings of want and need in her that she'd never experienced before. He fascinated her, luring her with his easy charm and good looks. She'd never yearned for any man as much as she had for Tucker.

He scared her to death.

"Gorgeous, isn't he?"

Emma jumped, gasping for breath as she swung around. She felt hot, achy and totally out of sorts and it was all Tucker's fault.

"Are you okay?" Her assistant, Callie Jones, was looking at her with a worried look on her face. "Maybe you should sit down."

"No." Her reply had been sharper than she'd intended and Callie looked even more concerned. Emma took a deep breath and tried again. "I'm fine. I think the heat is finally getting to me." That was as good an excuse as any. The weather had been unbearably hot and people were beginning to feel the effects. She could hardly tell her friend that she'd been lost in an erotic daydream, featuring a man that she was determined to avoid at all costs.

It must have worked because Callie became her usual cheerful self once again and pointed back to the new painting on the wall. "That is one hot dude."

"Callie!" She tried to sound stern, but the younger woman just cocked an eyebrow at her, daring her to disagree. In spite of her earlier discomfort, she found herself staring at the man in the picture again. A reluctant smile crossed her lips and she pursed them to try and hold it back. But it was no good, Callie had already seen.

"See, you think so too." Her light laughter filled the room and she slung her arm around Emma's shoulders. "It's okay to think he's hot, boss. Just because you don't like to date doesn't mean you can't admire the scenery."

"Admire the scenery!" Emma sputtered and began to laugh. She covered her face with her hands and tried desperately to control herself. "I'll have you know that that is a serious piece of artwork."

Callie shot her a coy look from underneath her heavily painted eyelashes. "He certainly is."

Laughing at her assistant's antics, Emma shook her head and turned away from the painting. She could always count on Callie to make her feel better. The younger woman was a gem as an employee and a wonderful friend. An aspiring artist, Callie looked the part with her multiple earrings and her nose ring. She wore mostly dark clothing with dramatic makeup. Her talent was undeniable and she worked hard at her art and at the gallery, but it was her bubbly personality that attracted Emma. It was so unlike her own more serious one. But the laughter was just what she'd needed to disperse the uncomfortable feelings the image had evoked. She needed to get back to work.

"I'll be in my office if you need me." She headed towards the small room in the back of the gallery.

"Don't worry. I'll certainly keep an eye on things out here." Callie's laughter followed her all the way back into her office.

Emma shook her head and sighed as she closed her office door behind her. Some days she wished she were more like her friend. Callie dated a variety of men, keeping it all very casual and enjoying life with a sense of vigor that she admired. Emma rarely dated at all and took life very seriously.

She sometimes daydreamed that things were different, but then her common sense would reassert itself and remind her why she didn't trust strong, good-looking men. Her father had been such a man, and she and her mother had paid the price. James Howard had swept Emma's mother, Sarah, off her feet when she was just eighteen. Emma had followed only five months after they were wed. Any idiot could do the math.

Her father had flitted in and out of her life for the first nine years before finally disappearing for good one day. She remembered his charming ways, his easily broken promises and her mother's tears. Emma refused to dwell on her own tears and broken heart.

Sarah Howard had always lived on the false hope that her husband would one day return, right up until she'd died of cancer three years ago. Emma hadn't even known how to contact him to let him know. As far as she knew, her parents had never divorced.

If her childhood had taught her one thing, it was not to depend on anyone, especially not a handsome, charming man. Emma refused to be weak like her mother. She'd worked her way through school and opened a small art supply store, Artworks. Once she'd started making money, she'd saved and planned, finally achieving the goal of owning her own gallery as well. With her two art-related businesses housed side by side in the small building on Summersville's busiest street, she was living her dream.

She'd picked the community of Summersville to settle in four years ago, deciding that it was the perfect place to open her business. It was a nice-sized town without being too big, a pleasant community where people said hello to each other on the street, but large enough to support her business ventures. It also got a good share of the tourist trade from early spring until the leaves finally fell in late fall. All in all, she was pleased with her decision to move here.

She'd made a couple of very close friends, but work occupied most of her time. Her apartment, which was in an older building, was close enough for her to walk to work. She was thirty-one years old and she'd built a good solid life. If sometimes she felt restless and discontent, she squashed those feelings.

Sure she dated. Sometimes. But she dated safe men, serious men, and plain-looking men. She'd made a mistake with Tucker and she regretted it ever since. From the moment he'd moved into the building, he'd made it known that he wanted to get to know her better. But she shied away from him, practically overpowered by his raw masculinity.

And yet, somehow he'd slipped past her defenses, charming her with his old-fashioned manners and his sense of humor. Even though he was so gorgeous that just looking at him was enough to make her drool, she hadn't felt threatened by him. It was as if he'd kept his entire masculine energy and testosterone harnessed while he was around her. In a moment of weakness, she'd accepted an invitation to go out to dinner with him.

One date had led to two and then to a third. They'd been totally normal dates, dinner one evening and a movie the next. Conversation had flowed easily between them as they discovered they had friends in common. It surprised her how easy she found it to make conversation with him. They talked about everything from politics to community matters to sports. Even their first kiss had been totally non-threatening.

Her guard had slipped slowly as she found herself drawn closer to Tucker, wanting to know all there was to know about him. The more she found out, the more he fascinated her. She caught glimpses that suggested there was much more to him than first met the eye. The heat still crackled between them, but he seemed content to let her take the lead and that had led her to a false sense of security.

It was only on that unforgettable third date that she'd seen the *real* Tucker for the very first time. He'd walked her to her apartment and, like a fool, she'd asked him in for coffee. It was if she'd somehow unleashed the sleeping giant. He'd practically oozed sex appeal and masculine determination when he'd bent down to kiss her.

She'd been swept up in the intensity of his kiss. With all his attention focused on her, she'd felt like the most desirable woman in the world. And what woman could resist that? What had happened next still kept her awake at night. And when she did manage to sleep she had long, hot dreams that left her sweaty and aching for fulfillment when she awoke.

That had been two months ago and Tucker had been true to his word. He didn't crowd her, but he always seemed to be around the building when she was. His eyes got a knowing gleam in them whenever he saw her, as if he knew that she was thinking about him. Then he'd give her a sexy grin that reminded her that they shared a secret that no one else knew. And always, she was aware of him as a man. His large, hot body standing next to her in the building lobby was enough to send shivers of desire coursing though her entire body.

He'd even sent her flowers once. She hadn't been sure they were from him as there had been no card, but she'd called her friend Lily Summers, who ran the only flower shop in town. Lily had confirmed that Tucker had purchased the lovely bouquet of wildflowers. She'd hung onto those damned things until they almost rotted, she was so reluctant to throw them out.

Sighing, Emma rubbed her forehead with her hand. That painting in the gallery had conjured memories that she been trying desperately to forget. Tucker was responsible for too many nights of lost sleep as it was. Now, he was affecting her work as well. And that just wouldn't do.

Shaking herself out of her sensual haze, she buttoned her jacket over her swollen nipples and checked her phone messages. The familiar voice of her friend Annabelle Sloan came over the speaker, reminding her of their lunch date tomorrow. Emma, Annabelle and Lily all got together for lunch at least once a week and she always looked forward to it.

But that was tomorrow. She still had to get through today, she reminded herself as she tried to concentrate on the bookwork on her desk. It was only eleven in the morning, but it had already been a long day.

Chapter Four

Emma stood inside the foyer of her apartment building and shuffled through the envelopes she pulled from her mailbox, glad to be inside and away from the stifling heat. A bead of sweat rolled down her temple, and she absently swiped it away with the back of her hand.

She lived close enough to the gallery that she walked to and from work every day. Usually, she looked forward to the pleasant fifteen-minute walk. It was nice to stroll through the town and mull over her day. Many times she'd stop and chat with friends that she met along the way.

But these days it was a chore just trying to get from one air-conditioned building to another. The summer heat wave that had Summersville in its grip showed no signs of abating any time soon, and after six days of the thermometer easily topping one hundred degrees, her temper was beginning to fray.

She hitched her purse higher over her shoulder as she headed towards the elevator, her sensible pumps tapping an impatient rhythm on the hardwood floor. Her only goal now was to get out of her cream-colored, linen suit and into a pair of shorts and tank top. It was only six o'clock in the evening and the sun still had a good three hours before it would go down. She planned to sip lemonade while lying in front of her air conditioner for the rest of the evening.

With a muted ring, the elevator door slid open and Emma pulled back the iron gate, eagerly stepping inside. Sliding the gate across, the doors were almost closed when she heard a familiar voice yell, "Hold the door!" She stabbed her finger on the button, the doors slid open again, and Tucker reached out and yanked the gate back, stepping into the cramped confines of the elevator with her.

If she hadn't already been hot, she most certainly was now. Tucker was six feet of prime male and filled the small elevator with his sheer masculine presence. Emma licked her suddenly dry lips.

Soulful green eyes, high cheekbones, and full lips gave his face a slightly exotic, yet sensual look. His short black hair stood up in spikes on top, just tempting a woman to smooth it down. Emma curled her fingers around her mail to keep herself from giving into temptation. She knew exactly how it would feel flowing between her fingers.

His body was hard. Everywhere. Tucker's shoulders strained the seams of his faded denim work shirt that hung open enough to reveal a skintight tank top stretched over a hard six-pack. His tight jeans emphasized the muscles in his thighs and cupped his tight bottom. In spite of her intentions to stay far away from him, she found herself drawn to him whenever they were together. And unfortunately, unlike most men, Tucker just seemed to get better with time and familiarity.

His lips were quirked up in a half smile and Emma realized that, not only had she been standing there staring at him like an idiot, but also her finger was still pressing the hold button. She had no idea when he'd closed the gate, but it was shut tight, and he was patiently waiting for her to select the right button as she was standing in front of the only control panel. She could feel the heat of embarrassment creeping up her face and quickly hit the button that would take them to the fifth floor.

"Hot day, isn't it?" She couldn't believe she'd asked such an inane question, and she felt her already red cheeks flush even more. To cover her discomfort she turned her attention back to the envelopes in her hands. *Pay attention to your male. No, mail,* she scolded herself.

"Hot is the right word." Emma shivered slightly as his low, husky voice washed over her. Glancing up, she swallowed hard when she saw the passionate gleam in his eyes as they skimmed up and down her body before stopping to linger on her legs.

She knew she was way out of her league with Tucker, as she'd always been drawn to quieter, low-key kind of guys. Tucker made her very aware that she'd been without a boyfriend for quite a while now. In fact, she hadn't even been on a date since their last fateful one, and the looks he was giving her were making her feel feverish and bothered.

Why, oh why, of all days, did he have to end up sharing the elevator with her? As it was, she'd had a hard enough time concentrating at work today after the episode with the painting and the subsequent memories that it stirred up. And nothing had *ever* distracted her from her work before Tucker.

"Oh my," she muttered before she could stop herself.

"Problem?" His deep voice rumbled close to her ear, his breath teasing the wisps of hair that lay there.

"It's nothing," she mumbled. She could barely breathe, let alone string together a coherent sentence. He was so close to her that he could easily trace the whorls of her ear with his tongue. The mere thought sent goose bumps down her spine and she shivered.

Totally disregarding her privacy, he peered over her shoulder and glanced at her mail. "You sure?"

If she didn't know better, she'd think that he was keeping tabs on her. But that was ridiculous. She'd made her position quite clear with Tucker, so he had no reason to be interested in her life.

In truth, she hadn't met a man who'd interested her in months, except for Tucker, and he didn't count as she wasn't about to pursue that attraction any further than she already had. He always left her feeling slightly wild and out of control.

And, for a woman who valued self-restraint, that was more than reason enough for avoiding him.

Emma glared at Tucker, but it was all for naught as he was still studying her mail and not her. "No, it's just a letter from a friend." Her voice was sharp, but she couldn't help it. His teasing was good-natured, but it left her feeling angry. Since their one time together, she had absolutely no interest in other men.

"You sure you're okay?" Tucker tucked his hands in his back pockets. She could hear the concern in his voice and knew it was sincere.

"I'm sure."

"If you ever need any help with anything don't hesitate to call or come knock on my door." His green-eyed gaze caught and held her captive. "I'd do everything I could for you."

She was touched by his offer, even though she knew she would never take him up on it. "Thank you." Impulsively, she reached out and briefly touched his arm.

He gave her a sharp nod before looking down to where her hand covered his denim-clad arm. She could feel the heat of his skin through the thin covering. Yanking back her hand, she hitched her purse over her shoulder, wondering why it was taking so long to reach their floor. The elevator was notoriously unreliable, but this was slow even for this relic.

She glanced up at the old-fashioned numbers over the top of the gate and frowned when she noticed the arrow wasn't moving. Damn, she hadn't even noticed that the elevator had stopped at the second floor.

Poking the button for her floor once more, she felt relieved when the elevator began to slowly rise. The faster she got away from Tucker and the hot fantasies he inspired, the better for her peace of mind. Absently, she tucked her mail into the outside pocket of her purse.

"Emma..." His voice trailed off as he reached out and touched her shoulder. It was the lightest of touches, but it seemed to burn right through the layer of her summer linen jacket, scorching her flesh underneath. She flinched from his potent touch, unable to stop herself.

Tucker swore under his breath, but released her immediately. Hunching her shoulders, she faced forward, wishing she were anywhere else at the moment. The man must think she was a complete nutcase. One minute she was practically devouring him with her eyes, the next she was acting like he was some kind of pervert.

Sighing, she turned to face him, knowing she owed him an apology. "I'm sorry." She rubbed her hand across her forehead where a headache was brewing from the combined heat and stress.

"Don't worry about it."

The lights flickered once, and then she was jolted as the elevator jerked to a sudden stop. Only Tucker's quick reflexes kept her from ending up in an undignified heap on the floor. One of his thick forearms was banded around her waist, keeping her upright.

The elevator went pitch-black and her fingers dug into his arm.

"Everything is okay," his deep voice steadied her. "I've got you."

Striving for some control, she released her death grip on his arm and forced herself to take a step away. She thought she heard him sigh, but couldn't be sure. "I wonder what happened?" Even though she knew it was useless, she stabbed at the buttons on the control panel.

"Rolling blackouts. The entire city has been having them all day." The tiny security light finally flicked to life.

"Great," she muttered. That's all she needed to cap off what had been a long, hot, frustrating day.

"Could be worse." Tucker's calm voice irritated her further.

"How?" she snapped back.

"The longest one today was only about a half hour. It shouldn't take them too long to get the power back on. We'll be fine."

Great, she'd practically snapped the man's head off and he was doing his best to reassure her. Taking a deep breath, she let it out slowly, before turning to face him. "Once again, I owe you an apology." Taking a step towards him, she held out her hand to try and find the wall.

Her hand was caught in his solid grasp as he drew her steadily towards him. "Apology accepted." Slowly, he raised her hand to his lips and kissed each knuckle slowly, one at a time, until he'd done the honors to all five of her fingers.

The tingles started in her fingers, ran up her arm, and eventually encompassed her entire body. His tongue licked the slight indents between her fingers, and she sucked in her breath as he slowly took one of her fingers into his mouth.

Her nipples tightened immediately and she could feel the dampness coating her panties. As much as she tried to fight it, her reaction to Tucker was like a spark to gasoline—explosive.

For a moment, she let herself enjoy the sensual heat flowing through her veins. It had been way too long since their one time together. And before that…well, she'd been in a sexual drought for quite a long time.

She'd always taken life seriously, first as a student, and then as a career woman, seldom taking the time to have a lover. The two times she had, she'd been left feeling disappointed and sorry she'd even bothered.

Both men had expressed their disappointment in her. One of them had even gone so far as to call her cold. After she'd gotten over her initial anger, she had been forced to acknowledge that maybe he was right.

Tucker had been the first man in over a year to even remotely interest her. But she'd been burned twice before and had long since decided that she simply wasn't the passionate type. Instead, she'd thrown herself into running the gallery and art supply store. Emma knew that it was her way of protecting herself against further disillusionment, but she'd made a life for herself that she was content with.

Regretfully, she tugged her hand away from his, breaking the tentative sensual bond between them. Instead of backing off, he slowly stalked towards her. She edged herself backward until her back touched the wall of the elevator. There was nowhere else to go. She swallowed as he came to a stop in front of her. Shuffling uneasily, she leaned against the wall for support.

Reaching out, he slipped his hands inside her open jacket. "Let's get you undressed."

Chapter Five

℘

Emma's screech of outrage bounced off the walls of the elevator. She shoved Tucker's hands off her, placed both her hands on his chest and pushed him away. He went easily, which reassured her slightly. But this time he'd gone too far.

"What do you think you're doing?" She tried to make her voice strong and authoritative. Her subconscious was urging her to get naked quick. Her breasts strained against the silk camisole that she wore under her jacket, making her regret that she hadn't worn a bra. Or maybe that was a good thing, she decided, as the soft material rasped her nipples, making them ache even as she imagined Tucker's hands covering the soft mounds.

"Just thought you'd be more comfortable in this heat." Tucker shrugged out of his work shirt, tossing it to one side, before crossing his arms behind his head and yanking his tank top off in one easy motion. The action was so totally masculine and natural it made her very aware of the differences between them. He made her feel very aware of herself as a woman.

He swiped at his chest with the cotton top before dropping it on top of his shirt. "I don't know about you, but I'm damned hot."

She curled her fingers tight against her palms in an effort to keep her hands off him as she feasted her eyes on his naked chest. Even in the dim light, she could tell it was finer than any sculpture she'd ever seen. His skin was tanned an even deeper bronze than it had been the night they'd had sex in her apartment. He did indeed have a perfect washboard stomach that tapered down to a lean waist, and even though she'd seen it before, it still left her breathless. A light dusting of dark hair covered his chest before angling downward and her eyes followed it until it disappeared into his jeans.

Raising his arms over his head, he flexed them, working out the kinks before lowering them back to his side. His low moan of relief as he stretched almost made her come in her panties. Swallowing hard, she watched him, totally spellbound. It was all too easy to imagine that groan of pleasure coming from him as he buried himself in her wet pussy and thrust into her willing body.

Emma could feel moisture running down her back and legs, a combination of arousal and sweat. She shifted her body and tried to unobtrusively flick her skirt back and forth to get a breeze, but it did no good.

"At least take off your jacket so you don't get heatstroke."

Emma's hands froze on her skirt as Tucker started towards her, his face all business.

Knowing she was being silly, she dropped her purse to the floor and eased the jacket over her shoulders. "Just so you know, I'm only doing this because it's the sensible thing to do given the circumstances." Folding it carefully, she bent down and laid it on top of her purse.

"Of course," he agreed easily.

She could tell he was doing his best to bite back a smile. He watched her for a moment and then sized her up in a speculative manner.

"You really should take off those pantyhose as well. Those things have got to be murder in this heat."

"I have to wear them for work, besides which they're thigh-highs, not pantyhose." Emma felt like sinking through the floor. What was it about Tucker that made her blurt out such totally inappropriate things?

"Really." He stared hard at her as if he was trying to see through her skirt.

She shifted as she felt another bead of moisture roll down her leg, and she bit her lip to keep from moaning aloud.

"Do you think we'll be here long?" Emma knew she was babbling, but the way he was staring at her was arousing her even further. She had to do something. Anything. She felt feminine, soft, and wanton. Not things she usually associated with herself.

Tucker shrugged, seemingly unconcerned by their predicament. "Why do you run away from me?"

His question caught her totally off guard. "I don't know what you mean."

Reaching out, he cupped her breasts in his hands and traced his thumbs over her swollen nipples. "I know you want me, so that's not the problem."

He moved closer to her until he stood between her legs. Bending down, he slowly lowered his mouth until it was level with hers. Using his tongue, he traced her lips slowly until her own parted. Taking advantage, he slipped his tongue inside and stroked the interior of her mouth. All the while, his hands continued to shape and mold her breasts until the ache became almost unbearable.

Emma moaned into his mouth, unable to hold it back any longer. Her whole body was afire with need. Her hands inched up until her fingers were digging into Tucker's shoulders. His skin was hot under her hands, and she stood on her toes so she could reach him better.

He pressed his body close to hers, rubbing his cock against her mound. Power surged through her. She'd never given any other man a hard-on so quickly before, not that she knew of anyway. And there was no doubt that Tucker was fully erect. Her inner muscles clenched in response and a thought flickered in the back of her mind that she could no longer ignore. Maybe it wouldn't hurt to give into her sexual needs just one more time.

Tucker pulled away from her mouth and left a trail of kisses as he made his way to her neck. He nibbled on her shoulder and she tilted her head to one side to give him better access. He murmured his approval as he nipped the sensitive skin where her neck and shoulder met.

"Let me pleasure you." His voice was little more than a hot whisper in her ear.

"Yes," she moaned before she gave herself time to think. She'd never experienced an orgasm as explosive as the ones she'd had with Tucker. Even when he was just kissing her, he gave her more pleasure than any other man ever had in her entire life.

Tucker's response was immediate. His hands dropped to her ass and pulled her tight against the front of his jeans and rubbed her mound across his cock. Clutching his hair in her fingers, she dragged his face up so that she could kiss him. Their lips locked together and he devoured her as if he couldn't get enough of her, tasting her mouth, and sucking on her tongue.

Shifting his hands upwards, he pulled the tails of her camisole from the waistband of her skirt and skimmed it up over her body, breaking their kiss long enough to pull it over her head and drop it beside her. His mouth returned to hers as his hands covered her bare breasts.

She cried out when his fingers plucked at her nipples, arousing them to greater sensitivity.

"Shhh," he calmed her as he kissed the corner of her mouth.

His hands cupped her breasts, plumping them in his hands, as he slowly lowered his face towards them. She caught her breath, waiting, desperately wanting what she knew was to come.

Tucker buried his face between the mounds and drew a long, deep breath. His moist, hot mouth nuzzled and licked the undersides of both breasts before he leisurely traced a path around each swollen nipple. The exquisite torture went on and on until she couldn't stand it anymore.

Part of her was screaming that she needed to stop this now. But a much louder voice was telling her to take what she wanted.

Grabbing his head in her hands, she guided it to one of the aching nubs. "Take it in your mouth." Her voice was low and husky, seductive in the dark elevator.

Her breath came out in a long hiss as his mouth closed over her nipple and sucked. Tilting her head back against the wall, she closed her eyes and let the sensations flow through her. Each time he suckled, she felt an answering tug between her legs. Her pussy was wet and throbbing and she was helpless to stop her hips from moving, seeking more.

"Beautiful," he whispered as he released her breast.

"No," she wailed, not wanting him to stop. Tucker simply placed a soft kiss on her nipple before moving to the other one. She almost wept with relief.

As his mouth continued to tease and torment her breasts, his hands slipped down over her torso, shaping her waist and hips before flowing down over her thighs. Clutching her skirt with both hands, he inched the fabric up until it was bunched at her waist.

One of his hands anchored the skirt, while the other skimmed up the inside of her thigh. Holding her breath, she waited for him to touch her. Tucker hesitated, raised his head from her breasts and shifted so that his mouth hovered over hers once again.

"You have to help me," he whispered as he nibbled on her lips.

"How?" She would do anything he wanted if it meant she could have him between her legs.

Smiling, he peeled her hands from his shoulders, brought them down by her sides and wrapped them over the handrail that was attached to the walls of the elevator. "Hold on tight."

Emma clutched the metal until it dug into her palms. Taking his time, Tucker stepped back and tucked the ends of her skirt into the waistband. When he was satisfied that they were secure, he knelt before her and hooked his fingers in the waistband of her panties. Ever so slowly, he tugged them down over her hips and legs until they were at her ankles. Carefully, he picked up one foot at a time and slipped her panties off. Wrapping his finger around one of her ankles, he slid one of her feet sideways until her legs were several feet apart.

Emma looked down at herself. Her breasts felt heavy and her nipples were fully erect, begging for Tucker's touch. Her high heels and thigh-high stockings were still in place, but with her skirt bunched at her waist and her panties gone, she was totally exposed to him.

She couldn't believe she was almost totally naked in an elevator with Tucker. For a moment, she almost panicked as her common sense threatened to reassert itself. She felt exposed and vulnerable and moved her hands to cover herself.

"No," he quickly admonished her. Pulling her hands away from her breasts, he placed them back on the rail and covered them with his own, much larger, hands. "Keep them here or I can't pleasure you."

It surprised her, but she was aroused at the thought of being captive to Tucker's sexual whims. Her pussy clenched with hunger. Her nipples throbbed in anticipation. She nodded.

Sitting back on his heels, he stared up at her and a slow, easy smile crossed his face. "Remember, if you move, I'll stop. It's up to you."

Starting at her ankles, he explored her entire body. His rough hands left goose bumps on her skin as he skimmed them over her heated flesh. Up over her calves and thighs, he stroked before covering both cheeks of her behind and squeezing them tight. "You've got a great ass."

Emma didn't know what to say, but thankfully he didn't seem to expect a reply as his hands continued up over her waist. His fingers were featherlight as they skimmed over her rib cage. He touched her everywhere except where she wanted to be touched. She squeezed the railing in frustration as his hand skimmed by her breasts and then trailed lightly down her thigh.

"Tucker," she cried.

"What, honey?" Leaning forward he ran his tongue up the inside of her thigh, licking off the moisture that dripped from her pussy. "Tell me what you want."

"Touch me."

"Here?" Slowly, he trailed his fingers through her damp pubic hair, just grazing her clit.

"Yes," she hissed and thrust her hips forward.

"Your pussy is so wet." He stroked several fingers over the swollen folds of her sex and held them up to her mouth. "Taste how good you are."

Tucker's fingers lightly traced her lips until she opened them. Slipping them inside, he moved them slowly in and out of her mouth. "Suck them. Hard."

She sucked and licked at his fingers, tasting her essence on her lips.

"Imagine if that was my cock you were sucking."

She sucked harder as his words made her hotter. She tried to close her legs to help ease the throbbing ache, but he stopped her immediately.

The minute she moved, he pulled his fingers from her mouth and sat back on his heels, waiting to see what she would do. She looked down at him, unable to believe he would leave her like this. His smile was filled with gentle understanding as he stared up at her. "It's up to you."

Emma licked her lips, needing his hands and mouth on her body, needing him to pleasure her. The heel of her shoe scraped along the floor of the elevator as she moved it back to its original position.

He just continued to sit there for a moment and stare at her. She couldn't stand the wait, so she flexed her hips, thrusting her pussy towards him. Reaching up, Tucker caught her nipples between his thumbs and forefingers and pinched them gently. Caught off guard, she cried out as her entire body clenched in pleasure.

"Doesn't that feel good?"

She nodded, unable to speak. Tucker pinched them tight again before reaching into the pocket of his jeans and bringing out two little strings of shimmering stones. "Do you know what these are?"

Emma shook her head, unable to take her eyes off him.

"I bought them for you several weeks ago and I've been carrying them around with me." Lifting one of the little strings to her nipple, he slipped it over the turgid nub before tightening it. "It's called a dangler. It'll help keep your nipples aroused, giving you more pleasure." Picking up the other one, Tucker pinched her nipple before securing the second one.

She looked down, enthralled by the wanton picture she made standing there. Although the strings of stones weren't overly heavy, the slight pressure was extremely arousing.

Reaching out, Tucker flicked the danglers with his index finger, making them both sway. She cried out immediately at the sharp arousal that shot through her body. Her pussy clenched hard.

Settling himself between her legs again, he traced the slick folds of her pussy. Emma clenched her teeth to keep from crying out. Leaning forward, he flicked his tongue against her clit as he slipped two of his fingers deep inside her.

"Tucker!" she cried, half afraid he'd stop and half afraid he wouldn't.

"Tell me what you want," he urged her as he continued to thrust his fingers in and out of her clenching pussy.

"More," she panted.

He slid another finger insider her, stretching her even further as he caught her clit between his teeth and held it captive while he flicked it with his tongue.

She arched back, causing the danglers to swing. The sensation shot straight from her breasts to her pussy. Thought was totally beyond her. She was drowning in the sensations of desire swamping her. Never had she felt this out of control.

"Reach for it, honey," he encouraged her. His mouth nipped at the inside of her thigh as his thumb pressed hard on her clit.

Emma let herself go, and as his fingers plunged deep inside her, she shattered. Convulsions shook her entire body. Her inner muscles clenched around Tucker's fingers as he continued to pump them in and out of her pussy. Clutching the railing for support, she screamed as waves of pleasure swamped her. It was even more intense than she remembered and more than she'd ever imagined it could be, more powerful and overwhelming.

Sobbing, she felt her knees give out. Tucker pulled her into his lap and cuddled her close to his chest. She could feel his heart pounding against his chest as his arms wrapped tight around her and he began to rock her gently in his embrace.

She flung her arms around him and held on tight. Both their bodies were slick with perspiration and her breasts slid against his torso. Moaning, she buried her face in his shoulder and kissed him. He tasted salty and male and absolutely delicious. She shivered when her pussy clenched hard in response.

Her knees were spread wide as she faced him and she clamped her thighs tight around his waist for stability. She could feel the hardness of his erection in his jeans and pushed her still-pulsing mound firmly against it.

Tucker said nothing, but his breathing got more ragged and his arms tightened until she could hardly breathe. She had to get hold of herself. Taking a deep breath, she slowly exhaled. Then she did the same thing again. It helped, sort of.

Just when she was finally beginning to feel calm, he loosened his grip on her and caught her chin in his hand. Tipping her face up so that he could see her, he kissed the tearstains on her cheeks.

"That was the most beautiful thing I've ever seen." The look on his face was one she'd never seen before. Tenderness, lust, possessiveness, and something she couldn't quite name were all displayed for her to see.

He opened his mouth to speak again, but the world suddenly exploded in a flash of light.

Chapter Six

∞

Emma flinched as the bright light hit her eyes. She felt Tucker's hand come up to cover her face even as he began to swear. The reality of the situation hit her like a slap in the face. What had she done?

Scrambling to her feet, she tugged her skirt down to cover herself and snatched her jacket off the floor. The elevator lurched suddenly and began to move upwards. Stuffing her arms in her jacket, her shaking fingers secured the two buttons just as the bell dinged. Reaching down, she grabbed her silk camisole and panties and stuffed them into her jacket pocket before seizing her purse and holding it like a protective shield against her body.

Tucker leaned down, plucked his shirts off the floor and slung them casually over his shoulder. For some reason, that little gesture made her blood boil. He didn't have a hair out of place and looked casually relaxed. While she felt hot, sticky, and totally emotional. She didn't know whether she wanted to kiss him or smack him, so she settled on just glaring at him.

He cocked his eyebrow questioningly, but she just sniffed haughtily and turned away as the door opened. It was just her luck that Mr. Meyers was waiting there in the hallway, leaning heavily on his cane, as he cast them a worried look.

"Are you kids all right?" The older man wore suspenders, a bow tie and glasses, just as he had every day since she'd moved into the building.

She reached out to slide open the metal gate, but Tucker beat her to it. She scowled at him before stepping out into the hallway and meeting Mr. Meyers' anxious gaze. Forcing a smile on her face, she reached out and touched him on the

181

arm. It was sweet of him to be concerned about them. "We're fine."

She could feel Tucker hovering behind her. "We just got caught in the elevator when the power went."

"I was worried. I knew you were in there because Mrs. Jacobs from the first floor called me and told me that she'd seen the two of you getting on the elevator. But I didn't know how to get the doors open and the building superintendent didn't answer his phone. I called emergency but they told me to call back in twenty minutes if the power wasn't back on." The older man barely paused for a breath as he continued. "Seems there was a bad accident at the intersection of Main and Anderson Avenue when the traffic light went out. And that's not the only one. The police and fire departments are all busy."

Emma felt her smile become genuine. Mr. Meyers was a good neighbor, more than willing to get involved and try to rescue someone in need, even though he was eighty years old. You didn't find that kind of caring in many large towns. "Thank you so much. But other than being hot and rumpled, we're fine." She felt the need to try and explain the state she was in.

Mr. Meyers laughed and nodded. "I imagine it would get extremely hot in that elevator after about twenty minutes."

"You have no idea," Tucker muttered behind her.

The older man cocked a questioning eyebrow, but Emma didn't want to give him a chance to ask any more questions. She could feel the moisture seeping down her thighs and between her breasts. Right now, she just wanted to be alone. "Shouldn't one of us call the emergency operator back and tell her we're fine before she sends someone here?"

"Right you are, young lady. I'll take care of that and then I'll give Mrs. Jacobs a call and let her know that you're both fine." He shooed them down the hall with one hand. "You two go and try and cool off." Turning, he walked back towards his apartment. "I find it even too hot just standing out here. Once I make my phone calls, I'm going to go and sit back in front of my air conditioner and read my newspaper."

"Thanks again, Mr. Meyers. I plan to do just that." She watched until he was safely in his apartment before hurrying down the hallway towards her own. Tucker was close on her heels. She could feel his large presence behind her.

She picked up her pace until she was practically running. Opening her purse as she went, she fumbled for her keys. Her hands were shaking so badly that she dropped her leather bag and all the contents spilled out onto the floor.

Swearing under her breath, she dropped to her knees and frantically began to scoop her wallet, papers, breath mints, and assorted cosmetics back into her purse. She stilled when Tucker's large hand covered hers.

"Emma," he began, but stopped when she stood suddenly and rushed to her apartment door. If she'd missed something, she would find it later. The only thing that was important right now was getting away from Tucker and all the unsettling emotions he'd stirred up within her.

Jamming her key into the lock, she turned it, pushing the door open with the same hand. Tucker grasped her by the shoulder and turned her to face him. "You forgot your mail."

Sighing with relief, she summoned a polite smile and reached out her hand to take it. "Thank you." She was pleased that her voice sounded even.

He passed her the envelopes and then grasped her shoulders in his hands. Pulling her close, he leaned down until his lips were almost touching hers. "You also forgot this." With that, his lips captured hers. When she gasped with surprise, his tongue thrust into her mouth.

Emma knew she could have stopped him simply by pulling away. Instead, she found herself leaning into his kiss. Her tongue stroked his and she felt the now-familiar heat rising in her body again. Liquid continued to seep from between her thighs and her nipples ached as the jeweled nipple danglers brushed against her coat jacket. Moaning, she raised her hands towards his chest and touched…nothing.

Tucker had stepped away from her and was watching her, his eyes blazing with passion. "You know where you can find me if you want more." After throwing down that provocative challenge, he turned away and let himself in through the door across from hers. She was still staring at him when his door closed with a thud.

She stood there totally stunned for a moment before shaking herself free from her enthrallment and hurrying into her own apartment. Slamming the door shut, she leaned against it for support, fanning herself furiously with her mail. The man was impossible! Tossing her purse onto the sofa, she kicked off her heels and dumped the mail on the kitchen table on her way to the bathroom.

Turning the shower on cool, she peeled off her sweat-soaked clothes, shivering as she remembered Tucker's hands shoving her skirt up and around her waist. She was still unbelievably aroused and just rolling her stockings down her legs became an act of pure torture. When she was finally naked, she glanced at herself in the mirror and barely recognized the woman staring back at her.

Her eyes were luminous, her skin rosy, and her lips were swollen from Tucker's kisses. With her short brown hair mussed up, she looked a little wild and certainly like a woman who'd been well pleasured. It was only when she looked a little lower that she noticed the little strings of jewels hanging from her nipples. She'd gotten used to them so quickly, she'd forgotten she was wearing them.

Carefully, she opened the loops and removed them both before taking a moment to examine them. They were beautiful. The strands of multicolored stones set into silver appeared small in her hands, and looking at them like this, it was amazing to think about how much pleasure they'd given her. She'd been startled and pleased when Tucker had told her he'd bought them for her. Placing them safely on the countertop, she climbed into the shower.

Stepping under the cold spray, she allowed it to pummel her heated flesh. When she started to feel human again, she grabbed her shower gel and quickly soaped herself from head to toe before rinsing off. Washing between her legs was pure agony as she was still unbelievably aroused. Not wanting to linger further, she turned off the taps and stepped out onto the bathmat. Grabbing a towel, she dried off and then hung the damp towel to dry before heading to the bedroom to dress.

The air was warm, as the power outage had shut down the air-conditioning. Even in that short length of time, the extreme heat had started to take control. Naked, she strolled across her bedroom and went straight to her dresser. Pulling out her lingerie drawer, she grabbed a pair of panties and tugged them on. Next she dug out her favorite denim shorts and paired them with a halter-top, not bothering with a bra.

Her breasts were fairly substantial and she usually wore a bra to work. It almost seemed prophetic in some way that she hadn't worn one today because of the unbearable heat. But around the house, you couldn't pay her to wear one. Besides, who was going to see?

Making her way to the kitchen, she poured up a large glass of lemonade, settled into a comfortable chair right in front of the air-conditioning unit, determined to put today's incident totally out of her mind.

Emma noticed the lack of cold air blowing on her parched skin before she noted the absence of noise. She'd been trying to lose herself in the latest erotic romance by Ms. Lillian, one of her favorite authors. It had been a mistake to start the book today, as it only conjured images of Tucker and her in the elevator. Desperately, she'd forged ahead, determined to block all thoughts of him from her mind, but it was futile. Marking her page with her bookmark, she tossed the paperback onto the small table next to her.

The silence was so complete that she knew the power had gone out again, at least in this building. "Great," she muttered as she heaved herself out of her chair.

Strolling to the kitchen, she opened her freezer door and dumped the last two ice cubes in the tray into her glass. She'd meant to fill up the trays she'd poured her drink earlier, but had gotten distracted. If the electricity was out for long, she'd have to venture outside in search of ice.

She went to the living room window, opened it and glanced outside. It was still light outside, so she couldn't tell if other buildings had lost their power too. The stoplight on the corner was still working, so Emma quickly closed the window to help keep in the cool air. It would be stifling in the apartment soon enough.

It was probably just a minor glitch in the power grid, but it wouldn't hurt to check. Padding back to the kitchen, she pulled out her portable radio and turned it on. Nothing. She shook it, but it did no good. The batteries were dead. How could that be? She'd replaced them...she thought for a moment and groaned as she remembered it had been Christmas when she'd done it.

Chewing on her lip, she pondered her options. Should she wait and hope that the blackout wouldn't last long, or should she go next door to Tucker's and borrow some batteries so she could listen to the news report? Tucker would have a portable radio, batteries and probably even more ice.

Besides, as an electrician, he might have an idea how long this situation might last. Another blackout so soon after the one in the elevator couldn't be good. With the heat wave they'd been having, everyone in the town had been running their air-conditioning on bust. They could be without power for an hour or even a day or more. It was only prudent to find out what was going on, and for that, she needed a radio.

Sighing, she shook her head. Who was she kidding? She knew she was just looking for an excuse to be with Tucker again. The man had whetted her appetite for sexual pleasure and she wanted more.

Not giving herself time to think about it, she hurried to the bathroom and tugged down her halter-top. Just thinking about Tucker had made her nipples hard, but she pinched them between her thumb and forefingers to make them even harder. Picking up one of the nipple ornaments, she slipped it on and tightened it, making herself moan. Her panties were wet by the time she finished securing the second one.

Watching herself in the mirror, she shimmied, making them swing. Shivering with pleasure, she pulled her halter-top back into place. You could see the outline of the danglers through the material, but only slightly.

When Tucker had put them on her, he'd mentioned that he'd bought them several weeks ago. It excited her to think about a man as large and strong as Tucker carrying around these delicate nipple danglers in his pocket for weeks.

Emma hesitated for a moment. Was she being wise in seeking out Tucker and risking a relationship with a man who could easily break her heart? Or was it already too late?

If she was honest with herself, she'd been drawn to Tucker's quiet, steady presence from their very first meeting. He had an innate strength and a kindness about him that she found very attractive. But now she also knew just how sexy and talented a lover he was.

"This is just silly." She glared at herself in the mirror, turned on her heel, and stalked to her front door. Jerking it open, she took two steps across the dark hall, and banged on Tucker's door.

The door opened just as she was about to bang it again. Her mouth dropped open at the sight of Tucker dripping wet and wearing nothing but a dark blue towel. The muscles on his chest glistened with moisture and she was gripped by the urge to lick off every single drop.

"Come in. You're letting out what's left of my cool air." Emma quickly stepped inside and allowed him to close the door behind her. He eyed her speculatively, but said nothing else.

"Do you have any ice and batteries?" she blurted out.

"Sure," he responded easily. "Give me a second to haul on some clothes." Tucker headed towards his bedroom as he spoke.

Emma almost drooled at the sight of those long muscular legs and tight buns as he walked away from her. The towel loosened as he walked. *Just a little bit more,* she urged the towel. She shook herself as he disappeared from her view and glanced around at his apartment, suddenly curious about Tucker and his home. Although they'd been out on several dates, she'd never seen the inside of his place. It was neater than she'd expected. Homey. Unable to resist, she wandered around the living room, nosing through the bookshelves.

Chapter Seven

ಬಿ

"Anything in particular you're looking for?" Tucker's voice made her jump as she realized she was no longer alone. She whirled around to face him.

Emma's eyes widened as she noted he wore only a pair of running shorts that covered even less than the towel had. There was a large bulge in the front of them, letting her know just how very aroused he was.

He ran a hand through his damp hair. "You've been running away from me for months. If there's anything you want to know about me, all you have to do is ask."

"I don't know what to say." Emma stared at him, at a loss as to how to proceed. Most men she'd known wanted to avoid conversation at all costs, but here was Tucker offering to answer any and all questions.

At that moment, she couldn't think of a single thing to ask him. None of her fears or uncertainties seemed to matter with him standing half-naked in front of her. She licked her lips as she stared at his wide, damp chest.

Tucker stepped up next to her until he was towering over her smaller frame. She tried to back away but came up solidly against the bookshelf. Slowly, his hands lifted to cup her face and he leaned forward to gently taste her lips.

In spite of her doubts, her hands crept up to his shoulders and she returned his kiss. Tentatively at first and then more boldly. He allowed her to take the lead, but when she opened her mouth to him he quickly claimed it for his own. His tongue swept inside, dueling with her tongue, sucking on it, tasting her until she was breathless.

He kissed his way across her jawline and down her neck. "Don't say anything. Just be with me." He nipped at the curve of her neck and then sucked the small sting away.

Emma could feel her breasts swelling. Her nipples were hard nubs against her top. They ached so badly that she rubbed them against the hard plane of his chest, hoping to find some relief. He groaned and pulled her tighter as his hands edged beneath the cotton halter-top and slid up to her naked breasts beneath.

"You wore them for me." There was both pleasure and satisfaction in his voice as he touched one of the strings of stones, making it sway.

"Yes," she sighed.

Sinking to his knees, he pulled her down to the floor with him so that she was sitting astride his knees. He lifted her top over her head and dropped it onto the floor beside her feet. His eyes flowed over her naked torso even as his large, rough hands cupped her breasts. Leaning forward, his tongue flicked at her engorged nipple while his thumb played with the other one, teasing it even tighter.

Moisture continued to flow from her core, soaking her panties, as she arched towards him, rubbing herself against his straining erection. She'd never wanted a man this much in her life. For months, she'd been deluding herself that she was over Tucker. Now she wanted to feel everything, do everything and anything with him.

As he continued to suck and lick her nipples, he wrapped his arms around her and pulled her closer to his arousal, urging her up and down his length. She grasped his shoulders and held on tight as she ground her mound against him.

Shifting her body so that she was lying on the floor, he unzipped her shorts and pulled them down over her legs. She kicked them away and arched under his hands as they skimmed the band of her panties.

Burying his face in her crotch he breathed deep and nuzzled her pubic hair through the thin fabric. Unable to help herself, she clutched at his head and pulled him tighter. His warm, muffled laugh vibrated through her body, arousing her to an even higher pitch.

"I want you to touch me everywhere. I want to feel your hands and your lips all over my body." She couldn't believe that the sultry command came from her mouth. Tucker tucked his fingers into the band and quickly skimmed off her panties.

He stood quickly and shucked his own shorts. Her pussy clenched hard as she watched him strip naked in front of her. She licked her lips at the sight of his hard, throbbing cock.

Lying there on the floor, totally naked and open before him except for her nipple adornments, she felt as if she was in the middle of an erotic fantasy. Emboldened, she opened her legs wider, planted her feet on the floor and arched her hips towards him. "Like what you see?"

"Oh yeah." The low, sensual tones slid over her skin making it tingle.

Dipping her hands between her own thighs, she stroked her fingers over the damp, sensitive flesh. "Well, what are you waiting for?"

His eyes gleamed with a mixture of desire and satisfaction as he knelt between her spread legs. Capturing her hands in his, he raised them to his mouth. One at a time, he licked and sucked her fingers, his tongue gliding over them. She pulled one of her hands away and wrapped it around his cock, squeezing it gently.

"You keep that up and I'll come before I have a chance to even start." He groaned as he sat back and his erection slid through her fingers.

He took a deep breath and then lifted her legs, draping them over his shoulders. His fingers spread her sensitive flesh wider so he could see and feel the moisture gathered there.

"You're so wet and ready for me. You want me to fuck you, don't you, Emma?"

"Yes. I want you, Tucker." Having made up her mind, she wanted to enjoy the entire experience. There was nothing she didn't want to do, to try, with him. She throbbed and ached, panting for breath as he continued to sit there, motionless, staring at her.

Suddenly, he leaned forward, his tongue tracing the slick folds of her sex from back to front. She gasped as the delicious sensation shot throughout her entire body. His tongue flicked her distended clitoris and she tightened her legs around his shoulders, trying to pull him closer.

His laughter was low and sensual as he caught the hard bud between his teeth. Slowly, he teased the nub with his tongue, sometimes barely brushing it and other times pressing down hard. Heat filled her, threatening to burn her alive. "I can't take any more," she moaned as her head thrashed from side to side.

Releasing her clit, he nipped the inside of her thigh. "Yes, you can." His voice was rough as he looked down at her. Lifting one of her legs from his shoulders, he started to nibble on her toes.

Emma sucked in her breath, unable to believe what he was doing. His tongue slid over her toes and around her ankle as his strong fingers massaged her instep. Her toes curled and her foot arched at his touch. *This man is incredible*, was her only coherent thought.

Taking his time, he continued his leisurely foray up her leg, lifting it so he could lick at the sensitive spot behind her knee. Emma nearly jumped out of her skin, but Tucker wasn't finished. Leaving a hot trail of kisses up the inside of her thigh, he licked the crease at the top. Every nerve ending in her leg quivered in anticipation of what he might do next.

Bending her leg so that her knee was pushed close to her chest, he lifted her hand and tucked it behind her thigh so that she could support her own leg in this position. He held his own hand over hers as he smiled down at her. "Keep your leg there."

Swallowing hard, she nodded. His eyes smoldered with desire as he picked up her other foot and began to nibble her toes. Her head arched back and she moaned when she realized he was going to do the same thing to the other leg.

By the time he bent her other leg into her chest and wrapped her hand around her thigh, she was gasping for breath. Her pussy was weeping with desire, the moisture flowing between the cheeks of her ass and pooling on the floor beneath her. Her nipples were hard nubs, aching for his touch. The danglers swayed with each breath she took.

She couldn't take any more of his sensual torture. "I need you, Tucker," she managed to gasp out. She started to lower her legs, but he stopped her.

Keeping her legs tucked tight to her body, he spread them as wide as they would go. "Just like this," he whispered. She shivered as he slid one of his long fingers inside her. Withdrawing it slowly, he then thrust two fingers inside her. She arched her hips up to meet them.

With his other hand, he stroked her throbbing clit, occasionally varying the pressure. She cried out as her inner muscles clamped down hard around his thick fingers. Tucker carefully worked another finger inside her, filling her completely. With her legs wide open, she was totally open and vulnerable to him, and that realization only served to heighten her passion.

As he continued to work his fingers in and out of her body, he never took his gaze from her face. She was right on the edge of climaxing when he pulled away from her. A cry of dismay escaped her.

"Shhh," he reached out and stroked her belly with one hand as he reached behind them, grabbed his discarded shorts and rummaged through the pockets.

He pulled out a condom, but before he could open it, she dropped her legs back down to the floor, rolled over, and came up on her knees in front of him. It was time for her to take control of the situation. He'd teased her and now it was time for payback.

His cock was huge as it rose straight up from his body. The dark veins pulsed as blood pumped through it, making it grow even larger before her very eyes. A pearl of liquid seeped from the tip as she stared at him. He had tasted her and now it was her turn to taste him.

He froze as she smiled at him, slowly bent her head and licked the red bulbous tip of his cock. Swirling her tongue around the head, she licked off the milky fluid and let his flavor fill her senses. Musky and salty and all male. She found it incredibly arousing.

"Yes," he hissed as he wrapped one hand around the back of her head, gently urging her closer.

Dipping down to the base, she licked her way back to the top before rolling her tongue around the head. Wrapping her hand around the base of his cock, she slowly pumped her hand up and down its entire length. More liquid seeped from the tip and she swiped at it with her tongue, savoring his essence, before taking him in her mouth and sucking.

He groaned and murmured encouragement as she continued to suck his swollen shaft. She'd never given a man a blowjob before. Had never wanted to. But with Tucker, she found that, not only was she enjoying doing it, it was enhancing her own pleasure. She found a rhythm with her hands and her mouth and was surprised when, without warning, he pulled his cock out of her mouth.

She strained towards him, but he stopped her. "This way," he urged her. Lying on the floor, he positioned her so that her legs were on either side of his face and her sex was spread wide over his mouth.

"Bend forward," he instructed. With his hands wrapped around her hips, she bent until her stomach was on his chest and his cock was right in front of her mouth.

Tucker's strong hands pulled her pussy down to his mouth and his tongue teased the opening before thrusting inside her. She instinctively pushed down to meet his thrusting tongue. His hands curled around the cheeks of her ass, opening them wide as he continued to pleasure her.

Sliding his tongue out of her, he thrust his fingers into her aching pussy. His tongue lapped at the cleft between her cheeks. She shrieked when his tongue grazed the opening of her bottom. Tucker just laughed and did it again.

His cock flexed, stroking the side of her face, reminding her that two could play this game. Closing her warm, wet mouth over the crown, she sucked. Hard. He instantly rewarded her with a loud groan of pleasure. Oh, she definitely liked this. Reaching down, she cupped his sac in her hand and rolled his balls between her fingers. She could feel them tightening beneath her touch.

Placing her other hand around his shaft, she stroked his entire length as she continued to suck hard on the tip. Occasionally, she swirled her tongue around the top before taking him as deep as she could into her mouth.

As his mouth and hands pleasured her, she continued to moan. The entire experience was unbelievable erotic and incredibly arousing. His entire body was shaking with need as she continued to touch and arouse him. Emma surrendered herself completely to the pleasure that coursed back and forth between them.

Her inner muscles clamped down hard on his fingers as she came in a rush. Pulling her mouth away, she buried her face in his groin, shaking uncontrollably as her entire body quivered with spasms of fulfillment.

Tucker seemed determined to wring the last drop of pleasure out of her as he continued to work her with his fingers and tongue until she gave one last shudder and relaxed in a heap on top of him. She didn't think she could move and would have stayed there forever, except Tucker shifted her carefully off him.

Languidly, she rolled over onto her back and watched him finally sheathe his cock with a condom and cover her body with his. With one hand, he spread her pussy lips wide, and with the other he guided his cock to her opening, pushing his way inside her swollen, pulsating sex.

Her inner muscles contracted around him, pulling him deeper inside, and they both groaned at the exquisite sensation. She was still so sensitive from her orgasm that every touch was magnified. Amazingly enough, arousal quickly sprang to life within her. One moment she felt sated, the next she wanted him again. Locking her legs around his waist, she urged him closer. Tucker clasped his hands around her waist and thrust deep.

Their sweat-slicked skin slid easily as he found a pounding rhythm that pleased them both. The slapping sound of their damp flesh and the panting of their breathing were the only sounds in the unnaturally quiet apartment.

Emma watched Tucker as he drove into her. His eyes were closed and his hair was tousled. His entire concentration was focused on their mutual sexual pleasure. A light sheen of sweat covered his torso and shoulders, making him look sexy and hot. Reaching up, she skimmed her fingers over his bulging biceps, reveling in his solid strength.

Tucker's eyes shot open and she was lost in the passion that smoldered there. She'd never seen such a look of naked desire and need on a man's face before. It scared her a little, but it also filled her with a sense of womanly pride and power. Tugging on his arms, she urged him closer to her.

As he lowered himself over her body, she wrapped her arms around his wide shoulders. Her hands traced the straining muscles, loving the way all that barely leashed power flexed under her hands. Pulling him closer, she buried her face in his shoulder and licked his salty skin before turning and biting his neck.

Tucker braced himself on his forearms for support and captured her face in his hands as his lips found hers and devoured them. His tongue plundered her mouth even as he drove his cock into her again and again.

Her body responded to his. His urgency fired her own. Arching against him, she met him stroke for stroke as she thrust her tongue wildly into his mouth, tasting his desire.

Tucker shifted, grasping her bottom with one hand as he levered her up to meet his downward stroke. Her clit rubbed against his pelvis and her body strained for release once more. Digging her feet into his butt, she met every pounding stroke.

Rearing back on his knees, he reached between their bodies and stroked her sensitive flesh once, twice, and then she was screaming in release. Her whole body contracted as she felt him come on one last hard thrust. He shouted her name as he shook with his release.

He managed to pull out of her before slumping to the carpet beside her. Dragging her into his arms, he cradled her close. She could feel his heart racing beneath her cheek as she curled into his embrace. As aftershocks of passion continued to course though her, Tucker ran his hands up and down her back and arms, soothing her.

Chapter Eight

ဆ

Emma didn't know how much time passed before Tucker finally moved. She didn't know how he could find the strength. Between the overwhelming heat and the sex, she felt lethargic and sleepy. Her entire body felt slick and her arms and legs felt like limp noodles. She figured that she might be ready to move by sometime tomorrow.

"Emma." She smiled as he said her name, but couldn't manage to open her eyes. He gave a rough laugh and a second later she felt his arms slide underneath her as he picked her up in his arms.

Her eyes popped open as she wrapped her arms around his neck for support. "That's better." Leaning down he planted a quick hard kiss on her lips. "I'm not done with you yet."

She just stared up at him in wonder. Surely he couldn't mean what she thought he meant. She'd already come twice and he'd just come a couple of minutes ago. He continued down the hallway and carried her into his bedroom, kissing her again before lowering her to the bed.

The sheets felt cool against her overheated skin and she stretched like a contented cat as she looked around the room with interest. The room was painted a rich cream color and filled with large pine furniture. The bed was king-sized and there was a matching pine armoire and chest of drawers. That was all she saw before her gaze was drawn back to Tucker. While she'd been examining his room, he'd removed the used condom and rolled on another one. Her eyes widened as she looked at the size of his cock. He was fully aroused and ready to go again.

"See what you do to me." His voice was rough as he came down on the bed next to her. Capturing her hands in one of his, he raised them over her head. Lowering his body over her, he covered her, trapping her legs under him. She struggled in his grip, but was unable to move as he held her gently but securely.

"No, don't fight me," he crooned in her ear.

In spite of her uncertainties, Emma felt herself responding to his gentling tone, and her body relaxed against his. Tucker nibbled her earlobe before trailing a line of kisses back to her lips. Gently, he moved his lips over hers, barely touching them. She strained towards them, wanting a deeper contact, but he pulled away so that he was staring down at her.

"Why did you fight the attraction between us for so long?" His voice was calm, but she sensed an underlying desire to truly understand.

"Because you scare me to death." The words flew from her mouth before she could stop them, but once they were out she felt as if a weight was off her shoulders. It was nothing more than the truth.

His eyes narrowed as he examined her face, searching for the truth of her words. He stared down at her for a long time, before sighing deeply. "You have to know that I would never harm you."

Emma sensed that she'd hurt him somehow with her words, and she was sorry for that, but if they were to ever have a relationship of any kind they needed to deal with this. "Physically, I trust you not to hurt me," her voice quavered as she spoke. "But emotionally," she swallowed hard and tried again. "Emotionally, you could — badly."

Her vulnerability lay before them, as she was now both physically and emotionally naked in this man's arms. She closed her eyes as tears threatened, and was unable to keep one of them from slipping down her cheek.

"Oh, honey," he groaned. His hold on her changed immediately. Releasing her arms, he used his thumb to brush away the lone tear from her face. "Don't cry. We'll work it all out."

Sitting back on his knees, he carefully removed the one nipple ornament that was still attached. It dangled from his fingers as he placed it safely on the bedside table. "We must have lost the other one in the living room. We can find it later." Bending down, he laved both nipples with his tongue. "I don't want you to get sore," he murmured between licks. "It's always supposed to be about pleasure."

Emma noticed that he hadn't given any indication about how he felt about their relationship. Instead, he'd distracted her with the physical aspect of it. And foolish as it was, she was more than willing to be distracted.

Deciding that she didn't want to talk as it only made her feel vulnerable, she just nodded at him as she felt the wetness between her legs once again. This man was making her insatiable.

As if he sensed her thoughts, he stroked his fingers between her legs making her gasp with pleasure. "We're good together." Leaning down, he nuzzled her damp pubic hair before licking her slick folds. "Very good."

"Yes," she moaned in agreement as he sucked on her engorged clit. No matter what else was between them, there was no denying the explosive physical connection that existed. His clever fingers skimmed over her warm, moist flesh before slipping inside. Her hips arched up eagerly to receive them.

"I want to take you from behind." His thumb stroked her clit as his fingers continued to slide in and out of her body. "I want you on your hands and knees with your ass in the air, offering your hot pussy to me."

His words stoked the flames of desire within her. Without giving herself time to think, she pulled up her legs and rolled over in the bed, coming up on her hands and knees. She was filled with a fierce need to satisfy this man. Bending her arms so that she was lying on her forearms, she arched her back like a cat, thrusting her behind in the air.

"Wider." Tucker was behind her now, his large hands caressing the fleshy cheeks as he urged her legs open.

She pushed her knees open until her legs were wide apart and she was completely open to him. His fingers dug into her behind. "You've got a gorgeous ass," he said as his teeth nipped at her flesh.

One of his fingers traced a line from the opening of her behind to her wet, aching pussy. Back and forth his finger stroked as he continued to place stinging little love bites on her bottom.

"Tucker," she wailed, wriggling her backside, needing more. Wanting him to fill her and ease the emptiness inside her.

"Tell me what you want." His fingers continued to torment her and he dipped one finger into her pussy before quickly removing it.

"I want you inside me."

"Your pussy is so hot and wet."

His deep voice washed over her, making her blood pump harder.

"Do you want me to fuck you, baby?"

"Yes."

"Yes, what?"

She knew then that he was going to make her say the words. Maybe even needed her to say them. Wanting to be sure it was her choice. Once she realized that, it was easy to give him the words. "Fuck me, Tucker. Please."

The words were barely out of her mouth when he pulled her tight to him and drove his cock into her waiting heat. Her muscles contracted around him as he filled her completely. He was so deep inside her it was almost painful, but it felt so good that she pushed back against him, wanting him even deeper.

He angled her slightly before he began to thrust. He set a pounding rhythm as he drove them both towards completion. Her breasts ached as they swayed back and forth with every hard thrust. She was mindless to all else but completion. It was so close now.

Wrapping one of his strong arms around her waist, Tucker fucked her hard and fast as the other hand spread her pussy lips wide in the front and he stroked her clit. It was too much for Emma and drove her over the edge. Screaming with release, she convulsed around him.

His hips pumped hard as he buried his cock hard and deep with each thrust. He let out a yell as he came. She could feel the pulsing of his cock deep within her as her pussy milked him dry. Finally, she slumped down onto the bed. Tucker managed to roll to the side before collapsing next to her. Emma had never felt more replete or exhausted in her entire life.

As they lay there in a sweaty, sticky heap, she couldn't remember ever feeling as content in her life. She'd had very deep feelings for Tucker. She wasn't ready to admit just how deep those feelings went, but they were there nonetheless. Yes, he was a gorgeous, charming man, but there was certainly more to him than that. The man had hidden depths that she'd yet to uncover, but she sensed they were there.

Now, that her breathing was back to normal, she felt slightly uncomfortable and shifted, trying to find a cooler spot. Her damp hair was plastered against her skull and her entire body was covered in a fine sheen of sweat.

Tucker grunted as he heaved himself up off the bed. Naked, he padded to the bathroom, and she could hear the faint sound of running water.

A minute later, he was back with a damp cloth in his hand. His black hair was wet and droplets of water rolled down his chest. Obviously, he'd splashed some water on himself to try and cool himself down. She didn't have the energy to drag herself out of bed yet, so she didn't even protest when he ran the cool cloth over her torso and between her legs, making her more comfortable. When he was finished to his satisfaction, he tossed the cloth on the bedside table and lay back on the bed, tugging her into his arms.

He heaved a large sigh, tilted her head up until she was looking at him, and pushed a strand of hair out of her eyes. Leaning down, he kissed her forehead. "I was going to give you until this weekend."

"I don't understand. What do you mean you were only going to give me until the weekend?" She was truly perplexed by his words.

He shook his head and sighed again. "I'd let you run away for long enough. It was time for me to do something."

"What would you have done?" She absently ran her hands over his chest and stomach. She didn't doubt for one minute that he'd have indeed concocted something to get her attention.

"I'd have come up with something," he paused for a moment. "Like maybe turning off the breakers to my apartment and yours."

Emma went still as she digested his words, hardly able to believe what she was hearing. "You didn't?"

He nodded and grinned, totally unrepentant. "It was easy, and the opportunity was just too good to pass up." He planted a hard kiss on her lips. "I had to do something after that amazing elevator ride."

"But what about the hall light?"

Tucker laughed. "I just turned off the switch at the end of the hall."

Emma wasn't sure how she felt about what Tucker had done. On one hand, she couldn't deny that she'd enjoyed their sexual encounters. But her stomach got queasy at the thought that he'd tricked her into joining him. She conveniently shoved aside the fact that she'd come to him and focused on his actions.

The way she saw it, he'd manipulated events so that he could get her into bed. The fact that she enjoyed herself here was irrelevant. A little voice in the back of her head was whispering that you couldn't trust a good-looking man like Tucker. He could charm his way out of any situation and would do whatever it took to get his own way. A man like that couldn't be counted on or believed.

The last thought sent a shaft of pain through her. So intense was the pain that she actually rolled out of Tucker's arms and curled her legs up into her chest. She realized then, that she'd begun to trust him and to hope. Visions of a future together had begun to sneak into her mind.

"Are you all right?" He rolled her onto his back and cupped her face in her hands. "What's wrong? Are you sick?" One of his hands caressed the side of her face and she couldn't resist turning her face into it. His touch felt so good.

"You planned this." He went still at her words.

"I had no way of knowing for sure if you'd come to me. You could have gone down the hall to Mr. Meyers," he reminded her. "But you came to me. That shows me that deep down you do trust me. I thought you must have after the elevator, but I know it for certain now."

Emma looked up into his piercing eyes that seemed to be trying to see all the way to her very soul. She closed her eyes, not wanting him to see how truly vulnerable she was to him. "I'm glad one of us is sure, because I'm not."

"You can't mean that."

She opened her eyes and met his gaze, careful to try and keep all emotion from her face. "Yes, I do."

Tucker sat up in bed and ran a hand over his face. "So where does that leave us?"

"I don't know."

"You don't know." His laugh was tinged with bitterness. "You let me know when you figure it out."

Her stomach clenched even tighter at his words. "What do you mean?"

Rolling out of bed, he grabbed a pair of jeans and hauled them on. Padding to the closet, he hauled out a T-shirt and dragged it over his head. "It means that I'm through playing games. You want to fuck me, but you don't want to have anything else to do with me." He shoved his bare feet into a battered pair of sneakers even as he grabbed his keys off the dresser and stuffed them in his pocket. "That's usually the woman's line."

"It's not like that." She sat up in bed and reached her hand out to him. She realized then that she'd wanted him to reassure her, to cuddle her, and tell her how he really felt about her. Instead, she was driving him away.

He looked at her hand and then at her face. The bleakness in his eyes shocked her. When he made no movement towards her, she reluctantly lowered her hand.

Without another word, he turned and walked out of the room. She stared at the open door, willing him to come back, but unable to make herself call out to him. Too many memories of her mother pleading with her father to stay filled her brain. She buried her face in her hands, trying to shut out the painful thoughts.

The sound of the front door closing echoed in the silence. It was the finality of it that finally shook her out of her stupor and made her move. Grabbing the sheet from the bed, she wrapped it around her as she hurried down the hallway. Maybe she could catch him and they could talk.

She opened the door just in time to hear the ding of the elevator, signaling its arrival to this floor. Hauling open the door, she stuck her head out just in time to see the door closing. Tucker stood in the center with his arms crossed, staring straight at her. Then he was gone from her sight.

The sense of loss was almost overwhelming as she stumbled back into his apartment. It no longer felt welcoming to her without him here. Dropping the sheet, she fumbled for her clothing that was strewn around the living room. She yanked on her shorts and top and grabbed her panties, wanting to make a quick escape.

Her only thought was to get home and try and sort out what had just happened. One minute they had been curled up in Tucker's big bed, happy and contented. The next, they had been fighting.

Men weren't worth the effort, she told herself as she balled the sheet up in her arms. She swiped at the tears on her cheeks as she looked down the hallway. There was no way she could face his bed. It would be mussed and warm and smell of him.

Burying her face in the sheet, she inhaled and was surrounded by the mingled scents of their lovemaking. Dropping the sheet, she backed away from it. She had to leave. As she turned, a sparkle from the living room carpet caught her eye. Knowing what it was, she still walked towards it, bent down and closed her hand around it.

She didn't look at it. Stuffing it in her pocket, she headed to the door. The apartment seemed to surge to life as the power suddenly came back on. Closing her eyes, she leaned on the door, knowing that Tucker had just flipped the switches in the utility room in the basement.

The fact that the power was probably back on in her apartment gave her no pleasure as she shut the door behind her, crossed the hall, and entered her own empty home.

Chapter Nine

ᔆᐣ

Emma sat in the cool interior of the restaurant and waited for her friends to arrive. She was glad to be inside and away from the oppressive heat still blanketing the town. Her right hand was tucked in her pants pocket, her fingers toying with the nipple ornament that Tucker had given her. She'd tossed it on her dresser last night when she'd gotten home, but had been unable to leave it behind this morning. It was practically burning a hole in her pocket, she was so very aware of it. All morning long, she'd been touching it, rubbing it like a talisman, as if somehow it could help her figure out what to do.

She felt tired and totally out of sorts as she'd hardly slept at all last night. She'd taken another quick shower and curled up on her sofa in total silence, listening for the sound of Tucker coming home. It had been late when she'd finally heard his footsteps in the hallway. When he'd hesitated in front of her door, she held her breath, willing him to knock. Disappointment hit her hard when she'd heard the sound of his door closing.

She rubbed her eyes with her hands, glad that she wasn't wearing any makeup today, otherwise she'd be a total mess. In a totally unprecedented action, she'd called in sick to the gallery.

The memory of Callie's surprise brought a faint smile to her face. Once she'd assured her young assistant that she was fine, but just needed a break, Callie had been enthusiastic with her support. "You deserve a day off to just enjoy and pamper yourself."

Callie's words were still ringing in her ears. Was she really that regimented and predictable? Unfortunately, the answer was a resounding *yes*.

Emma was glad that she had a lunch date already scheduled with her two best friends. She really needed to talk to someone about her dilemma. She'd met Annabelle Sloan and Lily Summers at a local luncheon for women in the local business community and the three of them had immediately hit it off. Annabelle was the local librarian and had gotten married just last year. Lily was the oldest of the three at thirty-eight, the mother of a nineteen-year-old son, and she'd been divorced for too many years to count. Seemingly, they had nothing in common, but the more they'd talked, the more ideas and views about things they actually found they shared.

Emma had never had close friends until she moved to Summersville, but it was yet another reason why she was glad that she'd chosen to move here.

The sound of laughter made her glance towards the door. She was just in time to see Mike Sloan bending down to kiss his wife goodbye. Annabelle's lips lingered against his for a moment before she turned and walked towards Emma's table, her hips swaying back and forth. Emma grinned as Mike's gaze seemed to focus on his wife's backside as she sauntered across the room.

"Is he still looking?" Annabelle asked.

"Oh, yeah."

"Good." Sliding into her seat, she turned, waved at her husband and blew him another kiss. He was still smiling when he disappeared from their sight. Annabelle swiveled back towards her, all business now. "Tell me what's wrong," she said as she hooked her purse on the back of her chair.

Emma didn't bother denying something was amiss. Over the course of their friendship, they'd all gotten really good at sensing when one of the others was troubled. "Can we wait for Lily? I only want to do this once."

"Of course." Her friend reached out and patted her hand before picking up the menu.

The waitress was already at their table when Lily hurried in. "Sorry I'm late." She plopped into the vacant chair and dropped her purse on the floor. Without missing a beat, she smiled at the waitress and gave her order. They'd eaten here so many times, they could all recite what was on the menu.

As soon as the waitress brought back their drinks, Lily got down to business. "What's wrong?" Picking up her glass of iced tea, she took a long sip before placing it back on the table.

"Having a hard day?" Emma was fascinated by the vibrant energy that always surrounded her friend.

"Don't change the subject," Lily admonished as she pointed her finger at Emma. "I could tell from the sound of your voice, when you called to confirm lunch, that something is seriously wrong." She hesitated. "Is it your business?"

Emma shook her head, trying to figure out where to begin.

"Not your health?" Annabelle reached out and gripped Emma's hand.

Shaking her head again, she took a deep breath and just spit it out. "It's a man."

The mouthful of iced tea that Lily had just taken sprayed over the table in front of them. As Lily choked and coughed, Annabelle thumped her on the back while Emma handed her a napkin. Lily waved them back to their seats as she gasped for breath. "A man?"

Emma smiled wryly. "Is that so unbelievable?" She guessed it was when they both nodded at the same time.

"Who?" Lily asked.

"Tucker Martin." She sat back in her chair and waited.

"He sent you flowers a few months ago." She tapped her fingers on the table. "But I thought you went out on a few dates with him and then called it quits?"

"I did."

"So what happened?"

"We got trapped in the elevator together when the power went out." Emma picked up her fork and toyed with it. "Things got hot and heavy pretty fast."

"Omigosh," Lily gasped.

Emma glanced at Annabelle who was watching her intently, obviously enthralled with her story. "That's not all."

"What else?" Lily waved her napkin in front of her face, as if trying to cool herself down.

"Mr. Meyers almost caught us, but I escaped back to my apartment. The power went again and I went over to Tucker's just to get some ice, and—"

"And?" Lily prompted when Emma was silent for a whole minute.

"It was amazing." Her voice was so quiet it was almost a whisper.

Finally, Annabelle spoke. "If it was so amazing, then why are you so sad?" Her friend had a way of going straight to the heart of things and that was one of the reasons Emma had wanted to see her.

"I don't know. We'd just had the most fantastic sex ever and then we were fighting. He accused me of playing games with him. Of wanting him only for sex and not for a relationship."

"Was he right?" Annabelle's soft words made her flinch. "How do you really feel about him?"

"I don't know." That was what had kept her awake all last night. "I don't mean to, but deep down, I don't trust him."

"Why not?" Lily's voice was suddenly harsh. "What's he done?" They both knew that Lily had little trust in men after her own ex-husband's transgressions.

"No, he hasn't done anything. He's been quite wonderful." The waitress walked up to their table with their orders, so they waited until she'd served them before continuing. "It's me."

"Why do you say that?" Annabelle shook out her napkin and laid it across her lap before picking up her fork.

"My father was a good-looking, charming man. He made people smile and laugh." She shook her head and picked at her salad with her fork. "He married my mom because she was pregnant, not because he loved her."

"He must have felt something for her if he married her," Annabelle pointed out.

"Yes, he felt he would like the small inheritance she'd gotten from her grandparents the year before. It was supposed to be for her college education. Instead it became money for him to fritter. Once it was gone, he started to stray."

"I'm so sorry, honey." Lily's sympathy washed over her.

Swallowing hard, she forced herself to continue. "He'd come back whenever he'd run out of money and sweet-talk my mother into taking him back. He'd promise her it was going to be different, but it never was. I was nine the last time I saw him."

"I still don't understand the problem?" Annabelle laid down her fork. "I'm sorry for what happened to you and your mom, but what does that have to do with you and Tucker?"

Couldn't her friend see? Hadn't she just laid it right out in front of them? Annabelle was still sitting there with an expectant look on her face. Emma opened her mouth, closed it, and then started again. "Tucker's good-looking and charming," she began.

"Yes, he is, "Annabelle agreed.

"So how can I trust him?" She buried her face in her hands. "How can I trust myself?" That was the real question. Emma was more afraid of being weak like her mother. She'd resented the fact that her mother allowed her father to disrupt their lives and make them unhappy. Just once, she'd wanted her mother to slam the door in her father's face and tell him to go away, that they didn't want him or need him in their lives. Just once, she wanted to be enough for her mother.

There it was. Emma sat up, shocked at her revelation. She was angrier with her mother than her father. Her mother's actions had left her feeling as if she wasn't enough.

"Oh, honey." Annabelle reached out and dabbed at Emma's face with her napkin, wiping a single tear that ran down her cheek. "Your mother was weak and that's not your fault. You were just a child. But Emma, you have to know that you're not anything like her. You're strong, independent and happy."

Emma considered her friend's words carefully. She was all those things Annabelle had listed. It was strange to finally come to the realization that she wasn't responsible for her mother's happiness or unhappiness, for that matter. It was sad that her mother had wasted much of her life on a man who wasn't worth it, but Annabelle was right. Emma was not her mother.

"And Tucker isn't your father," Lily added. "I know I can be cynical towards men, but I know that there are good ones out there."

Annabelle nodded. "Mike's worked with Tucker before." She stabbed a baby tomato with her fork, popped it into her mouth and chewed thoughtfully. "I like him. He's been out to the house a few times for supper and he was at the barbecue we threw earlier this summer. He strikes me as a straightforward kind of guy."

"You're right." Emma said it hesitantly, as if trying out the words. "I'm not my mother and he's not my father." Saying it out loud made it feel real. It was as if shackles she'd carried around all her life suddenly disappeared.

"Emma." Annabelle was very serious now as she reached out and took her friend's hand. "I almost lost Mike because I couldn't believe he'd be interested in someone like me."

"But you're beautiful and wonderful. Why wouldn't he love you?" Emma was shocked by her friend's revelation.

Annabelle smiled wryly. "But I didn't see it that way at the time. If you have feelings for Tucker then you owe it to yourself to see where your relationship might go. Maybe it won't last long, maybe it will." She shrugged. "But one thing I know for sure is that if you don't try, you'll never know." Annabelle's smile widened. "That means you have to acknowledge it publicly and not hold anything back."

Emma stared at her friend in horror. "I am not announcing to the entire town that I love him." Annabelle and Mike's story was well known by the town's inhabitants as she'd chosen last year's fair to announce it over the loudspeaker. Emma herself had witnessed the event and didn't think she was brave enough to do something quite that bold.

Lily muffled her laughter with her napkin, but Annabelle's filled the restaurant until tears flowed down her cheeks. "No," she tried to stop, but kept giggling. "It doesn't have to be quite so public."

Sitting back, Emma laughed with her friends. They were right. Tucker had let her know he was interested. It was up to her to make the next move.

The mood was lighter as they finished their meals. When they were sipping their coffee, Emma finally broached the subject. "Does anyone have any suggestions?"

Chapter Ten

ဆ

Tucker hauled open the front door and stalked into Art Inspired, determined to get Emma to talk to him. He'd waited all day yesterday, sure that she'd call him. But he'd waited in vain. His phone had remained silent. He hadn't even caught a glimpse of her.

The cold air struck him, helping to cool not only his body, but his frustration as well. The temperature was soaring to over one hundred degrees again today and people's tempers were beginning to fray around the edges. Taking off his sunglasses, he tucked them in his shirt pocket as he glanced around. Emma was nowhere in sight, and her assistant, Callie, was with a customer.

He thought about barging into her office, but decided to wait. After the way he'd stormed out of his apartment the other night, he figured he should try and show some restraint. It was probably better to talk to Callie first and try to find out what kind of a mood Emma was in.

He wandered around the room as he waited, looking at the artwork on display. Reaching into the front right pocket of his jeans, he stroked the jeweled dangler that he'd given Emma. She'd left it on the nightstand next to the bed. It had been the first thing he'd seen when he'd walked back into the empty bedroom that night because he hadn't wanted to look at the bed.

He'd already known she was gone because her clothes had been missing from the living room and the bed sheet had been lying in a heap on the floor. He thought about stripping the bed and changing the sheets, but he hadn't been able to make himself do it. They smelled like her. Instead, he'd spent the night on the sofa, unable to sleep with her sweet scent surrounding him without being able to hold her in his arms.

His thumb traced the stones on the nipple ornament and memories of her wearing it flooded his brain. His body reacted immediately and he could feel his cock begin to swell. Yanking his hand out of his pocket, he ran it though his hair. He had to get a grip on himself.

Giving himself a shake, he forced himself to look around the gallery. One thing he could say about Emma was that she ran a classy establishment. Paintings hung on the walls in pleasing arrangements. Pedestals topped with sculptures made of metal and stone were interspersed throughout the area. She even had one section that looked like an actual living room, giving people a better idea how certain pieces might look in their own home. It gave an overall impression of class without being stuffy.

Although he was trying to mind his own business, he couldn't help but notice that Callie's voice was getting louder and she was visibly becoming more upset. Working his way back around the room towards the main counter, he absently studied the man she was talking to. He was older, probably in his early to mid-fifties, but in good shape. He'd aged well and seemed to be doing his best to try and charm Callie into something. Tucker couldn't hear what they were saying, but he could hear the soft, pleading tone in the man's voice.

The man made a move towards Callie and she quickly stepped back. He'd seen enough. Sauntering over to the counter, he casually leaned against it and crossed his arms over his chest.

He made quite a contrast with the older man, who was dressed in an expensive suit and tie, his black leather shoes gleaming. The gentleman was the picture of suave sophistication. Tucker on the other hand was wearing a pair of worn jeans, a plain white cotton shirt and his dusty work boots.

Ignoring the man, he smiled at Callie. "Problem?"

She hesitated for a moment. "I don't think so."

The older man cocked his eyebrow and gazed at Tucker for a moment before dismissing him totally. The action amused Tucker, but he stayed where he was.

"I've come a long way and I wish to speak with Emma." The man straightened his jacket, reaching into his pocket as he spoke, and withdrew a folded twenty-dollar bill. He laid it on the counter in front of Callie. "I'd really appreciate it if you'd tell her I'm here."

At first, she paled. Then her cheeks flushed with anger. Tucker was surprised that steam didn't shoot out of Callie's ears. Obviously the man had no idea who he was dealing with if he'd thought she'd take a bribe. If he'd learned anything over the past few months, it was that she guarded Emma much like a mother lion guarded her cub.

The man smiled when she closed her hand over the money. It was more of a smirk really, but it quickly vanished when she tucked the money back into his pocket. Her voice was as frosty as the fake smile she gave him. "I told you already that Miss Howard is not available this morning. If you'll leave your name and number, I'll have her call you and set up an appointment."

A sound off to the side made Tucker glance over his shoulder. Emma took his breath away as she strode towards them. In her crisp white linen pants and jacket, she looked totally professional and untouchable.

There was just a hint of red peeking out from the top of her jacket. He speculated on whether or not it was a camisole or just a lacy bra she was wearing. She looked so restrained, but Tucker knew that it was that tiny splash of color that bespoke more of who Emma really was. For some reason, she seemed determined to hide that part of herself from not only herself, but the rest of the world as well.

She looked as cool as vanilla ice cream and good enough to eat. His mouth went dry at the thought of licking her from the tip of her cute little toes to the top of her head. He wanted to haul her into his arms and kiss her until she was mussed up a little. Just like she'd been when she'd been in his bed.

Just the sight of her bearing down on them had his cock starting to stand at attention again. He shifted, trying to hide his growing erection without being too obvious about it and settled back to see what would happen.

She ignored him totally. All her attention was focused on Callie. "Is everything all right out here? I could hear you in my office." Her eyes were cool as she glanced at the older man, but they warmed when they looked at her assistant.

"Everything is fine. This *gentleman* was very insistent that he see you, even though I told him you were unavailable for a meeting today." The emphasis that she put on the word "gentleman" left little doubt that she really didn't think the title applied to the man.

Amusement filled the man's face. "I didn't mean to upset anyone. It's just that I've come such a long way to see you, Emma."

Emma turned and really looked at the older man for the first time. She stared at him, a questioning look on her face. "I'm sorry, do I know you?"

He shook his head, sighed and looked hurt. Tucker wasn't buying the act and hoped that Emma didn't either. The man reached out with his hand pleadingly before dropping it back to his side. "You don't recognize me, Emmy."

Emma stiffened and all color left her face. "Don't call me that." She swayed on her feet and the older man reached out to grab her. Jerking away, she glared at him. "Don't you touch me."

All Tucker's senses went on full alert. He'd never heard such venom and anger from Emma before. Whoever this stranger was, she knew him and didn't like him. Not knowing what the threat was, but sensing it anyway, he moved to stand beside her, ready to help if she should need him.

"Is that any way to greet your father?" The look he was giving Emma made Tucker's skin crawl. It was calculating and slightly cruel.

Emma drew herself up and stared straight at him. "I haven't had a father since I was nine, James." She tapped a finger on her chin and paused for effect. "Come to think of it, I've never had a father. A sperm donor maybe, but not a father."

James Howard's face was suffused with anger for a brief second before he buried it. If Tucker hadn't been looking right at him, he'd have missed it. The man appeared to be very good at concealing his feelings.

"Emma, honey, I wanted to be with you, but your mother wouldn't let me. You were too young to know." He dabbed at the corner of his eye with his hand.

"Oh, please. You performed that tear-and-pity trick with my mother one too many times for it to be believable. She kept waiting for you to come back right up until the moment she drew her last breath." Emma's scorn was like a living thing and Tucker watched her with growing concern. "I couldn't convince her she was wasting her time with you."

James nodded. "I just found out about your mother." He shook his head and sighed deeply. "She was such a troubled woman."

"The only trouble she had was you." Emma stood her ground, not giving an inch.

"You've grown into a hard woman."

"If I have, it's because you helped to make me into one."

Tucker could feel her pain and wanted to reach out and touch her, to reassure her that he was here to help her if she needed him. But he forced himself to keep his hands by his sides, clenching them into fists to keep from hauling her into his arms to protect her. He didn't know how he knew, but somehow he sensed that it was very important for her to deal with this on her own.

"What do you want?" Emma broke the uncomfortable silence that had settled over the group.

James Howard looked affronted. "What makes you think I want anything from you?"

Her laughter was bitter. "Because you only show up when you want something." She took a step towards him and glared at him. "Enough of this show of fatherly concern. What do you want?"

"I was just wondering if your mother mentioned me in her will. Some small token." The older man shrugged, looking totally comfortable with his request. Tucker couldn't believe the audacity of the man. Emma's mother had been dead for three years and this son of a bitch had the nerve to come asking about the contents of her will.

"Money." Emma nodded knowingly. "I knew this was about money. Who do you owe this time? Or is it a get-rich-quick scheme?" She held up her hand to stop him before he could speak. "By the time she died, there was nothing left but medical bills. I don't suppose you'd want to contribute to those?" She continued on without giving anyone else time to speak. "I would imagine not. So why don't you do us all a favor and leave."

"I thought I might stay and visit you for a few days. We could talk about your mother." Tucker couldn't believe this guy. He just wouldn't take no for an answer. Even Callie was staring at the older man like he was some kind of idiot.

"You are not welcome and I will never give you a penny of my money. I am not my mother." She said each of her last five words slowly, enunciating each one so that there was no misunderstanding.

James stepped back and brushed a piece of lint of the sleeve of his suit jacket. "No, you're not your mother. She was a kind, gentle woman."

Tucker actually growled at this insult to Emma. Every muscle in his body was tense as he barely restrained himself from beating the older man to a pulp. "It's time you left." The harsh words were out of his mouth before he could stop them. But he didn't care. No one was going to get away with insulting *his* woman like that. Tucker didn't care who the hell they were. Emma laid her hand on his forearm and gently squeezed. Just her touch calmed him enough to gain control of himself.

"No, I'm not my mother." Tucker could hear the pain in her voice so he covered her hand with his own, silently offering her his strength. "She was a wonderful woman, but she was weak where you were concerned. She never understood that she could do much better than you."

"Your mother was a little nobody until she married me." The older man spat out, but quickly took a step back when Tucker broke away from Emma's grip and moved towards him. "I know where I'm not wanted." Sniffing haughtily, he raised his chin. "You could have used my help in your quaint shop, but I'm sure you've done the best you could." With that parting shot, he turned and strode from the gallery. No one else moved until the door closed behind him.

Emma began to laugh. It wasn't a pleasant sound, but had an edge of desperation about it. She clapped one hand over her mouth and the other over her stomach as if she could somehow hold in her pain.

Tucker wrapped his arm around her shoulders and shot Callie a look. Callie nodded and motioned him back to the privacy of the office. He guided Emma towards her office, knowing that they wouldn't be disturbed.

It bothered him that she let him lead her so easily. It was so unlike Emma, who was usually so full of life and so independent. As soon as the door closed behind them, he drew her into his arms and hugged her tight. He tucked her face into his chest and the laughter quickly became tears. Huge sobs seemed to rise from somewhere deep inside her and he was powerless to do anything but hold her close and rock her from side to side.

He had no idea how much time passed before her sobbing finally stopped. Swiping at her tears with her hand, she stepped back from him. Reluctantly, he let her go. He knew they had their own problems to deal with, but she hadn't deserved what had just happened.

"So that's my father." She gave him a watery smile.

"I gathered as much." He wasn't sure what else to say so he decided to follow her lead.

Shaking her head, she gave a small laugh. "The world is an ironic place, you know."

"How so?"

She motioned towards him with her hand and then just shrugged. "You. Me. Us." Sighing, she leaned against the edge of her desk, grabbed a tissue from a box that sat there and blew her nose. "I've done my best not to think about my parents' relationship, but in this last week, I've done nothing *but* think about it." She shredded the tissue in her fingers.

Tucker waited patiently, willing her to continue.

"I realized that the whole thing between us was tainted by their relationship. And when you left the other night, I began to think about how it had influenced me. Then there was lunch with my friends yesterday. I suddenly had a revelation that I had made too many choices in my life based on the fact that I was afraid of being weak like my mother. I felt that no good-looking man could be trusted to ever want me for myself. That I would never be enough."

He felt his stomach clench as she revealed her thoughts to him. "What does that have to do with us?"

"Don't you see? I was afraid that I was too much like my mother." She hesitated and then forged on. "And I was afraid that you were too much like my father. Charming, good-looking and not to be trusted."

Her words were like a knife in his heart. "You think I'm like *that* heartless bastard?" That she would think so poorly of him made him sick to his stomach. "You honestly think I'm like that sleazy bastard?"

"I was afraid, Tucker."

They were not the words he wanted to hear.

"But it seems as if the universe decided that it was time I dealt with these issues. They all seemed to come to a head in the last few days." She dropped the shredded pieces of tissue onto her desk and played with the button on her jacket. "I haven't seen that man since I was nine."

Tucker knew that he should be understanding and patient. Emma had been through the emotional wringer in the last hour, but so had he. His patience was at an end and he was desperately trying to deal with his own hurt. Although it was probably the hardest thing he'd ever done in his life, he forced himself to step away from her.

He didn't know what she saw in his face as she looked at him, but her eyes got wider and she reached her hand out to him. He looked at it and then looked away. "If you think that I'm like that man, then we have nothing to talk about. I won't bother you again."

She called out his name. But he ignored it, turned and carefully closed her office door behind him, and kept walking. Shoving open the gallery door, he stepped out into the oppressive heat and blinding sunshine, but somehow he still felt cold inside. He was through with playing games and waiting for Emma. It was time to move on with his life.

His heart pounded in his chest and actually hurt at the thought of giving up on Emma. He'd been sure that she was the right woman for him, but obviously she wasn't ready for a serious, committed relationship. And he had to face the fact that she might never be ready.

Given what he'd just seen and heard, he couldn't really blame her. But he wasn't fool enough to keep hanging onto a hope that didn't seem to be there. Maybe it had never been there. Maybe it had all been in his mind.

No. He wouldn't believe that. Emma had felt something for him. He'd seen it in her eyes and in her actions. She wasn't the type of woman who gave her body without giving at least part of her heart. It just didn't seem to be enough, though, for her to risk everything with him.

By the time he reached his truck, his shirt was plastered to his skin. He slipped his sunglasses back on his face, trying to cut down on the relentless glare from the sun. He cursed the relentless heat wave for the first time since it had begun. As he reached into his pocket for his keys, his fingers brushed the jeweled dangler. He closed his eyes and leaned his forehead against the side of the truck. Taking a deep breath, he forced himself to let it go and haul out his keys instead.

Pulling himself away from the vehicle, he climbed inside and drove away without looking back.

Chapter Eleven

ဆ

Emma stared at Tucker's back as he walked out of her office without a backward glance. She was an emotional wreck, but she knew that she didn't want him to leave. Didn't want to lose him. She'd already made up her mind to contact him and had been thrilled when she'd seen him in the gallery.

Then everything had gone to hell.

She shivered and rubbed her hands up and down her arms. Even though she was wearing a jacket, the air-conditioning was chilling. She knew the cold was coming from a place deep inside her. A place she'd been forced to examine the past few days. It hadn't been a fun experience, but a necessary one. This morning had just been one more unpleasant thing she'd had to face.

It had been a strange feeling to find her father standing in front of her after all these years. She remembered him as bigger and stronger than he really was. In truth, he was handsome in a superficial way, average height with a trim build. She could see how women found him attractive, but there was weakness in his face as well. It showed in his eyes.

She had changed. That was the biggest factor. Now that she was no longer a child, she saw him through much different eyes. Where before he'd seemed smooth and charming, now he just seemed manipulative and sly.

How in the hell had she ever thought that Tucker was anything like her father?

It now seemed impossible, even obscene, to have even imagined that. Tucker was as solid and dependable as they came, and he could be counted on. He wouldn't play games or try and manipulate her. From the beginning, he'd been straightforward and honest about what he'd wanted from her.

It was she who'd been less than honest, with herself and with him. But that was all about to change. And if it wasn't too late, she wanted a shot at a permanent relationship with Tucker. That is, if he still wanted anything to do with her after this morning.

She realized she'd made a mistake in trying to explain it all to him without reassuring him. The very first thing she should have done is to tell him she didn't think he was anything like her father. The explanation could have come later.

She'd hurt him badly. And not only this morning. There was still the incident from the other evening as well. She had a lot of explaining and making up to do with Tucker. But she was no quitter. No matter how long it took, if there was even a remote chance for them, then she would keep fighting for it.

He hadn't quit on her. In his own quiet way, he'd stayed in her life and let her take the lead. Well, it was past time for her to take it. Reaching into her jacket pocket, she withdrew the pretty jeweled dangler and wrapped her fingers around it. It had become a talisman of sorts, a reminder that he'd cared enough to buy these for her and carry them around in his pocket for weeks with no true expectation of ever being able to give them to her.

Carefully, she tucked the jewelry back in her pocket. A discreet knock on the door made her heart jump. Maybe he'd come back. "Come in," she called, even as she hurried towards the door.

She caught her breath as it slowly opened and then felt her stomach drop when Callie poked her head inside. The disappointment on her face must have shown because Callie looked at her and shook her head. "He's gone. Sorry."

"No, I'm sorry. Sorry you had to witness that."

The younger woman offered her a smile. "Hey, it's not so bad. You should see my family at Thanksgiving."

Emma just looked at her and then started to laugh. "I can always count on you to make me laugh and gain perspective." And that was the truth. Every family had its problems and hers was no different. It had just taken a little longer for all the problems to come out into the open.

But now that they were there, she could deal with them. And having them aired in such a public way made her realize they weren't such a big deal after all. Not as long as she faced them and didn't allow them to rule her life choices any longer.

Callie saluted her. "I aim to serve." Her saucy grin faded from her face, replaced by concern. "Seriously though, you should take the rest of the day off and go home." She hesitated for the briefest moment. "Maybe talk to Tucker."

"You're absolutely right." Striding back towards her desk, she shut down her computer, closed the file she had been working on and tossed it back into her in-basket. Grabbing her purse, she turned to see Callie still standing in the doorway with her mouth hanging open in surprise.

Emma laughed. "You didn't expect me to give in so easily, did you?" Closing the door securely behind her, she tested it to make sure it was locked.

Her assistant shook her head as they walked across the gallery together. "I figured I'd have to talk you into it."

"Well, how's this for a change? Put a sign on the door that says we're closed for the rest of the day, and go home. After this morning, we could both use some time off."

"Really?" Callie was already rubbing her hands together with glee as she headed towards the front counter.

"Yes, really. I'm the damned boss and if I say we close, then we close."

"All right." The younger woman had her cell phone whipped open and was hitting the speed dial as Emma walked out into the stifling heat.

Pausing, she rummaged around in her purse for her sunglasses and put them on. The sound of the door being locked behind her made her turn. Callie gave her a wave as she placed the closed sign on the door. Emma left work behind her and started towards home.

She only hoped that Tucker came home to his apartment tonight. Straightening her shoulders, she strode down the sidewalk. Well, if he weren't home tonight, she'd wait until tomorrow night or the night after that. But sooner or later, she would catch him home and then she would put her plan into action.

Tucker wrapped a towel around his waist as he stepped out of the shower. It felt good to wash away the dirt, grime and sweat of the workday. Now, if only he could take care of all his other problems so easily, he wouldn't care.

Grabbing another towel, he briskly rubbed it over his head. Slinging the towel over the shower rod to dry, he raked his fingers through his hair. He swiped at the condensation on the mirror with his hand, clearing a small patch, and stared at his reflection. His hair stuck up in short black spikes and his jaw was dark with stubble, but he couldn't be bothered to shave.

Sighing, he rubbed his hand over his face and turned away, padding down the hallway towards the kitchen. He looked tired. But, damn it, he hadn't had much sleep the past two nights. This whole thing with Emma was keeping him tied up in knots.

The cool air felt good on his skin as he opened the refrigerator door and took out a cold beer. Popping the top, he tilted his head back and took a large swig. It slid easily down his throat. Closing the door, he wandered over to the kitchen table and stared at the centerpiece in the middle.

Flowers. A great big bouquet of wildflowers. He recognized the white and yellow daisies, but that was about it.

He knew most of the rest of them by sight, but not by name. It was a huge splash of color in the middle of his table.

Taking another sip from the can, he felt a reluctant smile tug at his lips. He'd been working and had noticed the delivery van immediately, as it was very visible through the big picture window.

He'd been contracted to do the electrical work on a new home being built by Mike Sloan's company. He knew all the guys on the job, having worked with them many times before. They'd all paused, curiosity aroused, when the driver had started up the driveway with a large crystal vase filled with flowers. They'd all assumed that the driver had made an error.

Mike had met the deliveryman on the front porch. They'd all known something was up when Mike had started to laugh and motioned the man inside. He didn't know who'd looked more shocked, him or the guys on the work site, when the deliveryman walked right up to Tucker and handed him the vase.

He'd been so surprised, he'd almost dropped it. Carefully, he placed it on the floor and automatically reached into his pocket for a tip. The driver just smiled and shook his head. "Tip's been taken care of. Have a nice day."

The delivery guy was almost out the door before Tucker finally found his voice. "Who are they from?"

"There's a card attached." The voice drifted back. Tucker stood there staring at the flowers, almost afraid to touch them.

"You gonna read the card or are you just gonna to stare at them for the rest of the afternoon?" Mike had come up beside him and was staring at the flowers with interest.

Reaching out, Tucker snagged the card that was tucked inside the bouquet and walked over by the window for some privacy before opening it. It simply said one word. "Emma."

He closed his eyes, unable to look at her name. Why had she sent him flowers after he'd walked out on her this morning? It didn't make any sense. But still, he couldn't suppress the tiny glimmer of hope that sprang up within him before he squashed it. The flowers didn't necessarily mean anything. They could easily mean goodbye or thanks for the great sex. He wouldn't read anything into them.

Reaching out now, he rubbed his finger over the soft petals of the flowers. The guys had ribbed him for the rest of the afternoon, teasing him about his secret admirer, but he noticed that many of them glanced at the flowers with envy in their eyes. And they'd also helped him find a box and some newspapers to stuff around it so that he could safely transport the arrangement home without damaging it.

All the way on the drive home, his eyes had been drawn back to them time and again. And now they were sitting in the middle of his kitchen table and he knew he'd keep them there until they were wilted and dead. Lowering his hand, he took another sip of his beer as he wandered into the living room.

Dropping down onto the sofa, he propped his feet up on the coffee table and relaxed. He knew he should get dressed, but he just couldn't be bothered. He wasn't planning on going out, so he probably wouldn't bother. There was probably something in the kitchen that he could interest himself in for supper. But later. For now, he just wanted to sit in peace and unwind from the day.

Tipping his head back against the cushions, he closed his eyes and allowed his mind to drift. Suddenly everything went quiet. The hum of the air conditioner and the refrigerator were silenced. Another blackout.

He couldn't say he really minded. They hadn't lasted more than an hour or so each time and at least now he had an excuse not to bother with supper. If it kept up, he might call around and try and find a pizza joint that had power and order a large deluxe.

The knock was so quiet he almost didn't hear it. He really didn't want to get up from the sofa, but with the power gone, one of his neighbors could need help. Besides Mr. Meyers, there were also a few older ladies on this floor.

Opening his eyes, he planted his feet on the floor and heaved himself off the sofa. Placing his half-empty beer on the coffee table, he made sure his towel was secure as he headed towards the front door. He knew he should probably go and grab a pair of shorts, but the knocking was more insistent now. They could darn well take him like he was.

"Yeah," he said, as he pulled the door open, not bothering to check the peephole. Didn't matter who was there, he'd still open it. He was brought up short by the vision standing outside his door. He blinked once, not quite sure he could believe his eyes.

Emma was standing in the dim corridor wearing nothing but a skimpy white teddy. The silky fabric barely covered her breasts, clinging to her torso as it flowed over her body. It was cut high on her thighs, and left her long, luscious legs completely bare. There was a small red bow between her breasts and he was reminded of his earlier thoughts at the gallery. She might have changed clothing, but she still reminded him of a damned ice-cream sundae. And he still wanted to lick her entire body.

She shifted and her hands fluttered in front of her before dropping back to her sides. Her nipples were pebbled against the silk barely covering her breasts and her chest was rising and falling rapidly, her breathing shallow. Her face was flushed and he wasn't sure if it was because of the heat or because she was turned on. Probably a combination of the two.

His own body had reacted immediately, his cock going straight to attention as soon as he'd laid eyes on her. He wasn't going to apologize for his body's reaction to her. She knew that he wanted her.

She licked her lips and he couldn't take his eyes off her tongue as it stroked across them. "The power is out."

"So it is." He didn't know what she wanted, but he wanted her to spell it out for him. No chance of misunderstanding. No games.

She shifted slightly, seeming self-conscious as she pushed a lock of hair out of her eyes. "I was wondering if you had some ice."

He swallowed his disappointment. Obviously, the teddy was because of the heat. And truthfully, it covered more than most swimsuits did, but somehow it made her seem more provocative. She was just here because she needed his help.

"Sure. I'll get you some." He turned and stalked back into the kitchen leaving the door open. She could either come in or stay out in the hallway. It was her choice.

As he dumped all the ice he had into a bowl, he heard the front door closing. He hoped she'd take the ice and go. He didn't think he could take having her so near and not fucking her. He planned on another long, cold shower the second she was gone.

He turned and stopped. She was standing right next to the table staring at the flowers. "You kept them. I wasn't sure you would."

She looked so uncertain that he tried to smile. "Yeah, I kept them. Thanks." He cleared his throat. "No one ever gave me flowers before."

"Really?"

Her hesitant smile made his cock twitch. If she didn't leave soon, he was going to melt the ice with the heat from his body. "Really. The guys at work certainly got a kick out of it."

He could have kicked himself for saying that when her smile disappeared and she stared chewing on her lower lip. "I'm sorry. I didn't think about that."

"No problem. I think most of them were jealous." He held out the bowl of ice. It wasn't much, a few cubes and some smaller chips, but she was welcome to it. "Here you go. Is there anything else you want?" His tone was sharp and she flinched slightly, but he couldn't help it. He was so turned on he was going to explode if he didn't get her out of here. His body obviously had no sense and definitely had a mind of its own when it came to Emma.

She took the bowl and then set it down carefully on the kitchen table. "Yes. There is something else I want."

Tucker rubbed his hand across his face and sighed. "What else do you want?"

"You." She stepped closer and laid her hand on his chest. "I want you."

Chapter Twelve

%

She could feel Tucker's heart pounding beneath her palm and she almost wilted with relief. He wasn't quite as calm and removed as he seemed. Her courage had almost deserted her, he seemed so remote and almost cool towards her. She was used to the easy warmth of his smile and the invitation in his eyes and felt as if she'd lost something incredibly special when it was no longer there.

He hadn't budged, standing as still as a stone. Unable to resist, she rubbed her hand over his chest, loving the way the crisp hair felt against her palm and feeling the play of muscles flowing beneath the skin. Suddenly he covered her hand with one of his, flattening it against his chest and keeping it from its exploration.

"What do you want me for? If you want a quick fuck, I can probably accommodate you." Picking up her hand, he moved it from his chest to the front of the towel. There was no mistaking that he was totally aroused as she skimmed her fingers over the hard length that pushed against the towel, making it tent out in front of him.

His words were crude, but his touch was gentle. She knew she'd hurt him badly earlier today and that he was just lashing out. No, he wasn't going to make this easy for her.

Wrapping her fingers over his erection, she carefully squeezed. "I want you for that." She paused when he closed his eyes and tipped his head back. The strong column of his neck just begged to be kissed. Later. Right now, she needed to let him know exactly where she stood. "But I want you for so much more."

His eyes snapped open, a blaze of green fire, as he met her gaze. "What else?" he growled as he grabbed her hand and held it still.

Dropping all pretenses, she tugged her hand away from his and reached up and cupped his face. She loved the slightly scratchy feel of his five o'clock shadow. She loved the way he watched her, patiently waiting for her to talk. She loved the way he was with people and the fact that he was loyal and trustworthy. She loved his sense of humor and his sense of fairness. She just plain loved him.

"If it's not too late," she paused and his hands were suddenly at her waist, gripping her tight.

"If it's not too late," he prompted.

"I don't think you're anything like my father," she blurted out. As if a floodgate had opened, everything came pouring out. "It was never you, it was me. I was afraid. Afraid to be weak, afraid to need, afraid I wasn't enough. So I built walls around myself and pretended I didn't care. But you not only ignored my walls." She laughed. "You scaled them. And you did it so easily it frightened me."

She took a deep breath and stared into his soulful green eyes and saw herself reflected in them. "I was afraid to believe that you were for real. But you are. And I know that now. I'm no longer afraid. And I want us to have a chance."

Taking the biggest risk of her life, she took the plunge. "I love you."

Tucker was like a statue in front of her. Every muscle in his body seemed to tense at once and she wondered if she hadn't made a mistake. What if he no longer felt the same?

Suddenly, she was plucked right off her feet as his arms banded around her, and he buried his face in the curve of her shoulder. Wrapping her arms around his neck and her legs around his hips, she clung tight to him, needing the contact as much as he seemed to.

They fit together so perfectly, as if they were made specifically for each other. Standing in the kitchen locked in his arms, Emma finally felt as if she'd found where she belonged.

The stubble on his beard was rough against her shoulder and neck as he kissed his way up the side to her ear. She found it unbearably exciting and tugged him closer. His laugh was low and sexy in her ear as he nibbled her earlobe. When his tongue flicked into her ear, she could feel an answering pulse in her sex.

She didn't realize he'd moved until she felt her bottom land on the end of the counter, which separated the small kitchen from the eating area. Perching her on the edge, he spread her knees wide with his hands as he played with her ear.

Emma gripped his shoulders, holding on for dear life. She was wild for him, but she wanted to give to him. To let him take whatever he wanted. "Tucker," she moaned when he pulled back to stand between her spread legs. She didn't know what she was pleading for, only that she never wanted it to stop.

"You look like a damned ice-cream sundae." His fingers skimmed up the spaghetti straps that held up her teddy. "I thought so when you were wearing that white suit earlier today and I still think so." He slowly allowed his fingers to slip back down the straps and over the top of the fabric cupping her breasts until they came to rest on the red bow in the center. The teddy looked so very white and fragile next to his darker, rougher hands. The contrast was unbearable arousing and made her feel delicate and sexy.

She could feel her breasts swelling beneath his light touch. Her nipples tightened even more, sending another bolt of pleasure straight to her core. Moaning, she thrust them towards him, encouraging him to touch her.

"I wanted to lick you all over earlier." Removing her hands from his shoulders, he placed them on the counter so that they were supporting her. The movement arched her body towards him, making her silk-covered breasts an offering for him. "And I think I will."

Emma could feel the cream pooling between her thighs as he lowered his head and licked one of her straining nipples through the fabric. The heat of his mouth practically set her on fire. She wanted to wrap her arms around him, but knew she'd lose her balance if she did.

"Hmm," he murmured. "That's good, but I want to taste you."

"Yesss," she hissed between clenched teeth. Anything he wanted.

She wanted to cry out in frustration when his hands went back to the bow at the center of her teddy rather than to the shoulder straps. He traced the red tie one more time before gripping the fabric on either side and rending the material right down the center.

Emma froze in shock at the tearing sound. Looking down at herself, she was totally exposed as he pushed the sides of the torn fabric out of his way. He cupped her mound with his hand, allowing his fingers to sift through her pubic hair. With no warning, he slid two of his fingers past her slit and right into her heat.

Moaning, she tilted her hips, wanting his fingers deeper. She was so close to coming, but he withdrew his fingers and brought them to his mouth, licking them one by one. She shivered as he stepped back from her and tugged the towel from his waist, allowing it to fall to the floor.

"You're hot and wet for me already, aren't you, baby?" His words alone were like a stroke of pleasure.

"Yes. Don't stop, Tucker."

His fingers stroked the wet folds of her labia as he spread them wide. "But I don't want you to come just yet. I want you so hot, you're on fire." Her entire body clenched when his index finger stroked across her clit and he laughed. "I think we need to cool you down for a bit so you don't come too soon."

Standing between her thighs, he pushed his cock against her slit as he leaned down and kissed her. There was no hurry to his motions even though she was starting to feel slightly frantic. The pressure was building low in her belly and the waiting was making her crazy.

His tongue stroked over her lips and she parted them for him, but he took his time, tasting every inch of them before slipping his tongue inside. Again, he leisurely stroked her tongue and her mouth, as if he was savoring each and every stroke. She loved the feel of his tongue on hers and gripped his neck with one hand, wanting to deepen their kiss.

At the same time, she pushed her hips hard against his length, feeling it pulse against her clit. She lost her balance when he moved her other hand, but she trusted him to hold her and he did, carefully lowering her until she was lying flat on the counter. She closed her eyes and took a deep breath. She had no idea what he had in mind, but couldn't wait to find out.

He lifted her right foot and kissed her instep before placing her foot on the edge of the counter. Then he did the same thing with her left foot. He placed her feet as wide apart as they would go, so she was totally exposed to him.

She felt vulnerable, but powerful at the same time. Her eyes popped open when she felt something icy on her stomach. She shivered and tried to pull away from the cold, but with her back against the counter there was nowhere for her to go.

"Just feel how good it is against your skin." His movements were hypnotic as he stroked the small piece of ice across her belly and then lower. "The cold will make the heat even more intense." Water droplets formed as it melted, pooling on her belly before slipping down over her hips.

She gasped as he slid it over the folds of her sex towards her clit. "Tucker, I'm not sure about this."

"I am," he said as he lightly grazed the swollen nub.

"Oh god. Oh god," she chanted as he teased her with the ice.

"Trust me?" His question seemed simple, but everything she'd said earlier boiled down to this moment. He wanted— no, needed—her to prove her trust.

"Yes."

The word was barely past her lips when he slid the tiny chip of ice into her pussy and pushed it deep with his fingers. The contrast of heat and cold was too much and she came, her body jerking as she cried out. The intensity of her orgasm was amazing and unlike anything she'd ever experienced before.

Tucker's fingers were still deep inside her when the spasms finally subsided. The melting ice water seeping from her slit felt soothing against the heat. She could feel a bead of sweat trickle down between her breasts, but she didn't care. She was too relaxed to move.

Then he moved his fingers, spreading them wide as he slowly pulled them out of her. She could feel what was left of the sliver of ice still inside her. Tucker moved close so that his cock was against her sex again, effectively sealing it inside her.

Arching her hips, she gasped as her arousal began to grow yet again. And when he reached out and snagged another small piece of ice she didn't know whether to encourage him or scream for mercy.

Holding the ice chip steady, he leaned over her and rubbed it across her lips. The movement caused his cock to rub against her clit. She could feel the last of the ice crystals melt within her, the cool water both soothing and arousing the heated muscles.

The ice on her lips made her mouth feel dry. She wanted some in her mouth along with his tongue. When her lips parted, he smiled and popped the ice in his mouth and lowered his upper body across hers until his mouth was aligned with hers. He pushed the ice into her mouth with his tongue as he kissed her, and she accepted it eagerly. There was so much heat between them that the ice was soon reduced to water, which she swallowed.

"You are so damned sexy." His low growl made her heart beat even faster. He buried his face against her breasts even as he reached his hand out to the bowl again.

"I'm so hot." She felt almost feverish as she strained against Tucker, wanting to feel his body touching hers everywhere.

This time it wasn't as much of a shock when the ice stroked across her flesh. She anticipated it, even welcomed it as he slipped it over and around her breasts and swollen nipples. Again, the contrast of cold and heat almost pushed her over the edge, but this time she didn't want to go alone. This time she wanted Tucker with her, inside her.

She grabbed his hand and pushed it away from her breast. "Now, Tucker. Take me now."

"Fuck, yes." The piece of ice fell unheeded onto the counter as he gripped her hips, positioned himself and drove his cock inside her.

Chapter Thirteen

ഇ

Tucker gasped for breath as Emma's hot pussy clasped him like a tight velvet glove. His balls were drawn tight to his body. He was poised on the edge and had been since she'd whispered those three simple words that had completely rocked his world. *I love you.* They echoed in his mind even as his body craved release.

Until she'd spoken them aloud, he hadn't realized how much he'd wanted her to say them. Something inside him had relaxed at her words. Emma would never say those words to a man unless she meant them. And if she meant them, then she was serious about their relationship.

The strain of the last few months and especially the last few days slipped from his shoulders. All that was left was a burning need deep in his gut to claim her as his own. To fuck her so long and so hard she would never remember any other lover before him.

He'd never admit that to her though. He did have some sense. She'd think him a total Neanderthal. The thought made him grin. The woman did seem to bring out his more primitive side.

Deciding it was time to move, he bent forward and planted a quick kiss on her lips. "Wrap your arms around my neck." Her sexy, satisfied smile almost destroyed what small amount of control he'd managed to gain. He almost came undone when her hands stroked the hard planes of his chest, grazing his nipples before continuing their path up to his shoulders and finally around his neck.

"Hold on." Grunting, he stood. She shrieked at the sudden change of position, locking her ankles at the small of his back. Her fingers had his neck in a death grip and if he weren't so damned horny he would have laughed.

Supporting her back with one hand, he gripped her bottom with the other. The movement drove his cock deeper into her heat. He could feel the sweat on his body as he stood in the kitchen with Emma wrapped around him. The air in the apartment was quickly becoming warm, but it was nothing compared to the heat being generated between them.

"This feels good." She squirmed to try and get comfortable and began to nibble on his neck.

All his good intentions vanished. "I can't wait," he grated out.

"Then don't," she said simply.

He shoved her against the nearest wall, gripped her ass in both his hands and began to thrust. There was nothing gentle about him now. Every time he'd pull back, her body would suck at his cock, trying to keep it inside her, and when he'd shove himself back in, her inner muscles squeezed him tight. It was incredible.

The only sound in the quiet apartment was the wet slapping of skin as he pounded into her and their breathing as they both gasped for air. Tucker thought his lungs might explode, but he didn't slow his pace.

His hips pumped hard and quick as he held her immobile in his grip. Her fingers clutched at his shoulders and his hair as she desperately tried to meet his strokes. He'd waited so long that now it was taking him forever to come.

He had to have release. Now.

Emma cried out, her scream of release, raw and urgent. Her grip was almost painful as she clutched at him. He could feel her inner muscles milking his swollen cock. Clenching tight around it.

That was all it took. He came hard and fast then, letting out a yell as his hips jerked, and he emptied himself into her. As she went limp in his arms, he felt his knees buckle. But he didn't lose his grip on her as he lowered them both to the kitchen floor.

Keeping his arms around her, he rolled onto his back so that she was lying on top of him. He decided then that he could easily get used to this position. Neither of them felt the need to speak as they lay there catching their breath.

He pushed a lock of matted hair off her forehead. They needed a cool shower, just as soon as he could work up enough energy to move them. With the heat and the sexual release they'd just had, he was in no hurry to budge from the floor. Besides, it was cooler down here.

As she stirred in his arms, he kissed her temple. "Did I hurt you?" He knew that she'd come, but he also knew that he hadn't exactly been gentle at the end. Worry began to gnaw at his gut when she sighed but didn't answer him.

Rolling with her in his arms, he quickly had her flat on her back. Looming over her, he braced himself with one forearm as he stared down at her flushed face. "I'm sorry, baby. I didn't mean to hurt you." He rubbed his thumb over her cheek, noting the dark shadows under her eyes. She hadn't been sleeping well either.

"You didn't hurt me. I wanted you, too." Her brown eyes were solemn as she watched him.

She seemed to be searching his face for something, but he wasn't sure what. "You're sure?" He knew she'd had several orgasms, but there was an underlying sadness surrounding her that worried him.

"Yes, I'm sure." She turned her head away and started to chew on her bottom lip. "Can I get up now?"

Alarm bells went off deep inside him. No way was he letting her get away from him this time. Cupping her cheek, he turned her face back to him before using his thumb to sooth her abused bottom lip. "No."

Her eyebrows snapped together in a scowl. "No?"

"No," he reiterated. "Not until you tell me what's wrong." Sighing, he dropped his forehead down to hers. "Please tell me what's wrong."

"Was this just a quick fuck?" she threw his earlier words back at him. "Or did it mean more to you?" Her voice was barely a whisper, but her questions shocked him.

He reared back and stared down at her, barely able to believe what he'd just heard. "How the hell can you even ask that?"

She shrugged, trying hard to look nonchalant, but he could see the hurt in her eyes. "Because you never said if it was too late or not." She stared straight at him and tilted her chin up. "Because I told you that I loved you and you said nothing at all."

If he could have managed to kick his own backside, he would have been tempted to do so at that very moment. Since he'd met Emma he'd felt all kinds of emotions he'd never felt before in his life, and all to extremes. How in the heck had he managed somehow to forget to tell her anything?

He sat back, slightly stunned. Maneuvering around until his back was comfortably situated against the bottom kitchen cupboards and his legs were stretched out in front of him, he opened his arms wide. "Come here."

She hesitated before slowly rolling up onto her knees. She plucked at the remains of her teddy, trying to pull some of the fabric around to cover her. But it was a lost cause as the garment was in tatters. Finally, she gave up.

Tucker waited patiently as she came over and sat next to him. He patted his lap, wanting her closer to him. "Please." Reluctantly, she swung one of her legs over his hips and sat facing him, straddling his thighs.

"Did you know that you left one of the danglers that I gave you in the bedroom?" He could tell the direction of the conversation confused her.

She gave him a strange look as if she was trying to figure out the workings of his mind. "Yes," she finally admitted.

"I been carrying it around in my pocket ever since." The corners of her mouth tilted up slightly, but he didn't care if she found it amusing. "It made me feel closer to you somehow, having it in my pocket and being able to touch it occasionally." She laughed softly and he shook his head. "I know it's stupid…"

She touched her hand to his mouth to stop him from speaking. "No, it's not stupid at all. I've been doing the exact same thing."

"Really?" His own smile came easily and he chuckled as the humor of it settled in. "Both of us carrying them around with us." He shook his head. "Pitiful."

"No," she corrected him. "I think it's beautiful and romantic." Hesitantly she tugged part of the tattered fabric to the front. And there attached at the bottom of one of the straps on the inside he saw the glint of a row of stones. She'd fastened it to the strap with a piece of thread.

"I love you." The words were ripped from somewhere deep inside him. What he felt for this woman was overwhelming in its scope and intensity. He never wanted it to end.

This time her smile was wide and genuine. It was like a ray of sunshine brightening his life. "I love you, too." Throwing her arms around him she hugged him to her.

His arms banded around her, holding her so close that he could feel her heart pounding against his. He swallowed hard and kissed her temple, knowing he'd never get tired of hearing those words from her.

As she released him and sat back, he noticed that a single tear had slipped from the corner of her eye. Wiping it away with the pad of his thumb, he smiled at her. "This is more than just a quick fuck. This is so much more. This is today, tomorrow and the day after that. This is about forever."

"Forever," she repeated.

He wanted her again. His cock was standing at attention between them, his arousal impossible to miss. Emma looked down at his lap and laughed. "You're insatiable." She climbed to her feet, holding out her hand to him as she did so. "I want a shower before we do anything else. I'm sticky and sweaty."

Gripping her hand, he surged to his feet. "I wonder how long the power will be gone this time?"

"Omigosh." Emma slapped her hand over her mouth as she began to laugh. She laughed so hard that she doubled over and would have fallen if he hadn't caught her.

It was the guilty look in her eyes when she looked at him that finally gave her away. "You didn't?"

"I did," she gasped out as she tried to control herself. "I didn't know which switch to pull, so I asked Mr. Meyers."

"You didn't?" He tried to give her a stern look, but the corners of his mouth twitched upwards. "Emma, I'm shocked at you. Are you trying to give him a heart attack or something?" He shook his head at her in mock disappointment. "You didn't tell him why you wanted to do it? Did you?"

Standing proudly in the middle of his kitchen wearing nothing but a few tatters of silk, she nodded emphatically. "You're darned right I did. The man's old, not dead. Besides, he liked the whole idea of helping to bring us together." She chuckled again. "Apparently we hadn't fooled him for a second when we got out of the elevator. But he told me that there are just some things a gentleman doesn't mention."

"Is that so?" Swooping down on her, he scooped her up into his arms.

"Yes, that's so." She patted him on the chest. "I suggest you haul on a pair of shorts and run down to the electrical room before we both expire from the heat."

Carrying her down the hall, he went straight for the bathroom. "Shower first. Then I'll turn the power back on."

Emma lay sprawled on her back in the center of the mattress. She was so relaxed she felt as if she didn't have a bone left in her body. Stretching her legs, she tightened all the muscles before relaxing them again. Tucker grunted but didn't move from his position. Currently, he was lying facedown on the bed with one of his arms thrown over his head and the other one circling her waist.

She curled her toes and sighed with contentment. From her position, she had a great view of his butt. And Tucker had a prime example of the perfect male butt. In fact, she was sure that other women would pay good money to see an ass that fine. But it was all hers and she wasn't sharing.

The pillowcase rustled as he slowly turned his head and opened his eyes. "That was a deep sigh." He looked tired, but well sated as he yawned. The stubble on his jaw was even darker now than it had been. The sun was starting to come up and the early morning light was just beginning to brighten the bedroom.

"I'm just a little bit tired."

A wicked grin covered his face. "Are you now?" His arm tightened around her.

She closed her eyes as the mere thought of how they'd spent last night made her heart start to pound. After their quick shower, Tucker had raced down to the electrical room and turned his power back on in record time. By the time he'd returned, she been ready and waiting for him.

The matching nipple ornament had been sitting on the bedside table, so she'd gone back to the bathroom where the tattered remains of her teddy were dumped on the floor and carefully removed the one that she'd attached to the strap. Returning to the bedroom, she'd put both of them on her breasts before draping herself across the bed.

Stuffing a few pillows behind her so that she was on more of an incline than flat on her back, she'd arranged herself in what she hoped was a provocative pose. She'd felt daring and sexy with her legs spread wide and her arms thrown over her head. Her nipples looked dark and exotic with the small jewels flowing from them, just the feel of them pinching her nipples tight made her hot. Her cream had flowed easily from her pussy, which was aching for Tucker to fill it.

Closing her eyes, she'd lost herself in the erotic sensations, dipping her fingers into her core and stroking her swollen clit. Her hips moved sinuously as she withdrew her fingers and spread her labia wide. The cool air washed over her hot flesh and she moaned.

"I never did get a chance to eat you up like I wanted to." His voice was hoarse with need.

Somehow she'd known he was there. Had sensed his presence. She hadn't bothered to open her eyes, but had just tilted her hips towards him. "Taste me. Lick me," she taunted him as she continued to pleasure herself.

His clothes rustled as he undressed and then she felt the bed sink when he crawled onto it. Wrapping his hands around her ankles, he stroked his hands up the insides of her legs. Her hips arched in anticipation.

His next touch surprised her. The rasp of his thumbs across her nipples made her gasp and she opened her eyes. His hands were dark against her paler skin and he looked huge as he knelt over her.

She shivered when he lightly pinched the swollen tips. "You're so beautiful." His fingers traced the row of stones the flowed down the slope of her breast. Bending forward, he flicked his tongue across each one in turn. "I won't disturb these for now."

Having said that, he kissed and nibbled his way down her torso. His tongue explored her belly button and he seemed fascinated by her hipbones, kissing and nipping them until she'd finally had enough. Gripping his hair, she'd pushed his head lower.

He laughed. "Impatient, are we?" Spreading her thighs, he pushed them as wide as they would go. "Hold them open for me."

She immediately hooked her hands under her legs. Her sex was totally exposed to him. She sucked in her breath when his head dipped down and she could feel his breath feather across her slick folds. Then he touched her.

It was maddening, the way his fingers or tongue would lightly touch her, never quite hard enough or long enough in any one spot. Yet, at the same time, each touch sent her spiraling higher and higher until she knew she soon had to crash. True to his word, he licked her, tasted her, and consumed her.

His tongue flicked her clit softly and slowly and then hard and quick. He'd slip one finger inside her only to pull it back out quickly. When she moaned in disappointment, he plunged three fingers deep. She never knew what was coming next. There was no rhyme or reason to his movements.

"Tucker," she gasped. Her whole body was shaking, her arm strength giving out. She couldn't hold herself like this much longer. Couldn't take this sensual torture.

"Now, baby. Come for me now." He drove his fingers inside her pulsing core and pressed hard on her clit with his tongue.

Her body exploded. Thrashing her head from side to side on the pillows, she bucked her hips and cried out. Her body clenched so hard it was almost painful. She could feel the gush of warm liquid coat his fingers. Letting herself go, she dropped her arms and legs back to the bed, shivering as spasms of pleasure continued to rocket through her.

Tucker raised his head as he carefully removed his hand. As she watched, he licked his fingers one at a time.

"Better than ice cream."

His words had sent her into another spasm and before she could recover, he'd lifted her hips and slid his cock into her swollen pussy. She'd accepted him easily, feeling her desire rising again as he proceeded to drive her to yet another orgasm.

She'd lost count how many times they'd made love last night. Not that she'd minded, but she was feeling a little sore this morning.

Tucker shifted beside her, rolling over onto his side and propping himself up on one arm. "How do you feel this morning? Really?" The hand resting on her stomach moved in small circles.

She thought about it. "I feel amazing. Tired, but energized."

"I didn't use protection last night." His gaze was steady and amazingly unconcerned. "I've always used protection. Always."

She knew he was telling her that he was safe. "I'm on the Pill, so we're okay."

His hand stilled on her belly and he sighed. "I guess that's for the best. For now."

And what exactly did he mean by that? He sounded almost disappointed that she couldn't get pregnant. "So, where do we go from here?" She was almost afraid to ask, but she had to know.

"This is for keeps." He drew a finger over the side of her face in a soft caress. "I want to see you, to spend time with you, exclusively. I won't share you." His gaze was fierce as he glared at her.

She smiled softly up at him. "I don't want any other guy. Only you." Wrapping her hands around his neck, she tugged him closer. He placed a soft, gentle kiss on her lips.

"I'll try and be patient, but I already know what I want."

"What do you want?"

"I want you in my life every day and in my bed every night. I want a life together and eventually kids. I want marriage. I want it all." He gave her a gentle smile that melted her heart. "I've had longer to think about this than you have. So, I'll try to be patient until you get used to the idea. But that doesn't mean I won't do my best to convince you sooner." His smile turned wicked. "I really think that we need to buy some ice cream and cherries today."

Tucker's hand wrapped around her breast as he leaned down and planted a searing kiss on her lips. Her head was spinning as he continued to plunder her mouth. She thrust her fingers through his hair and pulled him closer.

Emma knew she'd found her man for now and always. And she'd tell him so. But later. Maybe after they'd shared some of that ice cream he promised her. For now, she simply wanted to love him again.

Why an electronic book?

We live in the Information Age — an exciting time in the history of human civilization, in which technology rules supreme and continues to progress in leaps and bounds every minute of every day. For a multitude of reasons, more and more avid literary fans are opting to purchase e-books instead of paper books. The question from those not yet initiated into the world of electronic reading is simply: *Why?*

1. *Price.* An electronic title at Ellora's Cave Publishing and Cerridwen Press runs anywhere from 40% to 75% less than the cover price of the exact same title in paperback format. Why? Basic mathematics and cost. It is less expensive to publish an e-book (no paper and printing, no warehousing and shipping) than it is to publish a paperback, so the savings are passed along to the consumer.

2. *Space.* Running out of room in your house for your books? That is one worry you will never have with electronic books. For a low one-time cost, you can purchase a handheld device specifically designed for e-reading. Many e-readers have large, convenient screens for viewing. Better yet, hundreds of titles can be stored within your new library — on a single microchip. There are a variety of e-readers from different manufacturers. You can also read e-books on your PC or laptop computer. (Please note that Ellora's Cave does not endorse any specific brands.

You can check our websites at www.ellorascave.com or www.cerridwenpress.com for information we make available to new consumers.)

3. *Mobility.* Because your new e-library consists of only a microchip within a small, easily transportable e-reader, your entire cache of books can be taken with you wherever you go.

4. *Personal Viewing Preferences.* Are the words you are currently reading too small? Too large? Too... ANNOYING? Paperback books cannot be modified according to personal preferences, but e-books can.

5. *Instant Gratification.* Is it the middle of the night and all the bookstores near you are closed? Are you tired of waiting days, sometimes weeks, for bookstores to ship the novels you bought? Ellora's Cave Publishing sells instantaneous downloads twenty-four hours a day, seven days a week, every day of the year. Our webstore is never closed. Our e-book delivery system is 100% automated, meaning your order is filled as soon as you pay for it.

Those are a few of the top reasons why electronic books are replacing paperbacks for many avid readers.

As always, Ellora's Cave and Cerridwen Press welcome your questions and comments. We invite you to email us at Comments@ellorascave.com or write to us directly at Ellora's Cave Publishing Inc., 1056 Home Avenue, Akron, OH 44310-3502.

erridwen, the Celtic Goddess of wisdom, was the muse who brought inspiration to storytellers and those in the creative arts. Cerridwen Press encompasses the best and most innovative stories in all genres of today's fiction. Visit our site and discover the newest titles by talented authors who still get inspired - much like the ancient storytellers did, once upon a time.

ELLORA'S CAVE

ROMANTICA PUBLISHING

Discover for yourself why readers can't get enough
of the multiple award-winning publisher
Ellora's Cave.

Whether you prefer e-books or paperbacks,
be sure to visit EC on the web at
www.ellorascave.com

for an erotic reading experience that will leave you
breathless.